DARK ROAD TO DAYLIGHT

Gary E. Parker

DARK ROAD TO DAYLIGHT

A JANET THOMA BOOK

THOMAS NELSON PUBLISHERS
Nashville • Atlanta • London • Vancouver
Printed in the United States of America

Published in Nashville, Tennessee, by Thomas Nelson, Inc., Publishers, and distributed in Canada by Word Communications, Ltd., Richmond, British Columbia.

The Bible version used in this publication is THE NEW KING JAMES VERSION. Copyright © 1979, 1980, 1982, Thomas Nelson, Inc., Publishers.

Library of Congress Cataloging-in-Publication Data
Parker, Gary E.
  Dark road to daylight : a novel / Gary E. Parker.
    p. cm.
  ISBN 0-7852-7785-4
  I. Title.
PS3566.A6784D37 1996
813'.54—dc20
96—42229
CIP

Printed in the United States of America.
1 2 3 4 5 6 — 01 00 99 98 97 96

Dedication

My two daughters, Andrea and Ashley, want me to dedicate every book I do to them. But, since this is the eighth book I've written, that gets old after a while. So, I want to dedicate this book to schoolteachers, particularly any teacher who encourages students to read and write. In my own experience, I remember three—my sixth grade teacher, Mrs. Williams, my eleventh grade English teacher, Mrs. Watson, and a college English professor, Dr. West—who inspired me to put words on paper. If not for them, I don't know if I would have had the courage to try.

Then little children were brought to Him

that He might put His hands on them and pray,

but the disciples rebuked them.

But Jesus said, "Let the little children come to Me,

and do not forbid them;

for of such is the kingdom of heaven."

And He laid His hands on them.

Matthew 19:13–15

Friday
August 22

CHAPTER ONE

2:20 P.M.

Sitting in a rusty, nine-year-old Chevy pickup under a pine tree as tall as a water tower, Rusty Redder exhaled a mouthful of cigar smoke. The smoke, hanging dead in the stillness of the 98-degree air, combined with a glaring sun and blurred Rusty's vision for a second. Rusty brushed the smoke away and focused his attention back on his target—a baby girl about fifty yards away, playing with a tan-colored cocker spaniel. The toddler had the dog by the tail, but the grip looked less than secure from what Rusty could see.

If his plans had been different, Rusty might have smiled at the sight. After all, he loved children as much as the next guy. Heck, he even had a child, a boy who must be at least seven by now. Not that he could really remember the last time he had seen his boy. Even so, he knew for a fact that kids did the craziest things—things that just broke him up with the giggles.

But Rusty couldn't laugh today. No, today he had a job to do. And the job involved the baby girl.

He sucked another drag of his cigar and fingered the looped earring dangling from his left ear. The glint of the sun lit up a tattoo on his bicep. The tattoo, stenciled into his flesh in bright red ink, spelled one word: *BEAST*.

Rusty grinned as he stared at the tattoo. When people saw it, they usually assumed it described his character—kind of like a warning label stamped right there. But he didn't see himself that way at all. *He* wasn't the BEAST. Bernardo was.

Bernardo the Beast—the World Federation Wrestling champion. A 400-pound hulk of wrestling mania. A beast with ears like pointed red horns and a black beard cut into the shape of an upside-down pyramid. Now Bernardo was a beast!

Rusty had Bernardo's autograph. Got it at the Coliseum one night last December, right after the Beast tossed that wimpy excuse for a wrestler named Terry the Whole Truth out of the ring and into Rusty's lap. Rusty kept the autograph in his wallet in the back pocket of his much-worn blue jeans. He loved Bernardo, loved him so much he tattooed the champ's nickname right there on his left bicep.

A bee buzzed through the cigar smoke, interrupting Rusty's thoughts. He blinked and remembered what he was about to do.

The baby girl. Yeah, there in the yard.

He knew the little girl—at least a little bit. Her name was Stacy Chapman. Mother named Bethany. Phone number, 585-2121. Grandmother named Lydia, but called Mee-Maw. No man in the house. Though not certain of the fact, Rusty figured a divorce best explained that. It didn't really matter to him. He knew all he needed to know.

He lived in the same trailer park as the baby girl, the Lincoln Family Trailer Park, a collection of almost a hundred rectangular boxes—tornado traps, he called them—situated on ten gravel roads that ran in parallel lines among the dwellings.

His place sat six gravel roads away from the spot where the little girl, her mother, and her grandmother lived. Their trailer sat on the corner lot at the end of the gravel road on the perimeter of the park. A field of pine trees blanketed the road opposite their spot, and one of the few empty lots in the park sat right next to them.

Rusty had seen the child and the grandmother as he drove past their trailer the day they moved in. With a quick glance, he sized them up—an old woman wearing a straw hat and carrying a baby of undetermined age and gender. Grunting, he sped on past. Another poor family, he figured. Here today, behind on their rent tomorrow, and gone the next day. Folks just like him.

Three days later, he had seen a row of azalea bushes in front of the blue-and-white trailer. A day after that, two newly planted dogwood trees sprang up. As he approached the place the next day, a Saturday, he saw a woman, considerably younger than the one in the straw hat, out in the yard. She had on blue jean shorts and a red

bandanna and a cutoff T-shirt the color of a robin's egg. Work gloves covered her fingers, and she held a pair of posthole diggers in her hands. The muscles in her tanned arms glistened as she jabbed the earth with the digging tool. Beside her lay a stack of chain-link fence squares. Sweat soaked through her T-shirt, and it stuck like Saran Wrap to her shapely body.

Swallowing hard, Rusty hit the brakes of his truck. *Maybe I should make this lady's acquaintance*, he thought, suddenly feeling generous, *see if I can help her put in that fence.*

The wheels of his truck scrunched to a halt. But then a warning light blinked in his head. Though he'd not seen a man at the place, it didn't make sense that a woman that good-looking didn't have a male companion lurking around somewhere. Must be out of town.

Rusty eased off the brakes and the truck inched forward. He heard a door slam, then saw the old woman step out of the trailer, a drinking glass in her right hand. He moved slowly forward, trying to decide whether to stop. The truck passed directly in front of the woman on the steps. She stared out at him for a second, then threw up her free hand in greeting.

Tossing caution aside, Rusty stopped the truck. The old woman, her straw hat so low on her forehead that he could barely see her eyes, waved at him again. He glanced over at the younger woman. Her head was down, the posthole diggers still chomping at the ground, the red scarf snug on her head, a wild mat of black curls dangling out of it over her forehead and down into her eyes.

As if suddenly frightened, Rusty ducked his head, trying to avoid the old woman's eyes. Yes, he wanted to meet the young one, but only after he had watched a bit longer, found out a bit more.

But the old lady's eyes stayed on him. He could feel them burning into him, lasers of high intensity. Reluctantly, he looked up. The woman never broke her stare. She walked toward him, her eyes steady.

"I'm Lydia Spicer," she called. "Friends and neighbors call me Mee-Maw. That's my daughter Bethany—" she pointed to the woman in the cutoff jeans— "and I'll pay you twenty-five dollars to dig the rest of those holes for her."

Caring less about the money than the chance to meet Bethany, Rusty had parked his truck, climbed out, and walked toward the trailer. "I'm Rusty," he said, glancing from one woman to the next. "Glad to help."

Bethany nodded but said nothing. He took the posthole diggers from her. Then, to his utter disappointment, she turned and walked away.

Working hard to hide his feelings, Rusty poured himself into the work. Lydia Spicer didn't disturb him. Within forty minutes he had completed the job. Tossing the posthole diggers aside, he took the glass of tea Lydia offered him and drank it down. When he finished, she paid him, thanked him for his hard work, and sent him on his way.

Too shy to push himself on Bethany, Rusty took the money and left. He'd get another chance to meet her, he decided. And soon. He'd see to it.

To that end, he paid close attention to Bethany's comings and goings over the next few weeks. She kept a regular routine, and he learned it well. She left the baby with the old woman at about 6:45 each morning when she drove to work—she was a nurse at Murphy Memorial Hospital. Rusty knew because he followed her there one day soon after he dug the holes for her fence. She came home a little after six.

Yeah, he knew her schedule, but that hadn't done him much good. No other opportunity to meet Bethany had presented itself. That is, until today, when the call came. Just a bit ago. An offer for a spur-of-the-moment job. An odd one, but one he accepted quickly, without giving it much thought. The job promised big bucks, bigger than he'd ever made in his life. So here he sat—ready to do the job. As much as Rusty disliked the nature of his assignment, he couldn't afford to reject the work. Dollars were tight and ten grand would go a long way. Heck, with ten thousand dollars he could buy tickets to see Bernardo fight any time he wanted.

Rusty chewed on the end of his cigar and played with his earring another moment. Man, it was hot. Though he wore only a pair of scuffed basketball shoes, without socks, his blue jeans, and a plain white T-shirt—one pocket in the front for his cigars—he still sweated like a live pig on a barbecue spit. He would be glad when this was over.

In the distance, he heard a rumble.

Thunder?

 6

He jerked his head to the left and checked the western horizon. A bank of brooding clouds hovered there—an angry scowl in the sky. Rusty shuddered. He didn't like lightning. Didn't like it a bit. He had seen a man get hit by it one day about five years ago when he was working on a highway construction crew.

The hair on the back of his neck poked upward and, for a split second, he reconsidered his plans. If a storm came up, he didn't want to work in it.

But then he remembered the money. His orders said he had to deliver the child today if he wanted the ten grand.

He grunted. Okay, he didn't like lightning, but he had to live with it from time to time. That's the way life shook itself out. Work was spotty—herky-jerky these days. When a job promised to pay him as well as this one, he couldn't afford to walk away from it—no matter how scary the storm.

Rusty sucked on his cigar. *Make the best of it*, he thought. *Go with the flow, deal with it.*

He took a deep breath, realizing that, as usual, he didn't have a detailed plan for what he was about to do. He never did. He didn't operate that way—with schemes and details and all that stuff. He liked spur-of-the-moment. Take a job, check out the situation, puzzle over it for a few minutes, maybe a few hours, then just do it. Like that shoe commercial said.

Rusty flicked his cigar ashes out the window and chuckled under his scraggly red beard. So far, his style had worked out just fine. Through twenty-nine years of a rough-and-tumble life, including almost six years of steady criminal activity, he had spent less than thirty days in jail.

Staring at the child in the yard, he saw the cocker spaniel's tail slap against her chubby thigh. The little girl grabbed for the tail, her tiny fingers opening and closing as if milking a cow. Shaping her mouth into a big circle, she cooed, "Scooo-er." Sounded like "Scooter" to Rusty. The dog's name, he figured.

Scooter dodged the fingers and twisted to face the baby. His tongue lolling out, the dog opened his cheeks and grinned. His teeth, yellowed by a steady diet of table scraps, glistened in the bright heat. Leaning forward, he licked Stacy on the lips.

She smiled hugely. Rusty watched as her eyes crinkled with joy. She reached for Scooter again. This time she caught him by the scruff of the neck and pulled him to her face. She stuck her tongue out and buried her chin in Scooter's tan fur.

Rusty took a deep breath and tightened his stomach. The time had come. If he didn't move now, the chance might pass.

He glanced at his watch. Just past 2:30. With school out for the summer and a couple of hours yet before most workers came home, the road was empty in both directions. Time to do the deed. His eyes, red-streaked and heavy-lidded, rolled sideways—leaving the child and landing on the grandmother, Mee-Maw Lydia. She sat in a creaky-looking lawn chair in the shade of the only grown tree in the yard—a full-leafed live oak. The oak stood close to the trailer, its leaves providing a touch of shade over the front windows.

Rusty studied the grandmother. At least seventy-five years old, he decided, and no more than a hundred pounds. Her straw hat covered her slim face, and she wore a pair of flowered shorts, a white loose-fitting blouse, and a pair of sandals that looked like garage-sale leftovers. Even from across the yard, Rusty could see spidery veins running up her pencil-thin calves. Lazily, she waved a fan in front of her face.

Reaching to the seat, Rusty picked up a phone and dialed Bethany Chapman's number. 585-2121. A couple of seconds later, the old woman in the lawn chair tilted her head to the left, toward the open window by the oak. The fan stopped waving. Through his receiver, Rusty heard the phone ring again. Mee-Maw Lydia pulled herself from her chair, stared at the baby for a moment, then lay the fan in her seat. A third ring sounded. Lydia tottered slowly toward the door of the trailer. The phone rang again and again. She climbed the three steps of the trailer, looked back at the baby one more time, then pulled open the door and disappeared inside. Tossing his cigar out the window, Rusty reached for the door of the truck.

In the rectangular living room of the trailer, Lydia Spicer dropped the phone into its cradle on the coffee table and stood still for a second. She wondered about the caller who had hung up on her. A wrong number? Must've been.

Shrugging, she wiped a ridge of sweat off her forehead, clicked her false teeth together, and stepped toward the kitchen. *A glass of*

Dark Road to Daylight

iced tea sure would hit the spot, she thought. She had made a pitcher fresh that morning. Sat it to cool in the refrigerator.

Passing the front window, she glanced out and saw Stacy standing by Scooter, her hand on the dog's back. All okay. Clicking her teeth, Lydia inched into the kitchen.

Moving quickly but cautiously, it didn't take Rusty long to reach the gate to the fence. There, he paused for a moment to check for traffic. None in sight. Aces. If the grandmother stayed inside just another couple of minutes, he would make his ten grand without a hitch. That's the way his employer insisted that it happen. No fuss, no muss, no one hurt.

He lifted the gate. It creaked. Stacy jerked her head around and her curls—as black as asphalt—bounced side to side around her ears. She pouted and a cloud rolled across her face. Scooter's tail paused in mid-wag, and he snuggled up against Stacy's hip.

Letting his imagination run, Rusty saw the next few seconds unfold. Like Bernardo the Beast in the middle of a championship match, he would grab the child in a headlock, lift her gently off the ground, and tuck her under his arm. Like that wimpy Terry the Whole Truth, she would yield quickly to his superior strength. He would win with ease, hustle back to his truck, deliver the girl, and pick up his money.

His pulse calm and his face serene, Rusty sprinted toward Stacy Chapman.

Scooter growled, and Stacy's blue eyes widened as she spotted Rusty. He bent over, his hands reaching for her. Scooter darted at him, barking and baring his teeth. Rusty kicked at the dog, but he quickly dodged away. Stacy's tiny face scrunched up into a fold of scared flesh.

Scooter pounced on Rusty from behind, grabbing a mouthful of shoe in his teeth. Rusty kicked out, his heavy leg tossing Scooter away, throwing him into the air. Scooter landed hard and yelped in pain. Stacy's eyes flooded with tears and she twisted away, her baby-fat legs waddling toward the trailer. Scooter sprinted past her in the opposite direction, headed back for another run at Rusty. Stacy tripped and fell. Her face scraped into the dirt of the dry grass. She wailed and the sound of it cut through the deadness of the scorched air.

Inside the trailer, Lydia heard the wail of her only grandchild and almost dropped the glass of tea she cupped in her bony fingers. With a speed that belied her age, she pushed herself up from the kitchen table and rushed through the living room to the front door. Jerking it open, she saw a man reach for her Stacy.

For a split second, Lydia froze where she stood. She recognized the man—the posthole digger—but she couldn't remember his name. What was he doing—?

Her blood pounded through her skull and the veins in her face stood up under her thin skin. The posthole digger was about to grab her grandbaby! But why?

Suddenly, Lydia felt faint. Still holding the tea glass, she blinked her eyes against the sun and fought to stay conscious.

About to grab the kid, Rusty spotted the grandmother at the trailer door and cursed under his breath. If she interfered, it would screw up the whole plan. One fly in the soup spoiled the whole bowl. He didn't want to hurt the old woman. Shoot, he didn't want to hurt anyone.

But that's the way matches sometimes worked out. Sometimes an opponent tougher than Terry the Whole Truth walked into the ring. These things happened.

But a good wrestler kept his wits about him when an opponent showed unexpected skills. Bernardo the Beast wouldn't back down now. Bernardo would fight through it, do the job, win the battle. If Bernardo could do it, so could he!

A half-step away from the baby, Rusty saw that Lydia couldn't do anything to stop him. She was still on the stoop of the trailer, a good thirty feet away. By the time she tottered down the steps, he would have long since hightailed it out of there.

Momentarily forgetting his instructions to treat the child gently, he grabbed for Stacy, catching her by the back of her dark hair. His

hands squeezed around her curls and he snapped her head up and back, pulling her off the ground. Clutching her to his chest, he turned back toward his truck. He could almost smell the fresh bills of his ten thousand dollars.

A set of teeth crunched into his right ankle and he swore again. The stupid, stupid dog. That dog was forcing him to get rough, forcing him to do something he didn't really want to do

Kicking again, he thrust the animal away. He reached inside the waistband of his jeans as he ran to the pickup and pulled out his pistol—an ill-kept .38 he'd bought almost three years ago at a pawnshop. He had never fired it.

He didn't like the thought of shooting the dog. His instructions said, "Hurt no one." But he didn't see any other option. Bernardo the Beast wouldn't let a dog chew on his ankle and go unpunished.

Twisting back around, Rusty's eyes searched along the ground for the cocker spaniel.

From the second step of the stoop, Lydia cast her eyes toward the heavens, said a short but intensely sincere prayer for accuracy, then cocked her left arm and let fly the tea glass. As true as a Nolan Ryan fastball, the glass whipped through the August air and smacked into the head of the posthole digger, who had scooped up her Stacy. The glass shattered against the man's right temple, and a spray of tea instantly gushed down his cheek. He staggered.

From behind him, Scooter sank his teeth into his right leg. Lydia heard him swear, his invective spewing like hot vomit from his throat.

Lydia never paused. She jumped the last step from the trailer and rushed toward the abductor. Two steps away she saw the gun in his hand.

Clutching Stacy against his chest, the man pointed his gun and fired. At first, Lydia didn't understand. He hadn't fired the gun at her! But then she heard a yelp. He had shot Scooter!

The dog dropped his hold on the man's leg and rolled over into the grass. Blood poured from Scooter's chest.

Her anger fueling her muscles, Lydia jumped onto Rusty's brawny back. With a whirl, he jerked left and right, out and back, up and down—a crazed bronco, trying to throw her off. But she didn't let go.

Instead, she held on. She rode him, her rage giving her strength she thought she had long since lost. She locked her arms around his throat, and her spindly fingers, nails and all, punched into the skin around his Adam's apple. She smelled cigar smoke on his breath. A wave of nausea hit her, and she felt a fainting sensation rushing over her again.

Desperate to stop the attacker before she lost her strength, Lydia squeezed harder and harder. He pulled his right arm away from his body, then rammed it back into her side, his elbow popping like a sledgehammer into her ribs.

Stunned by the blow, she grunted and lost her grip. She felt herself falling into blackness, losing consciousness. She gritted her false teeth and redoubled her efforts to hold on.

She grabbed for his throat again, but he slammed his elbow into her ribs a second time. She heard a crack, like a tree branch breaking. Darkness washed over her, and her blood pounded harder and harder in her skull. Her grip slipped even more.

Blindly, she reached out one last time. The fingers of her right hand closed on something round and solid. She clutched at it with all her might. For a full second she hung on, her hundred pounds fully suspended in the air by the earring in Rusty's left earlobe. She heard skin tear. Rusty screamed. The round object fell into Lydia's fingers. It felt wet. She clutched it to her side, her fingers like vise grips around it. She felt herself falling again.

Rusty's elbow pounded into her side one more time, and now she fell for good, her head hitting the ground at his feet. The roar in her head became a train rushing by, the sound of it throbbing and throbbing, a noise that hurt. The noise exploded in her skull and blew her away to blackness. Her fingers relaxed, and the earring in her right hand rolled like a tiny golden wheel into the dry grass under her cheek. For a full five seconds it rolled along the parched ground. Then, hitting the side of Scooter's doghouse, it stopped. For a split instant, it tilted there, as if deciding whether to stand or fall. Then it toppled onto its side.

   *Dark Road to Daylight*

Blood dripping from his ear, Rusty backed hurriedly away. His eyes blinked over and over, and torrents of sweat rolled down his chin. The ferocity of the gray-haired banshee had surprised him.

He squeezed his bloody ear, trying to staunch the flow. His fingers turned sticky with the red ooze.

He cursed his bad luck. What a mess. He might even need stitches. Worse still, he knew he had hurt the old woman. How bad, he didn't know.

Closing the fence and checking for traffic, he sighed with regret. This wasn't good. But, he assured himself, he couldn't help it. One thing led to another. To get the child, the grandmother had to suffer. The employer would just have to understand. Bernardo the Beast would have done the same thing.

Confident of his reasoning, Rusty looked down at the baby in his arms. In spite of everything, he had managed to grab the trophy, the girl named Stacy.

To his surprise, she had stopped crying. Now she looked up at him with a fixed stare, her blue eyes glazed.

Rusty grunted. *She's in shock*, he decided. *Good. Anything to keep her quiet.*

Across the road now, he climbed into his truck and placed Stacy in a baby seat he had bought at a second-hand store only an hour ago. As he snapped her in, she stayed still, her eyes never leaving his face.

A splatter of rain hit his windshield and he jumped, startled by the sound. Turning from the child, he leaned his head out the driver's-side window and scanned the sky. The storm clouds he had seen a few minutes ago had quickly moved closer. Now they stood directly overhead. The pine trees lining the road where he sat whipped and see-sawed as the wind picked up. A bolt of lightning cracked a couple of miles away.

Glad to have finished his work before the storm hit, Rusty reached into the glove compartment and pulled out a bottle of cough syrup and a tubular dispenser. Filling the vial with the purple medicine, he eased it over to Stacy's mouth. Though not exactly certain of the dosage, he wanted to drug the child so she would stay quiet.

To his relief, Stacy didn't fight the medicine. He squirted it into her throat and she swallowed it down. He wiped her lips with his bare hand, then quickly started the truck and pulled away. At the corner leading out of the trailer park, he paused to study his ear in the rearview mirror. The bleeding had almost stopped. Aces. Maybe he wouldn't need stitches after all.

Relieved, Rusty gunned the truck onto the highway and reached into his shirt pocket for a cigar. Lighting the smoke, he chewed on the end for a second, then inhaled. Instantly, he felt better. Sure, the ear hurt, but he had finished the toughest part of the job. Now only two steps left. Deliver the baby and pick up the money. A slight grin crossed his face. For ten thousand dollars he could stand a bit of pain.

In the dusty yard of her trailer, Lydia tried to pull herself off the ground, but every breath she took ripped at her lungs. Her ribs felt as if someone had smashed them with a boat paddle. She coughed, and blood trickled from her lips. Groaning, she lurched upward, then fell back down. Realizing she couldn't walk, she threw her hands forward and grabbed a handful of brown grass. She pulled with all her strength, and her body inched ahead. Another pull and she made more progress. A third pull and she covered almost a foot of ground.

Around her, everything grew darker. For an instant, she wondered if she were passing out again. But then a flash of lightning struck and several splats of water hit her on the shoulders, and she understood that storm clouds had moved in over her head. She pulled on the grass again and made another ten inches.

Slowly, ever so slowly, she crawled across the yard to the trailer, then up the three steps to the stoop. Bracing herself against the side of the door, she willed herself to stand up. Several drops of rain plopped onto her head. The cool water felt good, energizing. She pushed the door open and staggered inside. Within seconds, she reached the phone.

Sagging across the sofa, she searched for the numbers on the dial. 9-1-1. She punched them out.

An operator answered. Lydia tried to speak, but her tongue felt thick, unwilling to cooperate. She breathed heavily into the line, trying to force out the words. A mumbled gibberish sounded from her throat. She touched her lips, saw blood on her fingers when she drew them back. A wave of panic hit her. She couldn't speak! She shouted

   *Dark Road to Daylight*

into the line. Her voice croaked like a frog. She sucked in her breath, then exhaled slowly.

"Yes, this is 911," said the operator. "How can I help you?"

With an effort born of desperation, Lydia pushed her lips together and mouthed out the word. "Beast."

"Excuse me?"

Lydia took another deep breath. Her energy sagged. She moaned and it sounded like someone talking underwater. Air burst through her nostrils and her breath swooshed out.

"BEAST," she shouted. She thought she heard a giggle.

"I'm sure he is," said the operator. "But this isn't that kind of phone line. If this is a prank, you need to know it's a crime to call 911 without a legitimate emergency. If it's not a prank, give me your name, address, and situation and I'll get someone to help you."

Lydia tried one final time to communicate, but her tongue refused to respond. Frustrated, she slammed down the phone. The room began to spin, and she felt herself losing consciousness again. Frantic, she swept her eyes across the room. What else could she do? What if she died? Worse, what if she didn't die but couldn't talk when she regained consciousness? How long would she remain unable to talk? Long enough for the posthole digger to escape with her granddaughter?

Her gaze fell on a notepad and a pencil on the table by the phone. Her fingers trembling, she lifted the pencil and started to write. She scratched out two letters—*B-E*—and poised her hand to start a third.

The stroke hit her before the pencil touched the paper. Her tongue thickened, her right arm became numb, and the skin on her right cheek sagged downward. Dropping the notepad, she collapsed across the coffee table.

On the other end of the line, the 911 operator hung up the phone and leaned back in her seat. The call sounded like a prank—a kid doing heavy breathing exercises. Not the first time it had happened, and surely not the last.

The operator pulled a fingernail file from the desktop by her computer and rubbed it across her thumbnail. For a second, she considered skipping the next step in the process—activating the automatic identification system, the tracing mechanism the city had recently purchased and installed. The system traced all the 911 calls, and a dispatcher sent a policeman to the location.

The operator bit the end of her thumbnail. Such a silly call seemed hardly worth the effort. She swiveled around in her chair. But what if the woman truly needed help? Perhaps the 911 call was her only chance for survival.

The operator laid down the fingernail file and punched the computer keyboard. A series of prompts appeared; she answered them. The computer blinked, pausing for a second to bring up the information she sought.

In that instant, lightning cracked outside and the seat under her quivered. Overhead, the lights in the office blinked off. In front of her, the computer screen went blank. For almost ten seconds, she sat in the dark and waited. Then the electricity returned. The computer screen turned blue again and the lights switched back on.

The operator took a deep breath and refocused her attention on the computer. She really should get someone to check out the last call. The computer buzzed, then clicked—once, twice, three times. But when she looked at it, nothing looked back. The address of the last caller had disappeared.

CHAPTER TWO

5:52 P.M.

Unfolding her five-foot, eight-inch frame, Lieutenant Jackie Broadus stepped out of her unmarked police car. Though marble-sized raindrops splattered down on the shoulders of her navy blue blazer and through her raven-colored chin-length hair, she didn't reach for an umbrella. Her blue eyes peered through the rain, their concentrated focus soaking up the situation as thoroughly as the downpour from the dark sky soaked through the cuffs of her khaki slacks and the soles of her low-heeled black pumps. The only thing dry on Jackie Broadus was the white blouse she wore underneath the blazer and the Glock .17 strapped to her ribs in a shoulder holster on her left side.

To her right, by the side of the gravel road, sat an ambulance, its red lights flashing round and round, a beacon marking the spot of the bad news. In front of the ambulance two black-and-white squad cars were parked. Their lights were still.

Beyond the vehicles, a line of trailers bordered the gravel road on each side as far as Jackie's eyes could see. Behind the road where her car sat ran another line of trailers. Behind them a third row and beyond that another. Everywhere she looked she saw the trailers.

In spite of the pounding rain, a gaggle of curious neighbors stood huddled together just past the yellow crime scene tape that the uniformed police had already wrapped around the area. Several of them had draped garbage bags over their heads, and a cluster of five stood in mass under a sheet of clear polyethylene.

Surveying the scene, Jackie breathed deeply, as if trying to inhale everything she saw. She opened her hands, palms held up and slightly out from her body. For several seconds, she stood that way, her palms acting as receptacles, fleshy sensors drawing in the emotions, the atmosphere of the rain-slick yard where the crime had occurred.

Jackie, a detective for over fifteen years, knew she worked best through what she sensed. She paid attention to the details too—every good cop had to do that—but she didn't rely only on the bits and pieces of what she saw. She knew that facts alone tended to lead her down false trails, caused her to waste precious time and energy on what looked obvious but often wasn't. So she leaned most heavily on her intuition, that innate sense had never disappointed her. While others gathered the pieces of the puzzle, she saw the picture. That way, the whole puzzle came together.

From her right, a black policeman, covered from shoe to scalp in bright yellow rain gear, rushed toward her and interrupted her musings. "I'm Patrick," he called over the gushing water, raising his umbrella over her head and leading her through the gate. "Simon Patrick. I'm new. A month since I started at Longstreet. Haven't had the chance to meet you yet."

Jackie nodded to the man and followed him as he ducked under the crime scene tape. "Jackie Broadus," she said, her voice rich, like hot honey on bread. "I've only been at Longstreet Station for a week myself. Transferred over from Peachtree. Guess we're both new kids on the block."

Patrick extended his hand and Jackie took it. She dropped his grip, tilted her head toward the trailer. "What's the story here?" she asked. "Dispatcher didn't have many details."

"We're not sure just yet. Right now we've got a woman, seventy-six years old according to her license, down in the living room. Looks like a stroke." Patrick, stomping a skinny leg through a mud puddle, headed to the trailer. Jackie followed him, sidestepping the puddle.

"Dispatcher said something about a dog?"

Patrick grunted and, in one stride, climbed the three steps leading into the trailer. "Yeah, a cocker spaniel—he's been shot."

Patrick entered the trailer and snapped his umbrella closed. Water dripped off it onto the beige carpet on the floor.

"That's what got us here," he continued. "A woman heard a dog yapping. Ever since that Simpson trial, every time a dog barks, somebody calls the cops."

"The dog still alive?" asked Jackie, shutting the door behind her, automatically speaking louder to overcome the popping of the rain against the roof.

"Yep," called Patrick, his voice matching hers. "We've got him in the squad car, plan to get him to a vet as soon as we—"

Nodding, Jackie raised her hand, halting the thin policeman in mid-sentence. Without rushing, she ran her eyes over the room. Directly in front of her, the ambulance crew worked feverishly on a gray-haired woman.

The woman's face stared up at the ceiling. Her eyes were open. She looked quizzical, as if she were trying to figure out some pattern on the ceiling. Wispy hair crawled out from her scalp, and the skin on her forehead was as thin as waxed paper, thin enough for Jackie to see the skeleton underneath. A member of the emergency team lifted the woman's head and slid an oxygen mask over her nose.

Jackie looked away and examined the trailer itself. A neat place, she decided. A shelf full of violets, purple and pink, sitting on a table by the window at the front of the trailer. A row of five pictures on the wall directly across from the window. Tasteful frames bordered the pictures, frames obviously purchased with care. In the center of the pictures hung a cherry-red frame of intricate detail. The frame spotlighted the portrait of a cherubic baby girl—a girl blessed with black curls and chipmunk cheeks and eyes as shiny as the puddles of water that lay on the ground outside.

Jackie's eyes left the pictures and moved to the rose-colored sofa below them. The sofa, though well worn, was not a cheap piece of furniture. A quilt hung across the back.

Walking slowly, Jackie stepped past the ambulance crew and ran her fingers over the quilt, studying it intently. What a gorgeous piece of work! Rows of dolls adorned it. Six dolls down, six dolls across, each in the colorful costume of a different nation. Jackie held her palms on the quilt and breathed softly. If she knew anything at all about such things—and she did—someone had poured a ton of time and love into this quilt.

The emergency team dropped a stretcher next to the woman on the floor, disturbing Jackie's thoughts. She turned back to Patrick. "The woman's not shot," she said matter-of-factly.

"Nope, looks like a fall. Her ribs are bruised up pretty good. And she's got a cut over one eye. And like I said, what looks like a stroke. We called you because somebody shot the dog. Thought we might find a person shot too."

Jackie smiled. As the new detective at Longstreet—and as the only woman—she expected this kind of assignment for a while. One with no sharp edges. A puzzle, yes. A shot dog and an elderly woman with a stroke and a fall. But not a homicide. In spite of her years at Peachtree in homicide and missing persons, her transfer meant she would get the less enticing investigations until she proved herself. In one sense, she didn't mind. The lull would give her a chance to get a grip on the changes she had embraced in her life in the last few months.

Lifting the elderly woman from the floor onto a gurney, the ambulance crew stood up and moved toward Jackie. She edged to the side to let them pass.

"What's her name?" she asked Patrick.

"Lydia," he said, also pressing against the wall to make room for the stretcher. "Lydia Spicer. We found a purse in the bedroom. Had a driver's license in it. Can you believe, as old as she is, she's still driving?"

"Hope I'm so fortunate at her age," said Jackie, watching the emergency team rush out the door.

Patrick laughed, but Jackie didn't join him. He cut off the laughter in mid-chuckle.

"Any clue who shot the dog?" Jackie asked, stepping to the center of the room and squatting to examine where Lydia had been lying. "Or why?"

Patrick didn't answer. A shadow fell across Jackie and she sensed a weight entering the room. The rain suddenly let up outside, and the popping on the ceiling dropped to a gentle drumbeat. She raised her eyes and saw Patrick still squeezed against the wall. Beside him stood a second cop, this one much taller, so tall in fact that the trailer ceiling seemed to scrape along the top of his flat-topped blond hair. His width almost matched his height and his forehead seemed widest of all. It hung like a square awning over the blackest eyes Jackie had ever seen.

Slowly, she raised herself from the floor and extended her hand. "Jackie Broadus," she said. "Homicide."

"Chapman," the blond man said, his voice a rumble as deep as the thunder that had shaken the sky only a few minutes ago. "Cleve Chapman. Patrick's partner." He gripped her hand firmly, his calloused fingers dwarfing her own, squeezing her knuckles almost to the point of pain. Jackie didn't blink.

For several heartbeats, the two stood toe-to-toe, their eyes locked as if in silent combat. Watching him closely, Jackie couldn't decide if the man attracted her or threatened her. She did know he carried an enormous power in his tall, stout frame and pitch-black eyes. He had a charisma about him, an energy that exuded through the police uniform gripping closely to his tightly wound body.

Chapman dropped Jackie's hand, and though she wanted to rub the numbness from her knuckles, she refused to do it.

"Patrick get you up-to-date?" Chapman asked, his voice rolling through the small trailer.

"He told me about the dog and the woman," said Jackie, her words falling out just a bit quicker than usual. "Said you guys called me because of the dog. Just to be safe."

Chapman smiled slightly, but to Jackie he didn't look really amused. "That's not quite the whole situation," he rumbled. "Though at first, that's what we thought."

He stopped there, and Jackie knew he did so deliberately, his pause calculated to make her ask him what he meant. But she didn't move or speak.

Chapman studied her intensely, his black eyes focused like a gun sight at her face. She wondered if he tried to intimidate everybody or if he reserved this kind of attitude for women only. She glanced over at Patrick, saw him still squeezed against the wall, obviously deferring to his partner.

The rain outside picked up again, and a flash of lightning cut through the room. For a second, the lights in the trailer blinked off. When the zigzag of the electricity in the sky struck again, it illuminated Cleve Chapman's face and lit up his eyes—lit them up until they glowed with an inhuman incandescence. In that instant, his face contorted hideously and his black eyes seemed to bulge outward as if on loose stems that allowed them to crawl out of their sockets. Jackie shuddered, the rain that had soaked through her jacket suddenly ice cold on her shoulders.

She hugged her arms around her waist, struggling to calm down. The thunder outside rolled away like a convoy of trucks, and the lights overhead flickered back on. Jackie blinked, then spoke quietly to Cleve Chapman.

"So there's more than the dog now?" she asked, her voice as even as she could make it.

Chapman shrugged and relaxed his shoulders. The gesture seemed practiced, as if he wanted to ease her mind.

"Yeah, there's more than the dog now." He didn't go any further.

Jackie decided to let him play his little game. "And what is that?" she asked.

He smiled, and this time Jackie knew he didn't feel humorous. "This is where my ex-wife lives," he said.

Jackie blinked and eased a half-step away from Chapman. His words stunned her. Trying to clear up her confusion, she didn't respond for a moment.

Chapman spoke for her, quickly this time, as if anxious to fill the silence in the room. "Patrick and I got the call about fifty minutes ago. I recognized the address immediately. My ex-wife moved here a month or so ago. She and her mama and my little girl. Patrick and I got here immediately. Found the dog in the yard, Lydia in here, just where you saw her a few minutes ago."

"And then you called homicide."

"Yeah, then we called homicide."

Jackie's brow furrowed, and she tilted her head to the left. "I guess I'm still not following something," she said. "A shot dog and a grandmother with a possible stroke isn't a homicide."

Chapman walked two steps toward her. She found herself pinned against the wall. The air smelled stuffy, but slightly leathery too, and she realized that the aroma of aftershave flowed from Chapman's body, momentarily choking off her breath. His black eyes peered down at her from his towering height, blazing brightly as if trying to drill a hole right into her soul.

"No," he rumbled. "That's true. They don't make a homicide. But a missing baby girl just might."

Jackie blinked and stared past Chapman to the wall behind him, above the television. She saw the picture in the center of the wall, the one in the intricate frame. A curly headed, angelic-faced baby girl stared back at her.

She took a deep breath and nodded slightly. A man the size of a bear was threatening her, a dog was shot, a grandmother was in a coma, and a cherub of a girl was missing. Not a bad case for the first one in her new precinct.

Dark Road to Daylight

CHAPTER THREE

6:30 P.M.

Flicking her curly black hair off her forehead, Bethany Chapman passed through one last red light before she made the turn a mile up from her trailer. Glancing at herself in the rearview mirror, she saw a strong chin. Her brown eyes, though swollen from crying earlier in the day, were now dry.

Okay, she thought, *the worst is past.* She took a deep breath, reminding herself she could handle this.

It had been the worst afternoon of her life. At about two o'clock, just as she stepped out of the operating room, her ex-husband Cleve had called her. A surgical nurse, she still had on her bloody scrubs as she took the phone.

"I want Stacy," Cleve had said, as calmly as if ordering a pizza. "I'm going to marry Janette and I want custody of my daughter."

Hearing his smooth voice, Bethany's blood pressure instantly skyrocketed. Cleve had shocked her more than once during their three years of marriage and in the last four months since their divorce became final. It shouldn't surprise her that he had done it again. Squeezing the phone, she fought to stay calm.

"You'll never get her," she told him, her bottom lip quivering. "Not as long as I'm alive. Stacy belongs to me and Mom. You have no right to her."

Cleve snorted. "I got every right. And I'll do whatever it takes to make her mine again."

"You don't deserve her," Bethany responded, her fear of Cleve causing her voice to sound thin. "You ran out on both of us. Now you dare call me like this, in the middle of the day, and say you want custody? You can forget it!"

"I'm a changed man," Cleve said, staying cool. "Janette's made a big difference in me."

For a second, Bethany paused, remembering the first time she had met Janette. Then she shoved her lower lip into her mouth, biting off the bitter memory.

Get a grip, she thought, wiping her sweaty forehead with a trembling hand. *Remember what you learned in therapy. Don't give in to the anxiety. Breathe. Focus. You can deal with Cleve's manipulation.*

She closed her eyes, imagining Cleve on the other end of the line—his well-starched police uniform, his shoes so shiny you could see yourself in them, his gun holstered high on his hip. As he often said it, he liked to "look sharp, feel sharp, be sharp." Nothing sloppy about Cleve. Selfish almost always, but never sloppy.

"Maybe you have changed, Cleve," said Bethany, holding back her skepticism. "But that doesn't mean I'm going to cave in this time, just hand Stacy over to you. I've done that far too many times already. I'm not doing it again. Whether you know it or not, I've changed too. You can't push me around anymore." She nodded to herself. There, that sounded good. Not angry but not weak.

He grunted, dismissing her resolve. "Well, we'll see about all that. Either way, it doesn't matter a whole lot to me. I've already started the process to make her mine again."

"You've what?"

"You heard me. I've already started the process. You know me. I'll do whatever it takes."

"Take your best shot," said Bethany.

Cleve laughed, then hung up.

Bethany's knees buckled and she slumped to the floor, the phone banging once, twice, three times as she let it fall against the wall. A parade of legs passed her as people in the hospital went about their work, but she hardly noticed. For almost two minutes she sat there, struggling with a mixture of emotions—anger and fear, grief and despair, dread and loneliness. How dare Cleve try to take Stacy. After all he had done to both of them. He had no right to come back into

her life this way. No right at all! He had given up his rights, had forfeited—

Sitting under the telephone, Bethany suddenly heard it beeping. She blinked, then realized she had left it off the hook. Pushing herself up, she hung up the phone and refocused her thoughts.

Now wasn't the time for anger. Now was the time for cold logic.

Was she strong enough to face Cleve's latest insult, to keep him from getting Stacy? She didn't know.

She took several deep breaths, working to regain her composure. She had no clue what to do next—where to go, who to turn to for help. She knew she couldn't ignore Cleve. He would do exactly what he promised—would fight heaven and hell if necessary to get what he wanted. That's the way he was. Tenacious. An irresistible force. A man who refused to lose.

Bethany trembled. Worst of all, Cleve was a man who lived by a scorched-earth philosophy. If he couldn't win, no one else would either.

An overwhelming surge of tension bit through her throat, and her stomach flipped over. She was Cleve's enemy now. Not by her choice, but by his.

She tried to walk, but a swirl of black dots pushed up before her eyes and she staggered against the wall. Her heart pounded faster and faster, and a clammy sweat broke out in her palms. It was happening again! For the first time in three months—a panic attack—grabbing at her throat, threatening to squeeze the life from her.

She thought she had beaten them, that her therapy had gotten her past this helpless feeling, this sense of total weakness, total failure. But now the fear rushed at her again, a hyena gnawing at her body and soul, eating her alive. She hated feeling like this—that she was nothing, deserved nothing, should be nothing.

For an instant, she thought of the medication in her purse, how she could lie down on a bed at the hospital, swallow the pills, rest her head on the pillow, and cease to be. But she couldn't do that, she reminded herself, couldn't leave Stacy behind to face life alone.

No, where she went, Stacy had to go too. The two of them were inseparable. Cleve would never take Stacy from her. Better to die than to let that happen.

Bethany shuddered at the notion. She wouldn't do that for him. If anybody deserved death, he did, not her.

A fresh blaze of anger fired up in her stomach. Cleve did this! Like he had done almost from the day she married him. Maybe Janette Wilmer had done her a favor, though she didn't think so at the time.

A few months ago—right after Christmas—she had walked into her house on Azalea Court and found Cleve on the sofa with Janette, a bosomy redhead who worked at the health club where he worked out. Cleve's shirt was unbuttoned, and his holstered gun lay on the floor in front of the sofa. Lipstick the color of a peach smeared the side of his face, and his shoes were off. A dime-sized hole in the bottom of his left sock stared back at Bethany as she stood in stunned disbelief. Cleve and Janette didn't even pay her the courtesy of trying to explain. They just lay there, her arms locked around his neck, his black eyes wide.

Bethany didn't speak either. Amazingly, she felt guilty, as if she had done something wrong, as if she had somehow failed as a wife and caused this to happen. Like a trespasser, Bethany turned and stumbled out. Cleve didn't follow her. She was glad.

For the first few days afterward, she didn't even feel angry. Just shocked—stunned into an eerie silence. She and Cleve didn't speak of the incident. They didn't really have the time. He stayed gone close to sixteen hours a day.

Bethany walked around the house in a daze, unsure what to do or how to do it. Her husband of barely three years had broken the most basic rule of the marriage commitment. And he hadn't even bothered to apologize.

But she didn't know what to do about it. She thought about a counselor. Maybe a professional could save their marriage. But she knew Cleve wouldn't go.

She thought about divorce. But how? She had no money to get a lawyer. Sadly, she realized that Cleve had kept all their assets in his name.

Five days after the episode, Cleve solved her dilemma for her. He called from the precinct and told her he had filed for a divorce. A family had turned out to be more responsibility than he wanted, he said. At twenty-seven, he was too young to give up his freedom and settle down to one woman.

Worst of all, he informed her, she would have to move out of the house. He had stopped the payments on it, and since she had given up her work as a nurse when Stacy was born, she had no way to keep up the mortgage.

The suddenness of Cleve's action didn't surprise Bethany. He operated that way. Not an indecisive bone in his body. Handicapped by her natural inclination to back down when threatened, she let Cleve have his way. She left the house, dragging her baby to her mother's tiny apartment in one of the busier sections of northwest Atlanta.

For three months, they lived there while Bethany searched for a position at a hospital. Those months were the toughest. Finding a job took far longer than she had anticipated. She had to borrow money, first from her mother and then from a finance company. Depression and anxiety made sleep difficult. She chewed her nails to the quick and lost almost twenty pounds.

In those darkest months, she second-guessed her whole life—cried into the wee hours of the morning, put herself down, wondered why she couldn't please her man. More than once she considered closing shop for good, pulling down the shades, calling it quits.

The notion intrigued her, beckoned to her like a siren singing an appealing song. "Here," the siren called. "Here the pain will end. Here the silence will flow over you. Here the pain will end."

But Bethany didn't do it. Somehow she held on.

Then, just as she hit bottom, she found the job she wanted—as an operating room nurse at Murphy Memorial Hospital. The position carried only one drawback—the hospital was located thirty miles from her mom's apartment. She and Mom and Stacy would have to move.

That's how they ended up in the Lincoln Family Trailer Park. With no money for a down payment on a house and no apartment within their budget large enough for the three of them near the hospital, she opted for the cheap trailer. She didn't plan to stay there long, but until she could get her feet back on the ground and pay off her debts, it would do fine.

Fortunately, after she found her job and moved, everything seemed to turn for the better. The divorce was final. She loved her work. Her mom was unbelievably helpful. Stacy was growing like a weed, bringing incredible energy to both Bethany and her mom. With the insurance from her job paying for most of it, Bethany started seeing a professional counselor in early April.

The sessions forced her to dig into her past, to examine how and why she felt drawn to a man like Cleve in the first place. The therapy began to make a difference. She felt stronger. She almost stopped blaming herself for the divorce. Things definitely looked brighter.

Yes, the sessions made her stronger. But had they made her strong enough to stand up to Cleve's constant drive to control her? She didn't know. But she did know this—she wouldn't give in without a fight. This time, for the first time in her life, she would raise her claws and fight for herself and for her family.

Bethany gritted her teeth and straightened her spine against the wall of the hospital. She wouldn't allow another panic attack! To do so meant Cleve still had power over her.

The black dots in her eyes faded, and she slowed down her breathing. She could handle this, she reminded herself, she could deal with Cleve. But she couldn't do it right now, not here in the hospital. No, she needed a quiet place to focus and sort through it all.

She leaned back, her shoulders flat against the wall. She knew what she would do. She would take the afternoon off, leave the hospital, get some space to work out this problem. She had options. That's what her therapist kept telling her. She controlled her own destiny.

Her decision made, she walked to the nurse's station and told her supervisor she didn't feel well and needed the afternoon off. The supervisor nodded, letting her go without question.

Five minutes later, without a destination in mind, Bethany hustled across the rain-slick parking lot, climbed into her seven-year-old Toyota Camry, and pulled onto the highway. Passing through a red light, she considered her choices.

She didn't want to go home. If she did, she would have to explain the whole mess and that would upset her mom. Lydia didn't need that, not with her high blood pressure and all.

She thought about calling her counselor but realized he was probably booked with clients. Besides, she needed to handle this herself. That was a major lesson she had learned in her therapy—be more assertive. Don't let other people dictate to you what you should do. Trust your own instincts. She had what it took to handle herself, her therapist said, if only she would do so.

Sighing, Bethany vowed she would do just that. Even if it did feel so unnatural.

Her car tires humming over the highway, Bethany tossed several

ideas through her head. Go to a bar, have a couple of drinks? Stew through this latest mess in her life?

She turned a corner and stopped at a red light. She heard thunder rumbling to the west. No, she thought, a bar won't help anything. Besides, with her therapist's help, she had completely stopped drinking. It never solved anything anyway, and given her father's alcoholism, she feared she might have alcoholic tendencies herself. To take a drink today made no sense at all.

If not a bar, then where? A coffee shop maybe? A cup of mocha and a bit of time to mull through everything? The light changed and she turned left and headed to the Cross Branch Mall.

A coffee shop would do fine. It would provide a quiet place, a place where she could decide what *she* wanted to do.

She whipped through the traffic, passing a line of cars to her right. The sky darkened overhead and the rain began to fall harder.

What *did* she want to do? Cleve wouldn't give up easily. She knew that. Amazingly, his stubbornness had originally attracted her.

He was so unlike her own dad, a man who gave up on almost everything he ever started, a man with no strength to see a job to its conclusion. He bailed out on a succession of careers—most of them pretty good ones. Schoolteacher, manager of a mall, salesman for a computer company, part-owner of a bookstore. He left each job after about three years, moving the family from one place to another, a man with no root system.

He bailed out on his family the day Bethany turned sixteen, left the house without warning just after breakfast. He left no note, no birthday present, no explanation. He just vanished. Bethany had not heard from him since. She didn't even know if he was still alive.

Cleve seemed just the opposite of her father. He was the most decisive person Bethany had ever known. A tall man, almost six-five. Burly too, with a chest like an oak desk. When he strapped on his gun and pinned on his badge, he seemed invincible.

Bethany sighed. Now he had turned his power against her. A pair of tears climbed to the corners of her eyes. The tears exposed what she had been trying to camouflage since the moment Cleve called. She didn't have enough courage to stand up to him. If she had to deal with Cleve all by herself, she would never survive. It would take more than she had to fight this battle. It would take . . . well, she didn't know what it would take. A sense of hopelessness draped across her shoulders. She might as well give it up.

Suddenly, the idea of the coffee shop seemed ludicrous. What could that help?

More tears tumbled down her cheeks, and she licked the salty moisture into her mouth. But then, angry at herself for being so weak, she flicked the tears away and forced herself to bear up.

If not the coffee shop, then where? She turned right, still headed to the mall. Lightning flashed outside, and through the trees that bordered the highway, she saw a spire cutting through the falling rain. For a second, Bethany dismissed it. But the spire stayed in her view as she rounded a curve.

She knew the place. Trinity Lutheran Church. She passed it daily on the way to Murphy Memorial. A nominal Lutheran herself, she had grown up going to church but had drifted away from it during her college days and the marriage that followed. Religion seemed so . . . well, so irrelevant, and the God the church promoted felt remote, even nonexistent.

Squinting through the rain, Bethany quickly diagnosed the state of her religion and concluded she didn't really have any. An apathetic agnostic, she decided with a wry grin, that's what she was. She didn't believe in God anymore and didn't much care that she didn't.

A blast of lighting bounced off the church spire and reflected into Bethany's eyes. In spite of her indifference, the spire seemed to beckon to her. It towered in the storm like a lighthouse offering guidance to a lost ship.

As if by its own accord, her Camry slowed and turned right onto the street leading to the church. *Okay,* she thought, giving in to the compulsion, *a church is a quiet place, good enough for what I need.*

Feeling eerily keyed up, she parked under a pine tree and climbed out. She walked through the rain toward the white-bricked building to her left. At the door, she looked up. The spire seemed to wink at her, a secret joke between the two of them.

She tried the door handle. The door opened and she walked inside, her toes raised so as not to disturb the quiet. A carpeted vestibule led straight into a sanctuary and a row of glass chandeliers, each one at least five feet in diameter, burned overhead. Bethany took a seat on the back row. She shivered as her body took note of the building's air-conditioning.

 30

Snuggling down into the upholstered pew, she folded her hands and stared toward the front of the rectangular room. Windows lined the walls on both sides, and a grayish light from outside streaked through them. Up front, a communion table with a golden cross standing in the middle provided the centerpiece of the split chancel.

Staring at the cross, Bethany closed her eyes, bowed her head, and took a deep breath. She decided to try to pray. She cleared her throat and opened her mouth to speak. The sound seemed to scrape the walls of the silent room. But no words came out.

She thought maybe she needed to make her apologies to God for her long absence, but it felt unnatural to her, presumptuous even, to think that she could just walk back into a church and begin to pray as if she had never left. She had no right, she decided, no right at all to expect God to welcome her back so easily. Nothing came without a price. If life had taught her anything, it had taught her that.

She opened her eyes and saw the cross again. It dominated the room, drew her eyes no matter how hard she tried to look away from it. Wait a minute! Didn't God give her the right to come back? Was that what the cross was trying to tell her? Yes, exactly that. God didn't hold grudges! Instead, God waited—patiently—for missing sons and daughters to come home.

Bethany nodded to herself.

The cross. Grace. Forgiveness.

God was a big one for second chances.

So satisfied, she tried to pray again, bowing her head lower and squeezing her eyes tighter.

"Lord," she started. "Lord, . . . I don't know exactly what to say or . . . how to say . . . to say it. But if you're listening . . . well, if you're there . . . you know, well, . . . I'm looking for some direction. I'm here, asking for help. . . . So just, just show me what you want me to do. . . . Show me and I'll try to do it. . . ."

She paused, waiting for some answer. Nothing happened.

She waited again, expectantly, hoping to hear something—a roar, a word of some kind. But nothing happened—no visions, no voices. The storm rumbled outside, but other than that, nothing.

Clearing her throat again, Bethany wondered what the quiet meant. Did it mean that God was absent? Or was he gone, like in never was, nonexistent?

Or maybe God was silent because He didn't choose to speak. Maybe God was speaking but she simply didn't know how to listen.

Another thought hit her. Could it be that God was silent so He could better hear what *she* said?

Bethany opened her eyes and unfolded her hands. Okay. She didn't have the time or energy to figure it out right now. But the silence reminded her of one thing. Right now, she had to do something. And until God did speak, she couldn't count on anyone but herself. She would have to handle this on her own.

A clap of thunder boomed outside. The rain pounded harder and harder on the roof. Staring through the windows at the increasingly dark afternoon, Bethany slumped back against the pew, suddenly feeling exhausted.

She was weak and she knew it. Worse still, Cleve knew it. That's why he dared talk to her the way he did. She had never stood up to him, so he had no reason to think she would this time. For that matter, neither did she.

A streak of lightning sizzled and lit up the window directly to her left. For a second, Bethany turned and stared at her reflection in the glass. What she saw scared her. Frailty. Emptiness. Hopelessness.

Instantly, she knew what she needed to do. She would have to fight fire with fire. If Cleve lived by a scorched-earth policy, then so would she.

For the second time that day, tears crawled onto her high cheekbones. A dull ache drilled into her soul. What she had to do would take more courage than she had ever known. But she knew of no other choice. She had to do what she had to do.

Though frightened by her decision, Bethany also felt empowered by it. She could act, she decided. And the action would startle everyone who knew her. Her course set, she eased from the pew and walked out of the church.

As she crawled back into her Toyota, a surprising question came to her. Did the decision she had made come from God? Or from some other, less divine source? Well, she had no way of knowing. But time would surely tell.

Now, almost four hours later, she turned down the gravel road to her trailer. For the moment, the rain had stopped. A sliver of late afternoon sun peeked through the swiftly moving clouds as if to get

 **32**

one last glance before the day ended. The smell of wet earth filled Bethany's nostrils.

A hundred yards down the road, she spotted a white car. Tucked just inside the windshield, a blue light flashed. In front of her, a pencil-thin black man in a police uniform and a yellow rain slicker stood in the middle of the road, directing traffic, pointing the cars down a road to the right, one turn up from her place. As the cars detoured away, she inched forward.

Reaching the policeman, she rolled down her window. "What's going on?" she asked.

"Nothing to get alarmed about," he said. "You'll just need to detour here."

"But I live down there," she said, pointing to the end of the road, past the two police cars that blocked her view of her trailer.

The cop's face wadded up like a piece of crushed newspaper. "Down there?" he asked, gesturing past the cars.

"The last trailer on the end," she said.

"Are you Mrs. Chapman?"

"Yes, Bethany Chapman. I live—"

"Get out of the car, Mrs. Chapman," he said, interrupting her.

"But—"

"Don't argue with me," he snapped, the brown eyes in the middle of the wadded-up face rounding out as big as capital Os. "Just step out of the car."

Not wanting to fight, Bethany obeyed, unsnapping her seat belt and climbing out onto the wet road.

"I need to search you," the policeman said.

"Excuse me?"

"I need to search you."

"Not before you tell me why," said Bethany, her voice rising with tension.

The cop exhaled and his shoulders sagged for a moment. "Look, Mrs. Chapman, I don't like this anymore than you do, but I've got a job to do. I was told to search you and hold you if you showed up. That's all I can say."

Bethany pushed her hair back and stared hard at the cop. "Listen, Officer," she said, "unless I'm under arrest for something, you will not search me. I live in the trailer at the end of the road. I need to know what's happened there."

"I can't tell you," the cop said, his thin jaw firm.

"Then you need to step aside."

"I don't want to do this the hard way."

"You don't have to," she said firmly. "All I want to know is whether or not my child and my mom are okay. Is that too much to ask?"

The man sighed. He turned and looked around as if hoping someone would give him some direction. Seeing his indecision, Bethany started to walk. The gravel crunched under her hospital shoes. Momentarily defeated, he didn't stop her.

Bethany pushed past him and threaded her way through the traffic jammed into the road in front of her house. Sweat poured off her face. Her heart pounded under her green hospital scrubs. She spotted a square of yellow tape wrapped around the fence that surrounded her trailer. Twenty yards away, a pair of EMTs loaded a stretcher into the back of an ambulance. Though a white blanket draped the body, Bethany instantly recognized her mom's wispy gray hair sticking through the sides of the oxygen mask.

The EMTs shut the ambulance door.

Bethany started to sprint. Gravel sprayed under her feet, flying in all directions. She didn't head for the ambulance. Instead, she rushed toward the trailer. If her mom was receiving oxygen, she was still alive. Her question was about Stacy.

At the gate, Bethany unsnapped the latch and slipped under the crime scene tape. A blond-headed policeman with a flat-topped haircut ducked his head and stepped smartly from inside the mobile home. Seeing him, Bethany's heels dug into the gravel and she came to a quick halt.

"Your mom's alive," Cleve called, his face impassive, revealing nothing. "But just barely. It appears she had a stroke."

Bethany didn't move.

Cleve bounded down the steps as spry as a puppy chasing a bone. Bethany sensed instantly that he was enjoying the situation. He stopped right in front of her.

"Stacy is missing," he said, his voice calm.

Bethany shook her head quickly, side to side, as if trying to shake away the words. After a couple of seconds, she found her voice. "Where is she?" she asked.

 34

Cleve smiled slyly and his eyes danced. "I'm afraid you're going to have to answer that."

Quivering, Bethany took a step backward. "What does that mean?"

Cleve exhaled heavily and touched her arm. For a moment, Bethany thought he was being kind, gentle even. Her heart thumped faster, and she almost fell into his arms. His long fingers tightened like talons on her elbow.

"Don't you know?" he said, the smile still toying on his lips. "In the case of a missing child, the mother is always the first suspect."

CHAPTER FOUR

7:30 P.M.

Jackie Broadus couldn't remember a more depressing ride to the station. The whole scenario seemed unreal, beyond the pale of the possible.

Behind her sat Bethany Chapman, a woman seemingly as distraught as any she had ever seen. Helping her to the squad car a few minutes ago, Jackie thought she might collapse any second. And no wonder—her daughter was missing, her mother was in an ambulance on the way to a hospital, and she was in police custody for questioning.

Jackie tried to imagine Chapman's feelings but couldn't. Leaning her head against the seat, she stared out the window at the passing traffic. To her left, Officer Patrick drove. His partner, Cleve Chapman, would follow in a few minutes, after the lab crew began their inspection.

Overhead, a series of black clouds banked up—another line of storms passing through the city. A gust of wind momentarily threw the car off center. A crease of silver cut the sky, and a roll of thunder shook the highway. A sheet of heavy rain hit the roof of the car, ending the lull of the last half hour.

Jackie considered what she knew so far. They hadn't arrested Bethany Chapman, not yet anyway. But after a few minutes at the trailer, Jackie had decided that the best thing to do was get her out of the storm, go to the station, and let her make an official statement. That way, if Bethany satisfied her questions, she could get to her mother at the hospital before too much more time went by. Jackie had told Bethany almost nothing—only that her mother was in a coma and that Stacy was missing. Nothing about clues, leads, motives, or suspects. At this point, she didn't have much to tell. The only suspect was Bethany. And Jackie found that tough to swallow. What woman would hurt her own child? But she had to admit to herself, they did, far more often than she cared to consider.

Jackie shook her head, forcing herself to consider other possibilities. Who would abduct the baby? And why?

She pushed her hair out of her face and rested her chin in her palms. The rain dropped in sheets now, and the wind pushed the car side to side.

The baby could have been kidnapped, but that made little sense. From all appearances, neither Bethany Chapman nor her mother had any real money with which to pay a ransom.

Patrick turned the car to the left, going through a swaying red light. Not far to the police station now.

Jackie's thoughts returned to Stacy. If no one had kidnapped her, then what? Had Stacy wandered off by herself? A fence ringed the entire yard. Had someone left a gate open?

But if she had wandered out, where would she have gone? And why was the dog shot? No, it didn't seem logical that the child had left of her own accord.

Jackie sighed and wondered again about the attractive woman in the seat behind her. Who and what was Bethany Chapman? Why would she kidnap her own baby? And why shoot her dog?

In the backseat, Bethany chewed on her nails, first one and then the other. Since she had climbed into the police car, she had completely finished the right hand and started on the left. As she chewed, she wondered what Jackie Broadus thought of her, if she truly believed she could hurt her own baby.

Quivering with helplessness and suddenly chilled, Bethany dropped her fingers from her mouth and wrapped her arms around her waist. Her fingers dug into her sides, squeezing like vises into her ribs. Tears dropped down her cheeks, and she fought back a desire to scream.

The black-and-white squad car pulled into the parking lot of the station and stopped. Behind her, another cop piloted her Camry into a parking slot. She would need it to get home, Broadus had said when she asked for the keys.

Officer Patrick jerked an umbrella from the floorboard and jumped out. As polite as a valet, he opened Bethany's door and held the umbrella for her. Though she appreciated his kindness, Bethany ignored the umbrella and stepped out. Sheets of water instantly dropped onto her head, down her neck, and onto her scrubs. In a second, she was soaked. She didn't care.

With Broadus leading the way, Patrick herded her toward the police station—a square, red-brick structure. Four square windows in the front. None on the sides. Green hedges bordered the drab building all around but failed to dress it up much. The grass in the yard was brown.

Steeling herself, Bethany followed Broadus and Patrick as they ushered her through the familiar doors. Inside, Broadus quickly disappeared. Bethany stared around the precinct. She had been here scores of times. The Longstreet Station. Cleve worked out of this building.

In times past, it had seemed so safe. The place where her tough husband protected her and the rest of society from the criminal types who stalked the city of Atlanta. What a naive illusion that had been. Today, she knew differently. Nobody protected her. The building now felt ominous.

A flash of lightning cracked outside, and thunder vibrated the floor under her feet, startling her away from her memories. Patrick touched her elbow, indicating she should follow him. He led her to an elevator, then punched the button for the fifth floor—the floor that housed the interrogation rooms. Stepping out, Patrick pointed her to the last room on the right.

Still dripping wet, Bethany entered the room and plopped down in a straight-backed chair beside the only table in the cubicle—a 4-by-4 square one in the center of the tiny space. A recessed light hummed overhead, and the place smelled of an odd mixture of stale sweat and pine-scented air freshener.

Bethany leaned forward on the table, placing her head in her hands. Patrick stood over her shoulder near the door.

As the ex-wife of a cop, she knew the routine—the questions they

   *Dark Road to Daylight*

would ask, the games they would play, the verbal threats they would make. At least she held that advantage. They wouldn't surprise her.

She could do this, she assured herself. Just tough it out and go, do what she had to do, go—

She heard the door open. Jackie Broadus walked into the room.

Bethany stared at the tall detective, noted her khaki slacks, navy jacket, and white blouse. Her dark hair cut right at chin level. She had dark blue eyes and an athletic frame. About thirty-five or so, Bethany guessed. An attractive woman—the prettiest detective she had ever seen.

Broadus nodded to Patrick, and he walked out of the room. The detective took the seat opposite Bethany and tossed her a white towel. "This is a tough job sometimes," she said, her voice soft and reassuring.

Bethany took the towel and wiped off her soggy hair, but felt little sympathy for the detective.

"Like this situation," continued Broadus. "A missing child. The child's grandmother in the hospital. A dog at the vet, nearly dead."

Bethany dropped the towel onto the table. She hadn't even thought of Scooter. "What's wrong with the dog?" she asked.

"A gunshot wound. That's what brought us to your place. The dog's howling woke a woman near you from a nap. At first she thought the dog was just scared of the thunder. But he kept yapping—even when the storm calmed down. So she called the cops. Officer Patrick found the dog, then your mom inside. Thirty minutes later, I got there."

Bethany threw her head back and stared at the ceiling. It was white and bare and bleak.

"How bad is Scooter?" she asked.

"Not as bad as we first thought. The bullet cut through the thickest part of the hair on his chest. He's got a flesh wound but nothing vital was hit. The worst part was the bleeding. The vet gave him a transfusion and says he should make it."

For a moment, Bethany stayed silent. Broadus didn't push her. Seconds ticked by. Bethany fought to keep her fingernails out of her mouth. "Somebody took my daughter," she said finally, her tone flat, like a computerized voice.

Broadus nodded. "Apparently so."

"But who?"

Broadus grunted and stood up, moving to a soft drink machine in the corner. Pulling coins from her slacks, she dropped them into the slot and punched a button. A diet Dr. Pepper fell out. She repeated the process, then twisted back around, placing both drinks on the table.

"That's the mystery," she said. "Who took your daughter?" She sat back down. "You got any ideas?"

Bethany chewed a thumbnail before answering. "I have no way of knowing," she said. "But I can tell you it wasn't me."

Broadus popped the top of her drink. Bethany ignored hers. "I certainly hope it wasn't," the detective said, "but I'm sure you understand we have to check you out. Someone in the immediate family is always the most likely suspect."

Bethany nodded. "I understand. Since that South Carolina woman killed her two boys, people are even more suspicious of the parents, I expect."

"Sadly, in more cases than not, the mom or the dad *is* the culprit," Broadus said.

"That may be so, but you're wasting your time with me. I couldn't hurt my daughter. She and my mom are all I've got."

Broadus twisted the drink can in her fingers. "I want to believe you," she said. "I don't much like the alternative. But I still need to ask you some questions."

"Ask away. The sooner you ask, the sooner I can get out of here and start looking for my baby."

Broadus paused, took a sip of cola, then asked, "Where were you this afternoon?"

"I worked until just after two. Finished up a surgery, then took the afternoon off. I left the hospital and went to Trinity Lutheran Church."

"Trinity Lutheran?" Broadus arched her eyebrows.

"Yeah, I needed a quiet place."

"You in the habit of leaving work and going to church in the middle of the afternoon?"

"Nope," said Bethany, dropping her eyes. "Fact is, I've never done that before in my life."

"So what did you do at Trinity?"

"Oh, I sorted a few things out."

"What kind of things?"

"Personal things, you know, family things. I'm recently divorced."

Broadus twirled her drink can. "Anybody at the church see you? A pastor, a custodian maybe?"

Bethany considered the question for a moment, then shook her head. "Nope, no one I can recall. I was alone."

"Tell me about these personal things."

Bethany shifted in her seat, almost stuck a finger in her teeth, then pulled it away. "I don't know that I can."

Broadus shrugged as if Bethany's problems didn't matter. But she pressed on with her questions. "Well, you need to try—that is, if you want to clear this up and get out of here."

Bethany bit her lower lip, weighing her options. She didn't see any way but to answer Broadus directly. "My ex-husband called," she said.

Broadus leaned forward, her elbows on the table. "And?"

"He told me he wanted custody of Stacy. Said he would do whatever was necessary to get her back. Told me he had already started the process for doing just that."

"I'm sure that upset you," Broadus said.

Bethany grunted and her voice notched an octave higher. "*Upset* isn't a strong enough word. He left back in early January—right after I caught him on my sofa with a big-chested redhead. Said he didn't like the responsibility of a family. Then he calls me today, tells me he's going to get married again and he wants custody of Stacy. It's insane. He's got no business with my daughter, and if he tries to get her, I'll fight him every step of the way."

"Will Officer Chapman verify that he called you?"

Bethany paused. She hadn't thought of that. If Cleve wanted to play really dirty, he might not. "I don't know."

"You don't know?"

"Cleve's the most competitive person I've ever known. If he thinks lying about his call will help him get Stacy, he'll probably lie about it."

"Anyone else know he called?"

Bethany shook her head. "Not that I know of."

"Well, I'll have to ask him anyway," said Broadus.

"It'll be complicated, what with both of you working here and all."

"I know. But that goes with the job."

"You know him well?"

"No, barely at all. I've only been at Longstreet a short while."

"He's not somebody you want to know too well."

"Why's that?"

"Hang around him long enough and you'll see."

Broadus opened her mouth as if to speak, then paused.

"You'll ask him about the call, won't you?" asked Bethany.

"Sure I will," said Jackie. "Now, you say that after he called—that's when you left the hospital?"

"Yeah, right after. I was frantic, I had to go somewhere to think."

Broadus sipped her soft drink. The clock in the corner buzzed as the second hand twirled a quarter turn. Broadus set her drink down. "You've got blood on your clothes," she said, her nonchalant tone belying her deep interest.

Bethany popped back in her chair, the front legs of the seat rising off the ground. The statement sounded preposterous to her, but she knew immediately what it implied. For the first time since she sat down in the interrogation room, she felt her composure slipping away. She had done so well to this point. But this unnerved her. She stammered when she spoke. "I work . . . in the—the operating room. Blood isn't . . . isn't unusual there. I come home—more nights than not—with blood on my scrubs. I had just finished in surgery when Cleve called, I didn't have time to change, I left the hospital—"

"You went to the church in those bloody clothes?"

"Yeah, it never dawned on me to change. I was so upset, I didn't think about what I had on. I just got out of there, looked for a quiet place to get my head straight, I . . ." Her voice trailed off, sounding lame, like a killer trying to come up with an alibi. She buried her head in her hands.

"I'll need the clothes," said Broadus, her voice even in spite of the emotion in the room. "We can test the blood, make sure it matches that of your patient. They'll have a record at the hospital."

Bethany raised her eyes. Of course—the blood would verify her story. So would the hospital surgery records.

Broadus cleared her throat and stood up. She leaned over the table, peering into Bethany's face. "Look," she said, "I don't want to keep you any longer than necessary. I know you must be going crazy with worry. But these questions are my job. I'm sure you understand."

Bethany nodded, her mind numbed. "I do," she mumbled, "I understand. If I were in your place, I'd do the same thing."

Broadus walked away and stood by the only window in the room, a square one in the center of the bare wall across from the table. The rain had stopped momentarily, but clouds still hovered overhead. "Any enemies who might want to hurt you? Get at you through your daughter?"

"No one but Cleve."

Jackie stared out the window. "You really think he might have done this?"

"It's possible. If a mother could, why not a father? Besides, he did say he would do whatever was necessary to get her back."

"But wasn't he on duty?"

"Yeah, but he could have hired someone else to do it for him."

Broadus turned from the window. "He'd have to stoop pretty low for that, don't you think?"

Bethany nodded. "But it's possible."

Broadus shrugged. "Sure it is. Any other enemies in your life?"

"None to my knowledge."

"What about money? You got any?"

Bethany almost laughed. "Yeah, I'm loaded, that's why I live in a rented double-wide."

"What about Cleve? He have any money?"

Bethany sat up taller. Of course. "Cleve's family does," she exuded. That would shift the suspicion away from her, and it made some sense. "His dad owns a couple of golf courses. But Cleve is the black sheep of the family. Didn't follow his blue-blooded heritage."

"So he became a cop?"

"Yeah, something like that."

"But his family has money?"

"Not tons, but some. Enough for a ransom maybe."

"So kidnapping isn't totally out of the question?"

"I guess not."

Her pumps slapping against the tiled floor, Broadus stepped back to the table. "We'll need to set up a listening station at your place for a couple of days. See if anybody calls."

Staring up at the detective, Bethany forced a half-smile. "Whatever you need to do to find my daughter."

Broadus placed a hand on Bethany's shoulder. "We'll do all we can."

"Can I go now?" asked Bethany.

Broadus patted her shoulder. "For now, yes. But don't take any trips. I'm sure I'll need to visit with you again. And leave your scrubs."

"What will I wear home?"

"We brought your car, remember? You had some things in a gym bag in the backseat."

"How'd you know that?"

"The officer who drove your car told me. Change in the bathroom down the hall."

Bethany took a deep breath, stood, and walked from the room. In the hallway, Officer Patrick handed her a teal gym bag. Grabbing it, she turned, stared back at the interrogation room, and shuddered. Somehow, she suspected she would end up in that cubicle again.

Less than ten miles away, a swirling wind blowing west to east whipped a fresh set of chunky black clouds to a spot directly over Bethany Chapman's trailer. The clouds, heavy with moisture, sunk lower and lower in the sky. Lightning flashed and the clouds suddenly disgorged their contents, the rain splashing down in a torrent heavier than anything that had fallen all day. Instantly, it created rivulets and streams and rushes of foamy liquid. Within seconds, a swirl of the water lifted a golden earring off the earth where it lay at the edge of Scooter's doghouse. Gurgling and gushing, the water balanced the earring like a life raft, floating it on the top of a wave.

But the earring didn't float for long. Instead, its weight pulled it down and down, into a hole under the edges of the doghouse—a hole that Scooter had dug to bury a bone. The earring sank to the bottom of the hole, a buried treasure under a sea of turbulent water.

CHAPTER FIVE

9:00 P.M.

Leaving the police station, Bethany thought first about going straight back to her trailer. The last several hours seemed like an unreal nightmare that she could escape if she could only get home. At home she would find Stacy playing on the floor with Scooter. Lydia would be taking corn bread from the oven and placing a meat loaf on the table. That's what her emotions said—go home, nothing has changed. But she knew that as much as she wanted to ignore the truth, she couldn't. Everything had changed and she couldn't do a thing about it.

Right now, Jackie Broadus and a team of technicians were headed out to her trailer with a truckload of equipment. They would set up a listening post in her driveway and tap into her phone line to trace her calls. They would turn her quiet little place into a war room, hoping against hope that something would turn up to lead them to Stacy.

Speeding through the traffic since the rain had stopped, Bethany knew she would eventually have to deal with all that. But not just yet. First, in spite of her desire to get home, she had to go to the hospital and check on her mom. She had to hold her mom's hand and tell her she loved her.

A mile from the hospital, Bethany felt herself growing more and more despondent. Her mom had surely suffered a stroke. Doctors wouldn't yet know the extent of the damage. As a nurse, Bethany knew that no one could predict when or if Lydia would come out of the coma. She might die.

Bethany turned into the parking lot of Murphy Memorial and climbed out. Her shoulders sagged as she headed inside. She felt terribly alone. She wondered about Jackie Broadus. Did Broadus really think she had abducted her own child to keep Cleve from getting her? It certainly made sense. Or did the detective think a ransom call would come? Probably not. That wasn't rational. Thousands of kids in Atlanta had parents richer than Stacy's.

If not a kidnapper, then who would Broadus suspect? An itinerant molester? Some subhuman creature who drifted in and out of the big cities, preying on small children like a spider killing flies? A new Ted Bundy who happened by and saw her daughter?

In the lobby, Bethany climbed onto the elevator and headed to the intensive care unit. What about Cleve? she wondered. Surely if Broadus suspected her, she would also suspect him. Wouldn't she believe that he might have taken his own daughter? But why? If he planned on a custody fight, why announce it and then take Stacy? Why not fight it out in the courts?

But maybe Broadus would think that was a ruse. Cleve tells his wife he plans to fight in the courts to throw her off track about what he really planned. Perhaps Broadus would think he had Stacy right now, hidden away somewhere.

The elevator dinged, jarring Bethany from her thoughts. She clutched her arms around her waist, stepped off the elevator, and passed through the double doors into the ICU. She didn't have time for speculation now. Right now, she needed to focus on her mother.

Stopping at the nurse's station, Bethany asked for Lydia Spicer's room. The nurse, one Bethany didn't know, jerked her head to the left—room number nine.

Before entering, Bethany paused. She had stood in this spot many times with patients right out of surgery. She knew what to expect when she stepped inside her mother's tiny cubicle. But her previous experience didn't make this any easier. This wasn't a name on a hospital chart, an unknown person who came into her life for a few days and then disappeared. This time, her own mother lay in the 10-by-10 space, hanging on to a string of life as thin as a spider's web.

Bracing herself, Bethany pushed into the room. She saw Lydia stretched out under a cover of white blankets. Tubes protruded from her nose and throat. A heart monitor sat on the floor near her head and two bags of clear liquid pumped into her wrists from an IV stand.

 **46**

The smell of disinfectant drifted up from the body. Ignoring the smell, Bethany bent over and kissed her mother on the forehead. Lydia didn't respond. Bethany touched the top of her mother's right hand and rubbed it gently. Only the beep of the heart monitor disturbed the quiet of the room. Outside, a nurse walked by, her shoes shuffling along the tiled floor.

Bethany cleared her throat. "Mom," she whispered, "it's me, Bethany." Lydia didn't move. Bethany spoke louder. "Mom, I don't know if you can hear me or not, but I'm going to talk anyway. You just listen." She pressed her mom's hand harder.

"You were there, Mom, so you're the only one who knows what happened." The heart monitor clicked its rhythm. Lydia's chest rose and fell, the only sign of life in her body. Bethany suddenly felt tired, more tired than she'd ever felt in her life. If her mom didn't make it, she would have to deal with all of this on her own. She didn't know if she had the stamina to do it.

Still touching her mom's hand, she braced her elbows on the railings that surrounded the bed and hung her head. It just didn't make any sense. Why did this have to happen to her—just when she had gotten her life on track again?

A wave of helplessness slammed into her, and she felt herself going under. She would never get through this; it weighed more than she could bear. She was losing her grip. All day long she had fought to stay on top of it all. Now it just seemed so impossible, so incredibly impossible to bear up. The heart monitor beeped. Bethany stared at her mom. Her mom had borne up—over all those lonely years. In spite of all the seemingly impossible obstacles she faced.

Remembering her mom's stubborn survival, Bethany bit her lower lip and tightened her stomach. She had to make it. She took a deep breath and fought off the helplessness. She couldn't give in now, not when everything depended on her.

Bethany squeezed her mom's hand. She heard a slight moan. "Mom?" she called, her hopes rising. "Mom, can you hear me?"

Lydia's eyelids flickered, and Bethany leaned closer. Her voice quivered as she spoke, but she forced it to stay strong. "I need you, Mom. I'm all alone in this, and I don't know what to do or where to turn—so, Mom, if you can hear me . . . if you can hear me, squeeze my hand. Please, Mom, squeeze my hand." She paused to catch her breath and to give Lydia a chance to respond.

Silently, she waited. She glanced down at Lydia's hand, saw how tightly she had gripped her mom's fingers. She eased the pressure. Lydia moaned as if in relief. But she didn't squeeze Bethany's hand.

Bethany closed her eyes and dropped Lydia's hand. Okay, her mom couldn't respond. That's the way it was. She kissed her mom on the forehead, then turned and left the room. Outside the ICU, she paused to consider what to do next. She had no close friends in Atlanta. She trudged toward the elevator and punched the button. As the elevator door popped open, Bethany suddenly remembered. There was one person in Atlanta who cared about her. Her therapist. She would call him. He had helped her so much back when she had seriously considered—well, during the worst days of her depression. Yes, as soon as she got home, she would call her therapist. If he couldn't help her, no one could.

CHAPTER SIX

11:00 P.M.

His eyes darting from side to side, Rusty Redder stepped down from the cab of his Chevy truck and walked through the squishy mud to the passenger side. Overhead, clouds scuttled across the sky, carrying away the last of the summer thunderstorm. Distant lightning still occasionally flashed, but except for that, the night was quiet.

As if handling a Ming vase, Rusty opened the truck door and lifted Stacy Chapman from the seat. Under the influence of the cough syrup that Rusty had poured into her every two hours, her head drooped to the side and her eyes stayed closed.

Afraid to go back to his trailer after the kidnapping, he had stayed on the highways, waiting for the hour of delivery, stopping only to buy Band-Aids and a bottle of iodine for his swollen ear.

Now the time to hand over the child had come. He had arrived at the drop-off point—a deserted warehouse in a run-down industrial section of western Atlanta. He checked his watch—11 P.M. Right on time.

He grabbed a blanket from the front seat and wrapped it around Stacy's tiny shoulders. For a split second, he stared down into the child's face. *She'll be a looker one of these days,* he thought. *Like her mom.* A twinge of regret hit him as he wondered what would happen to the child, but he quickly pushed it away. It wasn't for him to know his employer's plans for the baby. His job was kidnap and delivery. He could live with that on his conscience. What happened later lay on somebody else's.

Holding Stacy close, he walked away from the truck, sloshing toward a windowless one-story building about twenty yards away. The building, a metal rectangle sitting on a concrete slab, appeared deserted. For an instant, Rusty wondered if he had the wrong place. But as he reached the tiny awning that marked the entry, the door of the building fell open. He squinted to see inside. The interior was dark, and the clouds rolling in front of the moon shut visibility down to nothing. Just as well, he figured. The less he knew, the better.

Taking a deep breath, he stepped inside. The floor felt hard under his basketball shoes. He waited several seconds, giving his eyes a chance to adjust to the darkness. He sniffed. The place smelled like oil and old rags.

In his arms, Stacy stirred. He glanced down at her. In the darkness, all he could see were her eyes. They were open, staring at him. The cough medicine apparently had just about worn off.

Rusty waited another second, not sure what to do. His instructions said to grab the baby and bring her to this location. After that, he would receive further directions.

Stacy whimpered. Rusty wished he had a cigar.

"Is the child as I requested?"

Rusty almost stumbled as the soft whisper cut through the dark building. He tried to locate the direction of the voice but couldn't. It came from nowhere, a sound not connected to anything he could see.

"She is," he said, his voice thin. "It's the girl, the one you wanted."

Stacy whimpered a second time.

"Is she perfect?" The voice was a woman's—the same one that had called him earlier in the day. It was gentle, the sound of leaves rustling in a slight breeze.

The question puzzled Rusty. But he didn't have the courage to ask what the speaker meant by it.

"I believe so," he said.

Stacy started to cry, softly at first, then louder and louder.

"The money is in your trailer." This voice came from a black corner to Rusty's left, a male voice, louder than the woman's, loud enough to be heard over the wailing child. "In your refrigerator. Cold cash, you might say."

Rusty squeezed Stacy tighter, hoping to quiet her. It didn't help. She wailed louder now, her voice huge in the square dark building. He

   *Dark Road to Daylight*

bent lower, moving his face near hers. "Shush," he warned. "It's okay." She stared up at him and her mouth opened for a second as if to smile. Her breath, sweet from the smell of the medicine, hit him, tickling his red beard. He grunted, confused by his feelings.

"Put the child down!" thundered the male voice.

Rusty almost stumbled backward at the sound. The voice reverberated through the cavernous building, echoing off the sides. "Leave the child!" bellowed the man again. "Leave the child and go!"

Rusty didn't need any further encouragement. Bending quickly, he set Stacy on the concrete floor and turned to run. He felt a hand on his shin. His heart rose in his throat. Stacy whimpered, and Rusty realized the baby had grabbed his pants leg.

For a millisecond, he thought about lifting her back into his arms and running out of the building, running from the voice that echoed like a demonic spirit around the black walls that encircled him.

"Go!" thundered the man.

Stacy whimpered and tugged at his jeans.

Rusty jerked away from the child's grip and sprinted through the open door. Outside, he scurried to his truck. Behind him, he heard Stacy squeal. Her sadness struck him right in the heart.

But it was too late now. He had finished his job. The ten grand waited for him at his trailer. What happened to the child now wasn't his business.

He climbed into the cab. Suddenly, the child's crying ceased, cut off sharply, like a knife slicing meat.

Rusty turned the ignition and reached to the dashboard for a cigar.

CHAPTER SEVEN

11:45 P.M.

Standing halfway between the head and the foot of the delivery table, Burke Anderson's brown eyes flipped like a tennis ball from his wife's face to the obstetrician's. Behind his mask, sweat rolled down his cheeks and his breath choked out in ragged gasps.

He felt out of place, like a slug at a Mensa convention. He didn't know where to stand. If he stood too close to Debbi's head, he couldn't see anything of the actual delivery. On the other hand, if he stood too close to her feet, he would see a lot more than he wanted to see. Not only that, he kept getting in the way of the doctor and nurse. No matter where he stood, it was the wrong place. So he kept sliding out and back, working as hard as he could to help Debbi. He didn't feel particularly successful. Not less than two minutes ago, he had taken her chin in his hands, looked lovingly into her eyes, and told her to breathe and focus, breathe and focus. She wanted none of it. She yelled at him, telling him his breath smelled like two-day-old pepperoni pizza.

Like the good husband he was, he bit his tongue, not reminding her that he had been with her in labor for the last fourteen hours and that, indeed, the last meal he had eaten was pepperoni pizza, which she had encouraged him to get for them both. For a second, he wished for the good old days, the days when the father stayed out of the birthing room, when he paced alone in a hallway, shut off from the arrival of his child. Those days seemed glorious right now, simple and—

"Push!" the obstetrician commanded. "Give it all you've got!"

Debbi obeyed, puffing out her cheeks in exertion, her normally clear green eyes bloodshot from her efforts. Gritting her teeth, sweat glistened on her forehead and a vein above her left eye stood up.

Though scared of what he might see, Burke eased to the lower side of the table. To his amazement, the crown of the baby's head had appeared. The hair looked dark, like his. A sense of awe washed over Burke. Beneath that hair was a head. Beneath the head, shoulders, a torso, legs and feet. He smiled. A head bone connected to a shoulder bone, a shoulder bone connected to a rib bone. . . . A child's song for his first child, his child with the most wonderful woman in the world. A woman with the body of a gymnast, the brains of a biochemist, and the beauty of a supermodel. Burke smiled. At least she seemed that way to him.

He stared at the baby's dark hair. It didn't seem possible that this moment had come. Not after all they had endured to get here. Debbi's pregnancy had taken every possible turn for the worse. She felt sick as a dog from the outset—nausea, high blood pressure, rapid heartbeat, dizzy spells.

Concerned that the baby would come too early, the doctors had put her to bed six months into the pregnancy. Burke smiled ruefully under his mask. Debbi hadn't taken too well to that. Said she didn't do invalid with a smiley face. The bed rest interrupted her incredibly active life. Made her leave her work as a reporter at the *Atlanta Independent* two months before she had planned.

Even on bed rest, she continued to have problems. She spotted blood over and over again. Then, three weeks ago, the child had flipped into a breech position. The doctor had turned it back in a tricky procedure on Wednesday. Finally, at about ten this morning, Debbi's water broke—five weeks early. She'd been fighting to deliver the baby ever since.

Burke blinked and pushed a strand of sweaty brown hair back under his cap. In spite of everything he and Debbi had endured, they had made it. Here he stood, thirty years old, about to become a father. He rubbed his palms on the legs of his blue hospital scrubs and watched as the baby's head edged farther out of Debbi's body.

His heart pumping in anticipation, he edged back toward Debbi's face. She paid him no attention. Her eyes were locked on the ceiling, her hands rigid at her sides, her fists clenched. The vein over her left eye looked like a mole run.

Though he knew Debbi was hurting, Burke couldn't help but smile. Even in pain, she looked beautiful. She had pinned her blonde hair into a neat bun on top of her head. Her high cheekbones glowed red—flushed from her strenuous labor. Her full lips were pressed together in concentration. Burke felt like bending over and kissing—

"Ease off," called the doctor.

Debbi collapsed on the table. Burke leaned over and kissed her lightly on the cheek. "Almost there, sweetheart," he said. "Our baby is almost born."

Debbi stared back at him, but her eyes weren't focused. The long labor had taken its toll. Gently, Burke wiped her forehead with a gloved hand. She took a deep breath and licked her dry lips.

"Almost finished, sweetheart," Burke repeated. "One more good push and you'll be done."

Her face wrinkled in pain as another contraction hit her.

"This is it! " shouted the doctor. "Make this one count!"

Debbi reacted instantly, throwing the full power of her well-muscled body into the effort. Watching her, Burke felt grateful that she worked out regularly through aerobic classes and some weight lifting. Though she generally refused to join him on his almost-daily five-mile runs, she still stayed in great shape. "Here it comes!" yelled the obstetrician. "Keep pushing!"

Debbi's back arched and she bit her lower lip. She moaned and a trickle of blood dripped out of the left corner of her mouth.

"Keep pushing!" yelled the doctor.

"Push, Debbi!" coaxed Burke.

The push exploded into a frenzy of activity. The baby's head slipped into the doctor's arms. The shoulders followed. The doctor grabbed the shoulders and eased them from the birth canal. The child's hips slid out and now the doctor held the whole body in his hands, the umbilical cord snaking back to Debbi like a diver's lifeline to the mother ship.

The child opened its throat and wailed. Debbi collapsed backward onto the table. Burke stepped away from her head and stared at the crying baby. The doctor nodded and Burke turned to the nurse. She held the child up for him to see. Then, from out of nowhere, she produced a pair of surgical scissors.

 54

Burke swallowed hard and a lump the size of a golf ball slid down his throat. With trembling hands, he took the scissors from the nurse and clipped the baby's cord. The instant he finished, the nurse took the child and sponged off its face. The baby wailed a second time. Within seconds, the nurse shoved a hat onto its head and a blanket around its shoulders. Finished for the moment with the child, the nurse handed it back to Burke.

He took the baby and held it up close to his face. A sense of gratitude unlike any he had ever experienced washed over him. This child he and Debbi had conceived, this child they had worried about for the last eight months, this child now lay alive in his arms. A tug of joy and relief pulled at his chest, and he felt like he wanted to cry.

But the baby beat him to it. A wail loud enough to wake the dead echoed through the birthing room. Burke smiled and his mask couldn't contain it. The grin creased up past his cheeks and crinkled the corners of his eyes. "Okay, little one," he said. "I know what you want. You want your mommy."

Easing back to Debbi, Burke lay the baby in her arms. "Here, precious, here's your baby girl." As if on cue, the child stopped crying.

Debbi snuggled her close to her chest and bent her chin to see her new daughter. "Joy," she whispered, her voice tired. "Elizabeth Joy, our baby girl."

Burke sighed, his sense of thanksgiving indescribable. He kissed Debbi on the cheek. "Our girl," he said. "We did it. We made a baby."

"You had the easy part," said Debbi, her eyes twinkling.

"Certainly the most fun," agreed Burke.

Debbi smiled at him, but tears also dripped from the corners of her eyes.

"I'd like to say a prayer," Burke said, his voice a whisper. Without a word, Debbi closed her eyes.

He placed one hand on Elizabeth Joy's tiny head and another on Debbi's shoulder. Quietly, so as not to disturb the others in the room, he spoke. "Lord, we're overwhelmed with feelings right now. We don't know what to say or how to say it. But one thought keeps coming to me—and that's how grateful we are. Grateful that you're a creator of life. And grateful that you allow us to help you do it. Thank you, O God, for Elizabeth Joy. Thank you for seeing Debbi through these last few months, as tough as they've been. And thank you for bringing this precious bundle of new life to us.

"As we become her parents, help us to do it correctly. Help us to show her what Jesus is like. Help her grow up to be just like her mommy—beautiful and healthy and smart. Help her to believe in you, O Lord, when the time is right for that to happen. And finally . . . Lord, if you can, help her like the Braves as much as I do. Amen."

He opened his eyes. Debbi pinched him on the forearm. "Forget the Braves part," she said. "Elizabeth Joy will pull for the Cardinals."

"No way, it's the Braves or—" His beeper went off, interrupting him. For a second, not realizing what it was, he didn't respond. The beeper sounded a second time.

Slightly agitated, Burke raised up from the delivery table. His pager—of course. He had forgotten to take it off. But he had left strict orders at the clinic not to be disturbed. He wasn't on call. His secretary knew the situation.

The obstetrician pointed past him. "You can call from outside," he said. "I've got a bit of work to finish here anyway."

"You okay, honey?" Burke asked Debbi, unsure whether to leave.

"Yeah, sure, I'm great," she mumbled. "You know, tired, but . . . fine . . . fine now that Elizabeth Joy is here. You go ahead. Check your page. And call our folks. I'll see you in a few minutes."

Grateful for Debbi's understanding, Burke kissed her one more time, pulled off his mask and stepped out of the room. What a woman he had married almost three years ago! A woman long on looks and brains, a woman who brought out the best in him and helped him overcome his innate shyness. A woman who could make twenty-five free throws in a row on a basketball court one day and win a Golden Keyboard Award for one of her newspaper articles the next. As Burke often described it, his marriage to Debbi showed that God still worked miracles. He didn't believe he could ever have won her on his own.

In the waiting area, he turned his thoughts from Debbi and spotted a telephone on the wall. Picking it up, Burke realized his secretary wouldn't have bothered him if it wasn't important.

He relaxed his shoulders. It was okay. Debbi had delivered their child, and both Mom and baby were feeling fine. If someone else needed him now, he could handle it.

Taking a deep breath, he leaned against the wall and dialed the number of the answering service for the Personal Care Clinic, where he had worked as a psychologist for the last three and a half years.

 56

CHAPTER EIGHT

12:35 A.M.

The conversation didn't last long. Molly, the secretary on call for the weekend, gave him a disturbing message—Bethany Chapman, a client of his for the last four months, desperately wanted to talk to him. She had put her off for over two hours, but the minute she found out from the nurses in the maternity ward that the baby was born, she beeped him.

Normally, Molly said, she wouldn't have called at all, but when Bethany called the office and explained the situation, how could she refuse? Her mother had suffered a stroke, and even worse, her daughter had disappeared. Besides, the woman said, Mrs. Chapman would meet him at the hospital in the chapel. Her mother was right there, so she needed to come back anyway. Her best judgment told her Burke wouldn't mind talking to Bethany for a few minutes since he wouldn't have to leave Murphy Memorial.

Listening to Molly, Burke quickly agreed. Molly knew about situations like these. His secretary at the clinic since he had started, she seldom disturbed him when he wasn't on call. About sixty, she treated him like the son she never had. Before he married Debbi, she often brought him food in clear glass dishes. She made a mean lasagna. And she made few mistakes. Though he needed to make some phone calls to announce his new daughter's arrival, those could wait a few minutes. A mother in a coma and a missing daughter took precedence over a couple of phone calls—as important as those were.

Hanging up the phone, Burke headed for the chapel, a cozy room with soft light and stuffed chairs two floors up from the delivery suite. On the way, he reviewed what he knew of Bethany. Separated from her husband in January, divorced in April. Mother of one small daughter. Living with her mother. Deserted by her dad on her sixteenth birthday. Low self-esteem, often thinking the worst about herself. In the past, she had suffered from periodic panic attacks, but recently she was getting those under control. Thought of suicide from time to time, but had never acted on her thoughts.

Getting off the elevator, he rubbed his palms on the thighs of his pants. He'd seen her about once every two weeks over the last four months. She had made good progress. No panic attacks in twelve weeks. She had started to get a handle on what had attracted her to her ex-husband—his strength, his sense of control. She had never felt any strength in her own father, had seen him as a man totally out of control.

She tended to give up her autonomy to others, to depend on them far more than she should. Though it would seem that her father's desertion would have made her more self-reliant, it had caused an opposite reaction, had made her feel inadequate, unable to deal with life. Her insecurities kept her miserable, indecisive, and guilt-ridden. Additionally, those insecurities led to her anxiety attacks.

At least now, as a result of the therapy, she knew all this. She recognized her patterns, understood her weaknesses. She also knew what she needed to do to get better. She needed to shape her own life, not let anyone else dominate her to the point that she lost her sense of self. Only when she learned to care for herself and depend on her own abilities would she be strong enough to stand up to her ex.

Yeah, thought Burke—she had come to those conclusions. But would she stick by them? Would she hold on to them when her emotions squeezed her by the throat and demanded that she give up and give in? Or would she let uncontrollable events shake her confidence and push her back to her former condition—a state that kept her hanging by a thread between coping and self-destruction? He wasn't sure how she would react to this crisis.

Burke turned left and entered the chapel. Bethany jumped to her feet like a startled deer, but Burke motioned for her to sit back down. She obeyed, dropping heavily on to a sofa that rested against the wall.

Burke pulled up a wingback chair and placed himself directly in front of her. Their knees almost touched. In the glow of the low lights, he noted her somber look. Circles wrapped around her eyes, and her lips curled downward into a grim frown.

He started to speak, but Bethany interrupted him. "I hope you don't mind my calling," she said, her voice barely audible in the quiet room.

Burke shook his head and leaned forward. "No, it's fine, I don't mind. Molly said you needed to talk to me."

"I didn't know you were at the hospital. I just called your office. Molly called me back, told me you were here."

"I've been here most of the day," said Burke, careful not to tell her he had left his wife and newborn child to visit with her. "So, tell me what's going on."

Bethany swallowed, then dropped her head into her hands. She pushed her right hand to her mouth, chewed for a second on her index finger. Burke saw a pinprick of blood where she had nibbled her nail down to the quick. Her old habit had reappeared with a vengeance. Burke waited, not wanting to rush her. After almost a minute, she sighed and raised her eyes.

"I don't know where to start."

"Start with the beginning," he encouraged.

She pushed her hair off her face. Her hands shook. "Okay, okay," she said. "At the beginning. This afternoon, just after two, Cleve called me. He told me he wanted custody of Stacy. . . ."

For almost fifteen minutes, Burke listened as she outlined the events of the day. As he listened, Burke thought how impossible this all seemed. These kinds of things happened to other people, not to people he knew, not to his clients, not to people he tried to help.

But then it dawned on him. Tragedies like the one Bethany found herself in the middle of happened almost daily in cities like Atlanta. Kidnappings, heart attacks, strokes, robberies, divorces, custody fights, murders—these kinds of experiences made up much of the fabric of the modern world.

Fact is, Burke had lived through a couple of experiences even more bizarre and unexpected than the ones Bethany now described.

Bethany's voice wound down as she concluded her account of the day. "So I called you. I didn't know what else to do. I needed someone to talk to me, give me advice, tell me something . . ."

She paused for a moment and dropped her head into her hands again. Her voice sank to a whisper. "I don't have any other family. Mom and Stacy are all I have, all I have . . ."

Burke waited before he spoke, giving her a chance to gather herself. "You did the right thing," he said. "I'm glad you called. You're not by yourself in this. I'll do all I can for you."

"You will?" asked Bethany, her eyes on Burke again.

"Yes, I will. I don't know exactly what that means right now, but if there's any way I can make a difference, I'll do it."

For an instant, a look of relief passed over Bethany's face. It quickly faded. "I don't really know what you can do either," she said. "The cops seem to believe I did this. They say the mother is often the first suspect."

Burke nodded. Having completed a Ph.D. in psychology, a dissertation that dealt with the role of the conscience in the development of the psychopath, and a number of clinical hours at the Atlanta Correctional Institute, he knew much of the data relating to criminal behavior. But no use pouring all that out on Bethany just now. "Who's working your case?"

"A woman, a detective at Longstreet. Her name's Broadus."

"Jackie Broadus?"

"Yeah, that's it. Jackie Broadus. You know her?"

Burke smiled. "Yeah, just so happens I do. But she used to work out of Peachtree."

"She said she just got a transfer."

"Yeah, some bad blood between her and a new captain at Peachtree."

Burke shifted to the chair's edge and rubbed his hands on his pants pockets, thinking about all the good things he knew about Jackie Broadus. She was a close friend. He and Debbi got together with her at least once a month. The last time she had brought a boyfriend with her, a guy named Aaron. Burke had introduced Jackie to him. Better yet, Burke had worked with Jackie through a personal crisis in the past year. After years of struggle, marked by guilt over a divorce and a sense of despair created by the constant evil she saw in the course of her work, she had become a Christian. She called him often, still dealing with questions about her new faith.

"I can talk to Jackie," Burke said. "We've worked together a couple of times."

 *Dark Road to Daylight*

Bethany tilted her head. "I don't understand," she said.

Burke smiled again. "It's complicated, Bethany, but you don't need to worry about it. I know Jackie from a ways back. I've—I guess you could call it 'consulted' with her on a couple of investigations. She's a friend of mine."

Her confusion still etched on her face, Bethany leaned back on the sofa. "So you think the investigation is in good hands?"

Burke shrugged, then stared at the distressed woman across from him. "Yes," he said finally, "I would definitely say that."

Bethany, her chin resting on her chest, wrapped her arms around her waist. Burke's eyes wandered above her head, saw a clock spinning the seconds off its rounded face, reminding him of how fast time clicked past. To the right of the clock, in the center of the wall over the sofa, was a wooden cross. Seeing that cross, he thought of something else he could definitely say. He could say with certainty that Bethany's situation was also in the hands of God. All of it—the investigation, Bethany, her mother, her daughter. Burke too, for that matter. They all rested in the hands of God. That's what he believed anyway.

But what if Bethany's mother died? And what if someone harmed Stacy? If they were in God's hands, how could Burke ever explain that?

With no answer to his own question, Burke said nothing else. Overhead, the clock ticked onward. Bethany sat on the sofa hugging herself. Burke leaned back in his chair and waited. He knew that soon he would leave her and go back to his lovely wife and little daughter. Then Bethany would face her problems all by herself.

Sighing, he glanced back up at the cross. As Burke stared at it, a realization came to him. Bethany didn't face all this alone. God walked with her through it. God offered her courage to face it. God extended hope even when she couldn't see any. But God didn't produce all of that in an unmistakable display of divine intervention. No, instead, God offered comfort and aid in human form. When God had a job to do, He chose a human to do it. Humans frail and feeble. But by the power of God, humans also strong and faithful.

Burke's eyes dropped to Bethany. He noted her slumped shoulders and shriveled posture. Gently, so as not to startle her, he leaned forward and touched her shoulder. God was with her, he thought. God was with her through him.

About seven miles away as the crow flies, Rusty Redder braked his truck and jumped out. Six big strides later, he yanked open the door of his trailer and bounded inside. Jumping over the pieces of a crossword puzzle that lay scattered on the floor of the living room, he hurried to the kitchen. With a jerk, he pulled open the refrigerator and then the freezer box within it. His eyes scanned the contents of the box, expecting to find a frosted Ziploc bag full of hundred-dollar bills.

That had been the agreed upon deal. He would deliver the girl and would receive ten grand. He smiled at the image of the frosted money. But then his smile faded. He didn't see a Ziploc bag.

Instead, he spotted a white index card sitting on top of his ice trays. Confused, he picked up the card and stepped back, shutting the refrigerator. The card felt cold in his fingers. A ridge of frost caked its edges. Rusty scraped away the frost and read the card. In black letters, three words stared back at him. "Your answering machine."

Rusty frowned. He didn't own an answering machine. He read the card again. Same words. "Your answering machine."

He scratched his head. It didn't make sense. He had completed his part of the bargain. Now he expected to get paid. Rusty believed in doing business that way. You do your job, the other guy does his. Everything depended on both fulfilling their part of the bargain. Anything else and the whole arrangement came unglued. That didn't do anybody any good.

As Rusty saw it, if you made a deal you kept your word. Even though he made his living by breaking the law, he still held to a certain code.

Hacked off at not getting his pay, he crumpled the card, dropped it into the trash can, and stomped out of the kitchen. This just wouldn't do. Gingerly, he touched the Band-Aid covering his left ear. His whole head still throbbed. He had done his job, even at great peril and continuing pain.

Plopping onto a sagging sofa in the living room, he thought for a second of Stacy Chapman, heard her cry out as he left her on the

 *Dark Road to Daylight*

concrete floor. He'd heard that sound ever since he left her. He'd heard it in the truck as he drove down the interstate. He'd heard it in a bar, over the music of the jukebox, when he stopped to swig down a beer. He'd heard it as he passed by the little girl's trailer on the way home. He'd heard Stacy's cry every second since he left her, and he didn't want to hear it anymore. He pushed his fingers into his ears as if to close out the little girl's cry, then threw his feet onto the top of the wooden coffee table resting in front of the sofa. He stared at his dirty basketball shoes. Beside them sat a telephone answering machine.

Rusty raised up from the sofa. Slowly, as if approaching a poisonous snake, he reached for the answering machine. A light on it blinked on and off.

Someone had brought the machine, then called him and left a message. His breathing growing heavier, he punched the play button. A heavy bass voice boomed into his trailer. He fell backward for an instant, the jarring voice making him wish he hadn't punched the button.

The message was simple. "Mr. Redder, you need to call when you get back. You know the number."

Rusty pulled a cigar from his shirt pocket, lit it, and stood up. For almost three minutes, he paced back and forth, back and forth across the tiny room. He didn't want to call back. Without knowing exactly when he reached this conclusion, he realized he didn't like this kidnapping business. Not that it scared him. It didn't. He'd faced tougher jobs in times past, jobs collecting money for loan sharks, jobs robbing grocery stores and private residences. Those held far more danger than taking a child. But kidnapping Stacy Chapman didn't seem right somehow; it didn't seem fair to steal a baby right out of her yard with no one but a skinny old woman to protect her.

Rusty sucked on his cigar, trying to decide what to do. He could simply ignore the message. Not call back. Move from his trailer, disappear, drop off the planet.

Rusty stopped pacing. He didn't have enough money to disappear. He scanned his trailer. Nothing of much value in the whole place. A used television and a small CD player. A stack of crossword puzzles he worked on at night. A few clothes in his closet in the bedroom.

Grunting, Rusty thought of the rest of his belongings. A rusty Chevy pickup and about a hundred dollars in a checking account he used to pay bills. All together, barely enough to buy a bus ticket out of Georgia.

He chomped on his cigar and stared again at the answering machine. Yeah, he knew the number. The number of the man and woman who had promised him big bucks. The couple who had broken their promise.

Yeah, he would call that number. He would call that number because if he didn't he would never get his money, and without his money he couldn't get away from all this—away from a boss man who welshed on his deals, away from a life of crime that suddenly left a bad taste in his mouth, away from a past that had brought little happiness and a future that promised even less. Worst of all, if he didn't call that number and get his money, he could never get away from the sound of Stacy Chapman's cry, away from the soft touch of that dear sweet girl who had grabbed him by the leg as if to ask him not to leave her behind.

Monday
August 25

CHAPTER NINE

4:00 P.M.

T he police left about an hour ago," said Bethany, her voice a dull monotone, her eyes black with grief. "They pulled out their equipment and left the trailer. No one called over the weekend—Detective Broadus is convinced no one will. Obviously, whoever took Stacy didn't do so for ransom."

Sitting across from her at the clinic, a hot afternoon sun burning through his window, Burke tilted his head to shade his eyes and kept quiet. Bethany looked devastated, her face as thin and lifeless as that of a stick woman drawn by a five-year-old. Her hair, usually curly, lay in strings across her shoulders and her fingernails were chewed so low Burke winced when he looked at them.

Burke knew much of what she told him from a phone conversation with Jackie Broadus earlier that morning. But he didn't tell Bethany that. Knowing it would help her to verbalize it all, he let her keep talking.

"On Saturday and Sunday, the cops canvassed every trailer in the park," she continued. "But they didn't find anything. They also searched the woods across from my trailer. Again, nothing turned up—no clues, no leads, no nothing. Detective Broadus alerted the FBI and the National Registry for Missing Children. They're doing all they can too, but so far, everything is coming up zero."

Burke leaned forward in his seat, feeling helpless. This was the toughest part of his job. He thought for a second about his role as a counselor at the Personal Care Clinic. His office was part of a corporation that had sixteen counseling centers scattered across

Atlanta and almost sixty more located in the other major cities of the South. Though the company was large, the PCC, Inc. administrators worked hard to keep their therapy centers cozy. They set up small operations—two or three therapists and a secretary or two in an office in a high visibility area. Larger therapy centers felt too impersonal for people. Polls showed it.

To Burke's satisfaction, PCC also worked hard to provide the counseling styles people wanted. That's why he fit in so well. A certain percentage of people—a particularly high percentage in the South—wanted a counselor who operated from a faith outlook. Specifically in the South, they wanted a counselor with a Christian background. Not that Burke only saw religious people. No, he had lots of clients who didn't have a single iota of religious leaning. But at the same time, his belief in Christian teachings actually gave him a built-in clientele PCC wanted to serve. Though the motives of PCC weren't necessarily his, he didn't really care. The company gave him freedom to live out his faith in his vocation, and he gave them a resource they wouldn't have otherwise had. The two fit well together.

PCC made counseling part of the neighborhood scenery. Like a dentist's office. Burke scanned his surroundings. They were comfortable, clean and neat. Green ferns in the corners. A brown leather sofa across from his chair. Rose carpet of high quality. Pastoral prints on the walls. Soft lighting. Subdued colors in the wallpaper. Only a couple of differences from the dentist's office—a couch instead of a dentist's chair. And no drill.

But a dentist could fix things more easily than Burke could. A shot of Novocaine, a drill, an extraction or two—a dentist could pull out the problem or clean out the problem or go around the problem. At times, Burke couldn't do any of that.

In the four years since he left the pastorate of a rural church in Cascade, Georgia, to do his Ph.D., he hadn't felt this way too often. But sometimes it did happen; he came to a dead end—a stone wall, a place where no answers came to him. He knew that it went with the territory. For that matter, it was just as common in life as it was in counseling. No matter what a person did, times came when he felt like a bug stuck to a windshield, unable to move in any direction.

For an instant, Burke wondered what would be worse—not finding Stacy or finding her dead. He shuddered at the thought and forced himself from it. "You must feel awfully frightened," he said, focusing on Bethany again.

"*Frightened* doesn't begin to describe it," said Bethany. "I'm numb, really, have been since Friday. I'm just going through the motions."

"Have you slept at all?"

"Just barely. I've tried, but I keep thinking about Stacy, keep thinking the phone will ring any minute and the police will tell us they've found her, they've found her and . . . well, that they've found her, that's all."

"I can get a doctor to prescribe a sedative," said Burke, glad to offer something.

Bethany pushed her hair out of her eyes. "No, I don't want any drugs. Not yet anyway. If I don't sleep in the next couple of days, maybe, but right now, I don't want anything clouding my thoughts."

Burke nodded. He leaned back and changed the subject. "How's your mom?"

"No change. Still in a coma."

"What's her prognosis?"

"No one knows. That's one of the worst things about all this. Mom knows what happened but she can't tell us. If she comes out of her coma, we might get some quick answers. But if she doesn't get better—"

Bethany paused, letting the statement hang in the air. Burke didn't take it up. He didn't know where to go with it if he did.

"I talked with Jackie Broadus," he said.

"Yeah, she told me."

"She said she was checking a couple of things on Cleve, but she has to be careful about it. Can't take the direct approach. She's new at Longstreet, plus she's a woman in a predominately male environment. She doesn't want to get off on the wrong foot. The uniformed guys can make her job tough if she does."

Bethany sighed. "Cleve certainly can."

Burke nodded. Bethany had told him about Cleve and his buddies. A couple of years ago, they had decided that a certain rookie—a female with a decidedly feminist attitude—wouldn't make it. Their method of intimidation took three forms. One, they "silenced" her and her partner—a male veteran of the precinct. No one spoke to either of them. This caused her partner to request a duty change. No one else wanted to work with her. Second, they contradicted her reports whenever possible. They made up minor changes, altered the facts slightly, made her look incompetent. Finally, and worst of all, they "inadvertently" walked in on her time and time again when she changed clothes at the end of her shift. She found herself with no privacy and no support. After six months she gave up and requested a transfer. Cleve and his crowd won.

At home that night, pumped up from an evening of drinking, Cleve had bragged about it to Bethany. She didn't find it the least bit funny, but what could she do, turn in her own husband? No way. "You really think Cleve might be mixed up in this?" Burke asked.

"I don't know, but he said he had already started the process."

"But where would he be keeping Stacy?"

"Has anyone checked Janette Wilmer's? Or Cleve's parents'?"

"Surely his parents wouldn't get mixed up in this?"

Bethany pursed her lips, thinking about it. "Maybe not. But they live in Montana in the summer. They may not even know Stacy is missing. Back at Christmas, before the divorce, we promised them they could keep her for a week or so in August. Maybe they think Cleve's just keeping his promise."

"So Cleve got someone to fly her out to Montana?"

"It's certainly possible."

"We need to get Jackie to check on it."

Bethany nodded, then glanced down at her watch. "My time is almost over," she said. "And I expect you want to get home. Molly said you and your wife had a baby last Friday."

Burke smiled. "Yeah, Elizabeth Joy, our first."

"You left her to come talk to me," said Bethany. "I want to thank you for that."

Burke dropped his eyes. "I wasn't much help in the delivery room anyway. Besides, when I got your message, the baby had been born. And you came to the hospital. How could I say no to a woman whose daughter had just disappeared?"

"Even so, you were kind to see me. I don't know if I could have made it through the night if you hadn't talked to—"

Burke's intercom sounded. "Dr. Anderson." Molly's voice cut through the room.

Disturbed by the interruption, Burke's face flushed for a second. Then he realized Molly wouldn't interrupt unless she thought it important. "Yeah, Molly, what's up?"

"Well, I don't know how to say this, Dr. Anderson, but, well, a couple of policemen are here. They say they need to see Mrs. Chapman."

"Okay, Molly, just a second." He turned to Bethany. "You want me to get rid of them?"

Bethany waved him off. "No, I better see them. It might be about Stacy."

Moving quickly, they both stood. Burke took her by the arm and walked her to the door. Maybe they had found Stacy, he thought. Or Lydia had come out of her coma.

His heart racing, he stepped out to Molly's desk. His heart sank.

Two policemen stood beside Molly. One with flat-topped hair the color of beach sand, the other a skinny black man with a face like a wrinkled newspaper. A sneer decorated the blond one's face. Instantly, Burke knew something bad had happened—or was about to happen.

"What can I do for you?" he asked, fighting to keep his voice even.

"We're here for Mrs. Chapman," said the guy with the sausage face, his voice not unkind.

Burke checked his name badge. Patrick.

"I don't understand," said Burke. "Is this about her daughter, her mother?"

"No, nothing new with them, unfortunately. This is about her."

Burke turned to Bethany. Her shoulders sagged and she seemed to have shrunk. The skin on her face hung like a snake's molt, lifeless, a shell without a body. She wasn't even nibbling on a fingernail.

"Are you okay?" he asked her, turning his back to the cops.

She nodded, but he knew she was lying. She wasn't okay, and from all appearances nothing would improve any time soon. He touched her elbow. It felt cold.

"What do you want with her?" he asked Patrick, his voice defiant.

"That's none of your business," replied the blond.

Patrick flicked a quick glance at his partner. "She needs to go with us," said Patrick, his tone gentle but firm.

"Tell me why," demanded Burke.

"You want me to answer him?" Patrick directed the question at Bethany.

Weakly, she raised her chin and nodded.

Patrick took a deep breath and hitched up his pants. "Well, I hate to say it, but she's under arrest in connection with the disappearance of her child."

Burke almost choked as he heard the words. Beside him, Bethany folded up like a dismantled tent and collapsed onto the floor.

CHAPTER TEN

8:00 P.M.

Not wanting the ringing to wake Elizabeth Joy, who had already fallen asleep for the evening, Burke hustled quickly to the front door of his newly bought house when the bell rang. Talking in a whisper, he welcomed Jackie and led her through the hallway to the den in the back of the house. There, he offered her a rocker by the dormant fireplace. He took a seat on the leather sofa that sat centered in front of the wide circle-topped windows that covered most of the back wall of the den. Overhead, a fan whirred, stirring the hot night air. Burke didn't like air-conditioning much so the windows were open. The sound of cicadas chirped through the window screens with a sweet regularity.

From the kitchen, Debbi and Burke's mom, who had come to help for the week, walked in. Mrs. Anderson, a stout woman with short gray hair and eyes that looked just like Burke's, carried a tray. On the tray sat four glasses of lemonade. Burke smiled at his mom. No matter what time of the day or night, if company came, she offered them food or drink or both. Fact is, she seemed to be offering someone food or drink all the time, whether they were company or not.

Mrs. Anderson offered Jackie and Burke the lemonade and both took a glass. Debbi took hers and sat down on the sofa beside Burke. Mrs. Anderson took the tray back to the kitchen. Probably to get some food, thought Burke.

"You've done some work on the house since I was here last," said Jackie, glancing around the den.

Burke nodded and sipped his lemonade. He and Debbi had leased the place for almost a year, then decided to buy it. An old two-story Tudor style with three bedrooms, it had needed a lot of fixing up. Since they purchased it, he had worked in the yard mostly, changing the flowers and shrubs, and on the front porch, painting it so he could enjoy sitting there with his wife and baby in his swing and two rockers.

"I'm getting there," he said, pleased that she had noticed. "But having a baby slows me down a bit."

Grinning, Jackie turned to Debbi. "I thought you were the one who had the baby."

Debbi shrugged. "To hear Burke tell it, you would never know. But it was me, I confess."

"You look mighty good for a woman out of labor less than seventy-two hours."

Debbi laughed lightly. "I'm about sixteen pounds away from looking mighty good," she said.

"She's already lost eleven," said Burke.

"But eight of that was the baby," said Debbi. "The other three the afterbirth."

"She's bound and determined to gripe about her weight." Burke grinned. "I keep telling her she looks super. She shouldn't expect so much so fast. The weight'll come off in its own good time."

For a second, the room fell quiet. Burke drank his lemonade and wondered if he should turn the conversation to the subject of Bethany Chapman, the subject that had caused him to invite Jackie over. Not that he needed a reason to invite Jackie to his home. He and Debbi and Jackie had history together.

The three of them had survived two murder investigations. Burke had played a big role in Jackie's recent decision to become a believer. He knew that since then she had seriously considered giving up her career. Knew that her faith caused conflict in her, caused her to want to leave behind the morbid crime scenes she visited so often. As she had put it, "I want to stop lifting bloody sheets."

Even more, she admitted to him—even if to no one else yet—she wanted to move beyond the dead to the living, to live her own life, maybe to find a husband and give birth to a child. Since her spiritual awakening, she had found this urge more and more insistent. Not because she thought that's what a "good woman" ought to do—give up her career to have babies—but because she felt that some part of her particular identity would come out only when she married and gave life to a child.

During her first marriage, she hadn't seen it that way at all. Back then, she wanted a career more than anything else. For fifteen years she had lived out that career. A good one. A fulfilling one in many respects. "But," she had told Burke, "a career can't sit by the fire with you at night. A career can't grow old with you. A career can't sit in your lap and play patty-cake or throw a ball with you on hot summer days."

As she saw it, she loved her work, but she had made a false god of it. With the discovery of the true God, her career now took less than first place. Now, she wanted more than what her job had to offer.

Watching Jackie, Burke realized that he felt obligated to her, protective even, like a brother to a sister. He knew Jackie felt the same way toward him. Burke rubbed his hands on the front of his pants. Jackie sipped her lemonade.

"You want to see the cause of my blimplike appearance?" Debbi asked Jackie, interrupting Burke's thoughts.

"I wondered when you would offer."

The three of them stood and made their way to the last room on the right end of the hallway that cut through the center of the house. Entering the nursery, Jackie surveyed the room in the glow of the night-light. A border of blue and pink rocking horses graced the top of the walls. Beneath the border hung wallpaper with matching colors. Paint the color of eggshells colored the space beneath the floor and the chair rail Burke had put up. In the corner by the crib stood a broomstick horse Burke's father had made. On one side of the white head, in a calligrapher's hand, he had written "Elizabeth" in pink paint. On the other side, "Joy." A black mane fell around the horse's face, and a pink ribbon knotted around its neck.

"It's a beautiful room," whispered Jackie.

"Burke did a great job with it," agreed Debbi, her voice also quiet.

"The least I could do," said Burke. "You were doing the hard part."

"Yeah," agreed Debbi, kissing him quickly on the cheek. "And you didn't have to gain thirty pounds to do it."

"Twenty-seven," said Burke. "You only gained twenty-seven. Don't make it worse than it is."

"Both of you be quiet," teased Jackie. "Let me look at this gorgeous child."

She stepped to the crib and leaned over. Elizabeth Joy lay on her stomach, her tiny hands tucked under her chin, her diapered backside covered by pink pajamas and protruding into the air. For several long moments, only the baby's breathing broke the quiet of the room. To Burke, the place felt like a church—holy, sacred. He loved the sound of a child at rest. Could anything sound as wonderful as that?

Jackie touched Elizabeth Joy on the forehead. The baby stirred, shifted her position slightly, then snuggled back into deep sleep. Jackie turned back to Burke and Debbi.

"You two must be thrilled," she said.

"Nothing else like it," said Burke.

"Even with the weight gain," said Debbi. "Nothing else like it."

The three of them walked quietly from the room and back into the den, taking their seats again.

"I hope to have one someday," said Jackie, lifting her lemonade glass to her lips. "Though my biological clock is winding down pretty fast."

"You will get married first, won't you?" teased Burke.

"I'm working on that right now."

"Oh?"

"Yep, you know that as well as I do."

"You and Aaron seeing each other that much?"

"Every time he's in town."

Burke leaned back in his seat. Aaron Hans, Jackie's boyfriend, worked with a computer firm as a consultant. Traveled a lot. Burke had met Aaron while studying at Emory. Had introduced Jackie to him. It pleased him that they had become this serious. Though Aaron was three years younger than Jackie, they had much in common. A sharp intellect, a keen sense of humor. A love for the outdoors. An intuitive spirit that made them sensitive to feelings.

"It's getting serious then?"

"You're being nosey, Burke," cautioned Debbi.

He held up a hand to stop her. "I can get nosey," he said. "It's the prerogative of a psychologist. I get paid to do it." He switched his attention back to Jackie. "So—tell me everything. It's safe with me, everything is confidential, remember?"

Jackie grinned and wrapped her fingers around her glass. "Not tonight, Dr. Anderson. When I know more, you'll be the first I tell. But you didn't invite me here tonight to talk about my love life." Her face turned serious and Burke understood. The time had come to deal with the tragedy that faced both of them. He instantly shifted gears.

"You arrested Bethany Chapman," he said.

Jackie sighed heavily. "Well, not me exactly. The district attorney's office told us to bring her to Longstreet on charges."

"And those charges are?"

"We're not sure yet. We haven't found the child, so it can't be murder at this point. But the DA thinks we have enough to believe the child has met foul play."

"You actually think she hurt her little girl?"

Jackie shrugged. "I know it's tough to believe, but mothers do it all the time. You know that. People who seem sane, compassionate, do the most horrible things. Something snaps in them, they come unglued, they lose whatever it is that makes them human, and they do the unthinkable."

"You think that's what happened with Bethany?" asked Debbi, interrupting Burke and Jackie. "She cracked up somehow?"

Shrugging, Jackie sipped her lemonade. "I'm not ready to say that."

"Then what's the basis for your suspicions?"

Burke leaned forward in his chair, anxious to hear Jackie's answer.

She said, "I'm not supposed to tell you."

Burke took a deep breath, but he didn't push. He knew Jackie well enough to know she would tell him if she wanted. But if she didn't, it wouldn't help to pressure her. Several seconds passed. Burke heard his mother banging around in the kitchen. Probably cooking something sweet.

Jackie dipped her finger in her lemonade, then licked it. A slight twinkle sparkled in her eyes. "You know I'm going to tell you, don't you?"

Burke shrugged and smiled. "It's up to you. But if you don't, I'm going to remind Aaron how young he is."

"You're a mean one, Burke Anderson," said Jackie. "Under that

kind of pressure, I don't have a choice. Here's what we've got. And this is serious, for your ears only."

Burke and Debbi nodded, their momentary levity forgotten.

"No one can account for Bethany's whereabouts Friday afternoon. She assisted in surgery from ten until about two, but from then until past six, she drops off the radar screen."

"Plenty of opportunity," said Burke, voicing the first line of a prosecutor's argument.

"Absolutely," agreed Jackie. "And we found bloodstains in her car. On the front seat by the passenger window."

Burke swallowed, not liking the implication of the blood.

Jackie continued. "Preliminary testing shows it's Stacy's blood. Bethany said Stacy fell last Wednesday evening, cut herself on her forehead, over her left eye. Said she took her to a drive-in clinic about a mile from the trailer park."

"They'll have a record of that," suggested Debbi.

"None there," said Jackie. "Bethany says the doctor on call that night knows her from the hospital, and since the baby didn't need stitches and he knew finances were tough for her, he didn't charge her."

"So he didn't chart it," said Debbi.

"Sounds reasonable to me," said Burke. "You can verify it with the doctor."

"Sure I could, if he were here. But he's not. He's on vacation in the Bahamas. Won't be back for two weeks. We're trying to reach him by phone right now, but no luck so far."

"Can't you wait two weeks before you arrest her?"

"We could except for one thing."

"The baby," said Debbi. "If she's still alive and you don't arrest Bethany, press her for information, two weeks is far too late to do anything."

"Exactly," said Jackie. "Besides, there's more."

"More?" Burke felt like a fighter hit with a series of heavy body shots.

"Yeah, one more thing, and it's the worst of all. We found a notebook, a kind of diary from all—"

Jerking up from his seat, Burke interrupted her. "A notebook?"

"Yeah, a journal of some type. Found it in Bethany's closet. She gave us permission to check the house the first day all this happened. Said she had nothing to hide."

Burke rubbed his hands on his pants and his spirits sank. He knew about the notebook. In fact, during an early counseling session, he had suggested to Bethany that she keep one, a journal of her feelings, a place to vent what happened to her and how she felt about it. Gritting his teeth, he set his lemonade in a coaster on a table by the sofa and eased up.

"She give you permission to read the notebook?"

Jackie dropped her eyes. "No, not exactly."

"But once she gave you permission to check the house you didn't need permission to read the notebook."

"You got it."

The room fell quiet. Debbi sipped from her glass. Burke walked over and stared out the window. The ceiling fan whirred overhead.

"So what's in the notebook?" asked Burke, sure he didn't want to hear the answer.

"She talked about her depression," said Jackie.

"And?"

"And about her thoughts of suicide."

"Go on," urged Burke, holding his breath for what he knew would come next.

"She said she couldn't kill herself because she didn't want to leave Stacy."

"And?"

"She said if she could take Stacy with her when she did it, maybe it wouldn't be so bad. Said maybe that would be best for everyone concerned. She and Stacy could die together, be together without all the pain and loneliness they had to face here."

Burke placed his hand on the wall beside the window and stared outside. A moth crashed itself against the screen, fluttered for a few moments trying to get inside to the light, then dropped down. Burke had heard these words before. Bethany had read them to him a few days after she wrote them, back in April, during the worst of her depression, at the time she first began to really face the reality of her divorce. He knew he could point that out to Jackie. He also knew it wouldn't matter. Jackie had little control over the situation now. The DA's office had the case. And knowing how the DA handled matters like this, he doubted that the date of Bethany's statement would make much difference.

CHAPTER ELEVEN

9:10 P.M.

In the last six years of his life, Rusty Redder had worked for a number of different people. His first criminal employment had come to him through an acquaintance he made while spending a week in the county jail on a robbery charge. Though the charge didn't stick—the judge tossed it out for lack of evidence—his jail mate had approached him in a bar on the south side of Atlanta three weeks later. The guy asked him to do a job for a wealthy patron who needed to stay anonymous. He assured Rusty that his particular skills were needed for the task.

Rusty felt good about that—someone thought he had particular talents. He had always believed it, but didn't know anyone else had noticed.

The job called for him to break into a palatial home in the Buckhead section of town and steal a confidential report on an Atlanta enterprise about to go public on the New York Stock Exchange. The security system on the house, though fairly modern, posed no real problem for Rusty. His street training and criminal experience had given him plenty of opportunity to learn about such devices and how to disarm them.

Rusty completed the job without a hitch, delivered the papers and computer disk that went with them, and collected his cash payment. A couple of smaller assignments followed that one—a delivery of a manila envelope, a threatening phone call. Both times, the employer paid up immediately.

His employment had always worked that way. Someone would call. Or a friend would introduce him to a client. He would do the job, then get paid. Do a job, get paid. Like a professional athlete. Like a wrestler—like Bernardo.

That pleased Rusty. He liked doing his job and then receiving the reward for it. But that hadn't happened this time. Rusty was furious. He had tried all weekend to call the number, but no one answered. Rusty let it ring and ring and ring. Nothing, no one. Not even an answering machine.

Now, sitting shirtless on the plastic brown sofa in his trailer, he didn't know what to do. He had no money to show for the most dangerous job he had ever attempted. He had no way to contact the man who owed him the money. Worse still, the one thing he did have he definitely didn't want—the insistent sound of the baby's cry pounding through his head.

Jerking his head side to side as if to throw the sound of Stacy's cry out of his brain, Rusty scanned his surroundings. A rented four-teen-foot-wide trailer. Chocolate-colored paneling on the walls. A poster of Bernardo the Beast centered in the paneling on the wall opposite the sofa. Blue lace curtains over the two windows behind his head. A television in the corner and three boxes of crossword puzzles sitting on top of the television. Not much to show for almost thirty years of life. Not much at all.

Cursing his predicament, he slipped into his basketball shoes and pulled a yellow T-shirt over his red hair. He had tried to do better. But life hadn't dealt him a particularly good hand.

He had no education to speak of. High school, and a half year at a tech institute. Nothing else. Parents divorced since he was thir-teen. Mother still in Atlanta, father God only knew where. A stepsis-ter on his mother's side. But he hadn't seen her in years.

With no education and no family, he had drifted from one job to another through his early twenties. A house painter, an electrician's helper, a mechanic at a truck stop. He had a knack for fixing things, but he couldn't ever settle on any one occupation. Drifting seemed to flow through his blood, drifting from one job to another, one town to another.

At the age of twenty-three, when he was working at the truck stop, he committed his first criminal act. He stole some gas—pumped

it for a couple of buddies who wanted to fill up their vehicles at a greatly reduced rate. Like for free.

No one ever caught him. He moved a few auto parts for cash a couple of months later. Again, no one caught him. It seemed easy. It seemed natural. It paid the bills.

Rusty left the truck stop. Drifted to a new town, then a second one and a third. Drifted into new crimes too. Primarily residential and auto theft. Nothing too large and nothing too dangerous. Just steady. So far, his illegal activities had kept a roof over his head and food on the table.

When the offer of the kidnapping came along, he didn't even hesitate. It seemed a natural progression. Still pretty safe, but much more lucrative.

Then he didn't get paid. And that burned his backside. That broke the code. He had to do something about that.

Rusty squared his jaw. He would find this deadbeat employer, force him to pay up the ten grand. He deserved his pay.

Shoving a cigar into his mouth, Rusty stood and headed for the door. Might as well get this show on the road. Just then the telephone rang.

As if grabbing a life jacket in high seas, Rusty jumped at the phone, eagerly pulling it to his uninjured ear. "Yeah," he said.

"Stacy is perfect."

Rusty swallowed hard. The woman.

"Good, now where's my dough?"

"Patience is a virtue."

"Yeah, well, so's honesty. You said I'd get my money when I finished my job. So where is it? I kept up my end. Now you got to keep up yours."

"Oh, I will, Mr. Redder, I will. In spades, you'll see. You'll see."

Rusty paused for a second and chewed on his cigar. Something about the tone of her voice made him nervous. It had an edge to it, a sharpness that seemed deliberate, almost as if the woman had tried to shave off any accent, to blend her voice in with everybody else.

Rusty shifted the phone to his left ear, then winced in pain. "You better," he said, the sore ear reminding him of the risky nature of his last job. "So where's my cash?"

"In a safe place, I assure you. You can pick it up soon."

"How soon?"

"As soon as you do one more task."

Rusty sucked on his cigar, not liking the suggestion. But he decided to hold his peace for a second, see what the lady meant. "And what's that?"

"I need one more child."

"That's not part of the deal!" exploded Rusty. "I signed on to snatch one kid, that's all, one kid for ten grand. One kid—a little girl—delivered safe and sound. That's what you asked me to do and I did it, and now I expect to get paid for—"

"Enough!" shouted the woman, interrupting Rusty. "Enough blather! You will get your payment as soon as you do one more task. One more child, but a boy this time, a boy with black hair and brown eyes, a perfect little boy. That is what you will do, Mr. Redder. And when you finish it, you will receive your payment." As if slamming on brakes, the woman suddenly stopped talking, as if no one could debate her, as if her word settled the issue once and for all.

For a moment, Rusty stood still, the phone slightly touching his sore ear. He didn't know what to do. He felt dumbstruck, almost hypnotized. He didn't want to take another child. Stacy Chapman's crying still haunted him. The sound of it kept him awake at night. The feel of her little hand on his leg still burned into his flesh. He didn't want to add another voice to hers, another hand touching his flesh and his soul.

But if he didn't do one more, how would he get by? He had no money to run, and no money to stay. He needed the ten grand. Needed it in the worst way. Ten grand would carry him far. Far, far away, far from the sound of Stacy Chapman's gut-wrenching cry and the feel of her soft hand.

"I want twenty-five for the two combined," he said, making his decision. "Twenty-five grand, paid the day of delivery."

He thought he heard a chuckle on the other end of the phone. "Don't sell yourself cheaply, Mr. Redder. I'll pay you thirty."

Rusty almost choked on his cigar. "Thirty?"

"Sure, as an act of good faith. So you will forgive me for the delay in payment. Call it a late charge."

A feeling of well-being swept over Rusty, and he momentarily forgot his earlier anger. A grin climbed onto his face as he imagined himself sitting on the beach in Daytona sipping a cold brew and listening to Jimmy Buffet. He chomped happily on his cigar.

"Yeah, well, thirty is fine," he said.

"I thought it might be. So, you'll get on this immediately?"

"Yeah, like the first one, immediately. You tell me who, I'll do the job, for thirty grand—remember, thirty grand is what you said."

"Thirty grand it is. A perfect child, safely delivered, and thirty grand it is."

"Yeah, perfect," said Rusty, shrugging. "Whatever you say."

"By tomorrow night."

Rusty quickly calculated the time. Tomorrow was too soon. Not much leeway. He started to complain, to ask for more time—but he knew instantly it wouldn't make any difference to the woman on the other end of the phone.

Sighing, Rusty nodded to himself. Okay, he could do it. If everything turned out well, he could do it. Get started early in the morning, check out the situation, do the deed, collect the cash, and head to Florida. Daytona—Bernardo's favorite city.

"Yeah, by tomorrow night," he agreed.

"Here's the name and address of the kid and the exchange point."

Rusty scanned the room quickly, looking for a pen. Saw a pencil on the floor behind the television. Grabbed it, pulled a piece of old newspaper out of the corner by the sofa, and jotted down the information.

"I'll deliver him right to you," he said, scribbling furiously. "You can count on it, I'll do my part."

"And I will do mine."

"So I'll get my thirty grand tomorrow?"

The line clicked. Rusty dropped the phone into the cradle and eased down onto his sofa. Chewing on his cigar, he thought about the thirty grand. My, my, that would feel good. Not a fortune, but more money than he had ever seen. All at one time. A pile of money. A pile big enough to get out of Atlanta and away from all the bad influences in his life.

He closed his eyes. His eyelids fluttered. Behind them flickered the face of Stacy Chapman. He saw her staring at him as he sat her down on the cold concrete in the warehouse on Friday night. She stared at him with her wide eyes, stared at him as if she knew him, as if she wanted to tell him something about herself, as if she wanted him to pick her up and hug her close and run away from the dark place, from the woman and the man who had come to take her.

But he hadn't done that and now the chance had passed. He couldn't do anything about what happened to the little girl. All he could do was make enough money to get away from it all. And that's what he would do. One more kid, then out of it. Out of it forever. Yeah, that's what he would do.

Tuesday
August 26

CHAPTER TWELVE

8:00 A.M.

Kissing his mom, Debbi, and Elizabeth Joy, Burke left his house and headed straight to Murphy Memorial Hospital to see Bethany Chapman. The cops had taken her there instead of the police station because she never regained consciousness after her collapse in Burke's office. Hearing of her condition, the judge assigned to her case had ordered the DA's office to take her immediately to the nearest psychological facility for observation and analysis.

Leaving his car and heading across the pavement, already blistering in the heat, Burke shook his head at the irony. Lydia Spicer in the intensive care unit. Bethany in the psyche ward on the eighth floor. All at the hospital where Bethany worked.

He stepped into the elevator and pushed the button. His shoulders slumped and he leaned against the back of the wall. What an awful situation. But not much he could do about it.

The elevator stopped and he stepped out. As Bethany's counselor of record, the judge had given him unlimited visitation privileges until further notice. The judge wanted her conscious and coherent. Until she became so, the wheels of justice would stop grinding.

At Bethany's room, Burke nodded to the uniformed cop standing by the door. "I'm Burke Anderson," he said, opening his wallet to identify himself. "Her therapist."

The cop studied his driver's license for a second. "You're cleared," he said. "Go on in. But don't expect much. She's still out."

Stepping past the man, Burke pushed open the door and walked inside. A still form lay on a white-sheeted bed by the back wall. One chair, a straight-backed one with a cover the color of guacamole dip, sat at the foot of the bed. A phone rested on a small table by the chair. A door leading into a tiny bathroom stood ajar beside the chair. Nothing else cluttered the room. Not a television, not a plant or a painting, nothing else. Only a sliver of sunshine slicing through the window over the bed redeemed the room from total bleakness. If you weren't insane when you came into this room, it might make you so before you left, thought Burke.

Glancing at the window, Burke wondered if it was shatterproof. Probably so. Shatterproof glass kept psyche ward depressives from jumping out.

Sighing, he walked to the bed and stared down at Bethany. He could hardly believe what he saw. Her usually lovely black hair was matted to her head. Her face was thin and pale, as white as computer paper. Her eyes were closed but surrounded by circles the size of saucers. She looked emaciated, as if she had a carnivore inside her gut gnawing away.

Burke touched her forehead. It felt hot and dry. He leaned closer to her face. "Bethany," he called quietly. No response.

He stepped away from her and moved to the bathroom. Pulling a paper towel from the rack above the sink, he wet it and walked back to Bethany. Gently, he rubbed her forehead and face with the towel. "It's Burke, Bethany, Burke Anderson." Nothing. He rubbed her face a touch harder. She stirred under his hand.

"It's Burke Anderson, Bethany. Can you hear me?"

Her eyelids flickered and Burke quickly looked over his shoulder. He wondered if he should call for the cop, then decided against it. If Bethany regained consciousness and wanted to tell him something, he didn't want any interference. Once the police took her back to Longstreet, it might get tough to see her, at least until they finished their interrogation. He wanted to talk to her first, give her some support, before she faced that frightening ordeal.

"I'm the only one here, Bethany," he said. "No one else but me."

She stirred again, her eyelids fluttering and her mouth twitching. "Bethany?" He spoke a bit louder. She opened her eyes and blinked at him.

He swallowed hard and wiped her forehead again. Not knowing how much she would remember, he didn't know exactly what to say.

If she didn't remember her child's disappearance and her subsequent arrest, a sudden reminder might plunge her right back into a coma. Burke decided to play it slowly. "You're okay, Bethany," he said. "You've been unconscious for a while but you're okay now."

She licked her lips. "I'm thirsty," she said. Hurriedly, Burke looked around for a cup but found none. "Hang on a second," he said, rushing to the bathroom. Cupping the water in his hands, he moved back to her and dripped the liquid onto her lips. Greedily, she licked it up.

Worried about the policeman outside, Burke didn't wait until she finished before he started talking. "We need to talk," he said, his tone urgent. "And I don't know how much time we have alone. Tell me what you remember."

Bethany took a deep breath and closed her eyes. For a split second, Burke thought she had drifted away again. "I remember everything," she said, her eyes still closed. "Everything."

Burke sighed with relief. "Okay," he said. "Okay. Then you know you're under arrest. There's a cop outside your door. The judge gave me visitation privileges. He wants you competent for arraignment as soon—"

"What about Stacy?" interrupted Bethany, her eyes now open, frozen in concentration on his face. "Tell me what they've found out about Stacy."

Burke broke her stare by dropping his eyes. "No word on Stacy. Jackie Broadus is working as hard as she can, but no one has found anything."

"It's got to be Cleve," Bethany said.

"Jackie is checking him," said Burke. "But she has to go slowly."

"While she goes slowly, I'm under arrest and don't know what happened to my daughter."

Burke started to defend Jackie, then decided against it. It wasn't the time.

"Is there anything you want me to do for you?" he asked. "Anything I can check out?"

For several moments, Bethany said nothing. A cloud rolled over the sun outside the window and the room darkened.

"What can I do to help you?" he repeated.

Slowly, as if afraid to move, Bethany pulled her arms from under the covers. Her hands reached for his arm. She grabbed him by the wrist. Her fingers dug into his flesh.

"Several things you can do," she said.

"Tell me."

"One, check on my mom. If she dies, I don't want her to die alone."

"I can do that. I've got a therapy group at the hospital twice a week. I'll see her at least that often, more if I can work it in."

"Good, thank you."

"What else?"

"Take care of Scooter."

"Scooter?"

"Yeah, our dog. He's at the Precious Pets Clinic. He's okay, but I need somebody to pick him up, keep him until all this gets settled."

Burke took a deep breath, remembering his now-deceased golden lab. Biscuit was his name. Biscuit had died saving his life. Burke loved dogs, but hadn't had one since Biscuit.

"I don't have anywhere to keep a dog."

"Scooter's easy," countered Bethany. "There's a doghouse at our trailer, his food is in the kitchen. You can leave him outside or keep him in, either way—he's trained."

Burke nodded, unable to turn her down. Bethany's nails cut deeper into his flesh. He wondered what else she would ask. "Two more things," she said.

"I'll do my best," he offered.

"Don't tell the police I'm conscious. I need a couple of more days to think through all this, to come to . . . I don't know, to come to some conclusion about what's going on. If I'm in jail, I don't think I can concentrate. I'll be too afraid."

She paused as if to give him a chance to say no. He didn't. He didn't blame her for not wanting to go to jail. He'd seen enough of that himself to know how scary it was. Even innocent people panicked at the prospect.

"The fourth thing?" he asked.

Her fingers tightened on his arm.

"I want you to find out if Cleve did this."

He stepped back from the bed. She clung to his wrist. For a beat, he didn't respond. "Can you do that for me, Burke?" she pressed. "Can you find out if Cleve had any part in this?"

He stood immobile, his arm stretched between her fingernails and his still body. What she asked of him went far beyond what a

counselor should do. All of it did. The care for her mother and her dog. The request to stay quiet about her consciousness. He should say no to all of it. The first two requests took him across the line between professionalism and personal involvement, and he knew all the arguments against doing that. The third one, well, if he accepted it, he might actually be breaking the law. He didn't know if his confidentiality privileges as a therapist covered this kind of thing or not. He'd have to find out. But the last request bothered him the most. That moved him back into a realm he had visited twice already in his life and didn't like either time. It took him straight into the heart of a police investigation. The last time had almost cost him his life.

"I think we should leave the investigation with Detective Broadus," he said finally, hoping to escape the responsibility. "I know her pretty well. She's a good cop."

"But you said she had to go slowly."

"That's true," he agreed, his spirit heavy. "But if Cleve is involved, she'll find out."

"I'm not sure I can trust that," said Bethany. "And I'm not sure I can wait as long as it'll take her."

Something in her voice scared him and Burke stared hard into her eyes. At that moment, he knew what she meant. She might not make it if it took too long to find Stacy. She seemed so distant, a human being fading away, disappearing into a cavern, a husk of a person dying from the inside out. If somebody didn't do something soon, she would cease to exist, either from a self-inflicted wound or from the simple fact that she would pull farther and farther inward until, like a black hole that sucked in all the light and life, she would collapse upon herself.

Sucking in his breath, he stepped toward her again and bent down over her face. "Listen to me, Bethany. Listen good. I'm going to find out what I can as quickly as I can. You hold on to that. Don't give up on me. You hear me. Don't give up on me. Okay?"

Her grip on his wrist loosened and she closed her eyes.

"Bethany," he called, panic in his voice. "Bethany?"

She didn't answer. Instead, she turned onto her side and shriveled up in a fetal position. For several long seconds, Burke stood beside her—not knowing if she had truly sunk into a coma again or if she was merely faking it for the sake of those who wanted her alert and ready for arraignment.

CHAPTER THIRTEEN

6:48 P.M.

All day Tuesday, Rusty Redder kept thinking about his next assignment—Taylor Bradford. Taylor Bradford—a boy under two with dark hair and brown eyes. He didn't know why his employers wanted this boy. It didn't really matter to Rusty. One kid or the other—no difference so far as he could see.

Amazingly, the boy lived with his mom and dad right under his nose, just like Stacy Chapman—six gravel roads over from her.

Sure, taking another kid from the same trailer park created certain dangers. It would stir up the cops, make the heat on the families who lived in the park hotter.

But Rusty had thought of a way to deal with that. He wouldn't go back to his trailer. He had called his employers, told them his plan. He wanted his money upon delivery, he said, right at the drop spot. They agreed.

Happy with his idea, Rusty packed up the belongings he planned to take and tossed them into his pickup. Deliberately, he left a few things behind—his television, a few well-worn clothes, the food in the refrigerator. If the police did a house-to-house search, he wanted them to think he still lived here, not that he had suddenly deserted the place.

All he needed now was to get the boy. The boy under two with black hair and brown eyes. The boy, Taylor Bradford. The twenty-thousand-dollar boy. The ticket-to-Florida boy.

Checking over his trailer one last time, Rusty considered what he knew about the boy. Taylor had lived in the park for almost three years, ever since his dad had come to Atlanta to help construct the new football stadium for the Falcons. Tim Bradford, Taylor's dad, worked hard, loved his wife, and had big plans. According to Tim, he and his family would soon move out of the Lincoln Family Trailer Park and take up residence in a real home—a place with brick on the sides. He'd been saving for a house like that ever since he'd gotten married seven years ago.

He and his woman needed a new house, said Tim, because of the second child they expected in early October. Every day Tim marked off another number on his calendar, anxiously looking forward to the day he would find his new home and buy it.

Rusty Redder knew all this because he'd joined Tim and four other guys in a card game on a Friday night back in early July. Tim had mouthed off all night about his big plans. Until that night, Rusty had never met Tim Bradford. He'd not talked with him since, but he had thought a lot about his big plans. Thought about them every time he drove by his trailer, every time he saw his kid playing in the dusty yard and his slightly overweight wife sunbathing by the plastic pool they had set up by the gravel driveway. Rusty had decided he didn't like Tim Bradford. Didn't like him precisely because he did have plans. Because he did have a future. A future with a reasonably attractive wife and a handsome child and a steady job with a construction company that kept him on even after the stadium work ended.

In other words, Tim Bradford had everything Rusty didn't have but desperately wanted, and Rusty resented him for it. Which made it all seem to fit. Tim Bradford had exactly what Rusty now needed to satisfy his employer—a boy under two with black hair and brown eyes.

Sitting in his truck, sucking on his half-smoked cigar and watching the sun begin to drop, Rusty again considered the dangers of snatching another child from the same neighborhood. Over the weekend, people in the trailer park had been on a higher alert than normal. The commotion from Bethany Chapman's trailer made everyone skittish. Fewer kids played outside.

But yesterday, well . . . yesterday, the cops took Bethany Chapman into custody. The newspapers said the police considered her a primary suspect. That calmed everyone down.

All morning Tuesday and into the afternoon, Rusty watched carefully. For the most part, life in the trailer park appeared normal again. The cops had pulled out the listening post from Bethany's place. The moms and dads returned to work. Dogs barked again, their growls echoing through the hot August air. Children played in their yards, rushing through sprinkler hoses, swinging on monkey bars, wheeling in and around their homes on bicycles. In the back corner of the park, on a square, flat area of dirt, a group of older boys without shirts tossed a basketball at a netless rim. Tossing out his cigar, Rusty took a deep breath. The day had finally just about passed. He could do the job as soon as the opportunity presented itself. Maybe even now.

About fifty yards away, in an unfenced yard, Taylor Bradford rolled a green-and-red soccer ball, then toddled after it. Pick up the ball, toss it, chase after it. Pick it up, toss it, then chase after it.

A few feet from the kid, on a plastic deck chair, lay Susie Bradford, her body glistening with suntan lotion. To her left sat a Ford Mustang—old but not a classic model. Behind the Mustang was a blue plastic swimming pool, about four feet high and approximately twenty-five feet in diameter. For several seconds, Rusty studied the layout, particularly the mother.

She was seven months pregnant. But still working on her tan. Wearing a pair of short, blue, spandex-type shorts and a halter top that seemed about to burst from her excessive bustline. Nothing covered her rounded belly.

Rusty shook his head. He didn't know much about Susie Bradford. Only what the trailer park rumor mill said. A bit uppity, said the gossip. As if the job Tim worked and their plans for a house gave her cause to put on airs.

Rusty fingered his sore ear. Word on the street had it she was lazy and spent too much money, that Tim would already have had a house if she had only helped a little.

As he watched her, Susie shifted in her seat, picked a bottle of lotion off the ground, poured it into her hands, then rubbed it onto her naked stomach. Rusty felt himself annoyed with her. At seven months pregnant, the woman should have more dignity. She shouldn't expose herself that way. It wasn't proper for a woman. Rusty knew he was bad in a lot of ways, but he still believed in certain things. And one of the things he believed was that a pregnant woman should act like one.

A feeling of rage pushed through Rusty and it felt good. He needed to feel anger at Tim and Susie Bradford. Anger gave him an excuse to take their son from them, reminded him that they didn't really deserve such a handsome boy, they shouldn't find happiness if he couldn't.

Rusty smiled a crooked grin. The anger soothed him. He realized it would keep him from hearing another child crying in his head. He had felt no anger toward Stacy Chapman and the lack of it had cost him dearly. He wouldn't make that mistake again. It hurt too much to hurt someone without anger.

Tightening his hands into fists, Rusty pounded his thighs. *Do something woman*, he thought. *Do something stupid. Go to the bathroom to empty your bladder. Walk to the backyard. Get a drink from the kitchen. Anything. Just leave the kid for a minute. That's all I need. A couple of minutes and he's mine.*

For a second, he thought of calling her like he had Lydia Spicer. But he decided against it. Even though the news reports said the old woman had a stroke, he didn't know what, if anything, she had said to the police. No reason to give them a pattern.

He could wait. He would stay patient. Not rush anything. Go with the flow, stay with his basic strengths, size up a situation, make his move, just do the job. Yeah, he could wait—

Susie Bradford was hauling herself from the lounge chair. Hauling herself up like a crane lifting cargo. Rusty glanced quickly at Taylor. His ball had rolled to the edge of the yard, and he toddled after it. Not sure of Susie's plans, but wanting to get in position to act if the opportunity presented itself, Rusty opened the truck door and climbed out. Slowly, but steadily, he eased around the side, step by tiny step, closer and closer to the boy. Better to be ready if the chance came than to sit asleep at the switch.

As he crept closer, he kept Susie in his sights. She slipped off her shoes, a pair of sandals, and dropped them to the ground. What was she doing? She stepped past her chair, and Rusty suddenly understood. She was going to get into the plastic pool, which sat behind the Mustang.

He watched as she lifted a leg, hoisting her heavy body over the side. It didn't go easily. Susie's condition made the climb into the pool something of a chore. She grabbed the side of the plastic pool and pulled herself up. Her front leg splashed into the water—a log of dead weight. Water sloshed over the side.

With one leg in and one leg out, she tugged again and twisted her backside. Her trailing leg split the water, and she lost her balance for a second, almost falling. Grabbing the side of the blue plastic, she managed to hang on, righting herself just before she tipped over. Her legs solidly under her finally, she lifted her nose into the air and cautiously squatted down into the water.

Not more than ten yards away, Rusty quickly sized up the circumstances. Taylor had picked up his ball but hadn't moved from the edge of the yard. Susie had closed her eyes, obviously enjoying the feel of the clear liquid lapping at her chin.

Rusty crossed the last few yards that separated him from Taylor. The child looked up and saw him. A big grin broke out on the boy's face, and he shoved his arms out from his body, extending the ball to Rusty. Rusty bent over, hunched like a baseball catcher about to receive a pitch.

He glanced back at Susie. Unable to see her through the Mustang, he leaned to the right. She hadn't opened her eyes. Pleased, Rusty focused on Taylor again. If he couldn't see Susie because of the car, she couldn't see him either.

He reached for the ball Taylor offered him. For an instant, he stared into the boy's brown eyes. So innocent, so sweet.

A pang of conscience sliced through Rusty; he took the ball hurriedly and looked away from the child, back around the Mustang at Susie. She still had her eyes closed, the water up to her chin, the sun playing on her face.

Anger washed over Rusty again. What a terrible mother! She didn't deserve this child! Paying her son no attention!

His anger a hot poker driving him, Rusty reached for Taylor. The boy didn't resist. As easily as lifting a sack of sugar, he pulled the child into his arms and twisted away. Then, carefully but hastily, he walked to his truck.

Within thirty seconds, he started the engine and pulled away. Going around the corner, he glanced back at Susie in his rearview mirror. Her eyes were still closed.

CHAPTER FOURTEEN

7:30 P.M.

Shadows cast by pine trees taller than telephone poles splashed across the hood of his Cavalier as Burke Anderson drove down the road to Bethany Chapman's trailer. A couple of vehicles zipped by him from the opposite lane, their wheels throwing up a white powder, but he barely noticed. He was too preoccupied.

The shadows from the pine trees danced a soft waltz as a touch of late afternoon breeze swayed them to and fro. Watching the shadows, Burke suddenly felt eerie, a detached observer of what he was about to do. The pine trees beside the road seemed to reach out for him, their talons gripping from the left of the road, reaching over his car to the row of trailers to his right.

For an instant, he stared at the stand of pines. Had the kidnapper come from there? Had he hidden among the tall pines, watched Stacy play, plotted how and when to grab her? Had he darted out of the woods like a wolf rushing after prey, taken her by the throat and hauled her back into the dark shadows?

The hair on Burke's neck stood up, tickling the collar of his starched white shirt. He shook himself, his shoulders rolling forward, trying to cast off the sense of unease that draped over him. He slowed down and looked to the right, checking the trailers, trying to find a number, trying to orient himself—367 . . . 363 . . . 355 . . .

What did Stacy's grandmother know? . . . 347 . . . 343 . . . 339— that was Bethany's. There. At the end of the road.

"That's the one, Scooter, right there," he said, turning slightly to the dog lying on the seat beside him.

Scooter whimpered and slapped his tail against the seat. Burke patted him on the head. The vet had released Scooter with a clean bill of health. A shaved chest and a gauze bandage just below his throat provided the only evidence of the dog's wound.

"We're going to get your doghouse, boy," said Burke, stopping the car. "We'll put it right beside the door in my backyard. You'll do great there."

He climbed out of his Cavalier. Scooter raised up and barked at him. "You want to go with me?" asked Burke. Scooter barked again. "Okay, boy, just a second."

Shutting the door, Burke walked to the trunk, flipped it up, then moved to the passenger side. He opened the door and snapped his fingers. Scooter bounced onto the road at his feet. Burke turned away and opened the fence gate, scanning the yard as he entered. For a second, he wondered about the absence of the yellow tape the police used to cordon off a crime area. Apparently, the investigators had finished their work.

He shrugged, then noted the azalea bushes bordering the front of the trailer and the dogwoods to the left of it. With Friday's rain, the grass had greened up somewhat, but still not enough to completely eliminate the parched look that came to Atlanta yards in late summer.

Burke closed the fence and paused. At his ankles, Scooter stopped too—his nose twitching, his tail snapping side to side.

Leaning over, Burke scratched the dog behind the ears. It seemed so unreal. Everything in the yard looked so much in order. If someone wanted to make a brochure to advertise the amenities of trailer-park living, they could do no better than to plaster a picture of this place on the front. But that picture would be deceiving. Deceiving because nothing was really in order here. Everything had been tossed upside down, lives had been scrambled, torn apart. Police had parked their cars here, tramped across this yard wearing their rubber gloves and holding their plastic bags, searching for evidence. They had scanned the premises with every technological gadget available, hoping to find something to lead them to Stacy Chapman. The yard that seemed so serene was anything but.

Forcing himself to get on with the job at hand, Burke stood. One doghouse. Hauled into his car and carted to his house. He had already asked Debbi for permission. She had given it—so long as the dog stayed outside. No dog, no matter how gentle, in the house with a newborn baby, she had said. Burke had agreed.

He saw the doghouse—sitting by the last of the azalea bushes. A small, igloo-style structure. It looked like it would fit in his car trunk if he kept the lid up. For a second, he wondered what the structure weighed, if he could carry it. Only one way to find out. He stepped across the yard, Scooter at his heels.

Grabbing the doghouse, he lifted it slightly, testing its bulk. Hey, not too bad. He could carry it, if awkwardly, to the car. Spreading his feet to get the weight onto his legs, he tugged the doghouse up and off the ground. With a grunt, he moved toward his car. At the gate, he paused, pushing it to the side with his right leg. A second later, he eased the doghouse down into his trunk. It fit, but just barely, the top turned sideways and wedged into the bottom of the old Cavalier. *That's one good thing about a cheap, beat-up old car*, he thought. Doesn't really matter how you treat it. With a piece of cord he had brought for just this purpose, he tied the trunk lid to a hole running through the license plate on the car.

Rubbing his hands on his pants, Burke turned around, ready to go. He looked for Scooter, then spotted him back in the yard, digging in the spot where the doghouse had been. Burke smiled. At least Scooter could act normal.

He whistled and Scooter raised his head for a second, then resumed his digging. "Here boy," called Burke. "Time to go."

Scooter ignored him, his paws scratching rhythmically in the ground. Dirt flew up in tiny batches, landing beneath his hind legs. Burke snapped his fingers and whistled. Scooter never looked up.

Slightly irritated, Burke stepped back through the gate and over to the dog. "Come on, boy," he urged, squatting down to pick up the animal. "We'll get a bone for you at your new home." Scooter dug his nose into the ground, then grabbed at the dirt with his teeth. His tongue flicked out as if scooping up a morsel of food. Burke lifted Scooter off the ground, shaking him to knock the soil off his feet. The dog wiggled in his hands, trying to jump out. Burke snuggled Scooter to his chest. "Easy boy," he soothed. "Easy."

The dog kept jerking, twisting his body side to side. A low growl rolled from his throat and Burke squeezed him tighter, surprised by his strength.

Scooter opened his mouth and barked. Something shiny fell from his teeth. With a quick twist, he lunged out of Burke's grasp, landed hard on the ground, and scooped the metal back up with his tongue.

Agitated by the dog, Burke instantly reached again for him, this time getting a solid grasp. "What you got, boy?" he asked, holding on tightly. "What's in your mouth?"

He took Scooter's face in his right hand, his thumb across the dog's nose and his fingers wrapped under his chin. "Let's see what we've got here."

Burke pried open Scooter's jaw and leaned him forward. Saliva dripped from the dog's mouth onto the ground. Right behind the saliva fell a round metal object. It hit the ground with a tiny thud and fell onto its side, disappearing in the weedy grass.

Shifting Scooter to the side so he couldn't scoop up the object again, Burke bent to his knees. With one hand on Scooter, he tapped the ground, feeling for the metal piece. Tap, tap, tap. Hold the wiggling dog still. . . . There, he found it, felt it in the grass.

Parting the grass with his free hand, Burke saw the rounded object nestled like a jewel against a backdrop of green velvet. It glistened there, still moist from the spittle of Scooter's mouth. Burke picked it up and rolled it in his palm. An earring.

A gold earring as round as a half-dollar. A gold earring with the clasp still fastened, a piece of odd-looking tissue stuck like a chunk of fuzz to the top of the clasp.

Dark Road to Daylight

CHAPTER FIFTEEN

8:29 P.M.

When Jackie Broadus walked into Danny's Doughnut Shop, she headed instantly to the booth she always used when she met Burke and Debbi here—a blue booth by the back wall, close to the jukebox. She scanned the place again, grateful for such a homey diner in the midst of the Atlanta metropolis. Danny's was a ramshackle but extremely successful spot favored by truckers, construction workers, and environmentally conscious yuppie types who wanted to mingle with people with mud on their boots. Burke had introduced her to it a couple of years back. Jackie liked Danny's because it had the atmosphere of a doughnut shop, but it was open all day and served delicious sandwiches in addition to its locally famous doughnuts.

The smell of coffee hung in the air, and the sound of a Garth Brooks ballad poured out of the jukebox. Jackie saw Burke and Debbi waving at her.

She took a seat across from them. "You left the baby?" she asked, somewhat surprised to see Debbi.

"Burke's mom is still with us," said Debbi. "I figured I could break away for a couple of hours."

Jackie nodded and smiled. She had known Debbi as long as she had Burke. Met them both through a murder investigation. Debbi had covered the story for the *Atlanta Independent*. She started to develop her reputation as a tough, no-nonsense reporter with that coverage. Since then, in spite of new ownership at the paper, she had risen to the top echelon of Atlanta journalism. Known for her drive. Her peers, reporters in both print and electronic media, called her "Super Glue" because she stuck to every story she attacked.

"I wondered when you would become a part of this," Jackie said.

"I'm not in on this" Debbi said, her tone teasing. "I just wanted to get out of the house for a few minutes and have a cup of coffee with my husband and my friend."

"But you don't drink coffee, remember. Too health conscious."

"Well, maybe I do now."

A waitress appeared from around the corner, breaking up their banter.

"What for you?" asked the waitress.

"A chocolate eclair and a diet Dr. Pepper," said Jackie. "You guys?"

"Already ordered," said Burke.

The waitress moved away. Jackie turned to Debbi again. "The newspaper hasn't called you in to work this story?"

"No, they know better. I have another six weeks of maternity leave. I plan to stay with Elizabeth Joy as long as I can."

"You going back after that?"

Debbi lowered her eyes. "I think so, at least that's my plan right now. But I don't know . . . as it gets closer, I might change my mind."

Jackie nodded. "It's a tough decision, isn't it?"

"The toughest. I love my job and my baby."

"If anybody can do justice to both, Debbi's the one," said Burke, patting her hand.

Jackie studied her friend Burke. A handsome man. About four years her junior. Hair the color of mahogany, eyes almost the same. A strong chin, like a block of ice. Not too big, but an athletic build. A runner, a former marathon runner in fact. Amazingly, he thought as well as he looked, if not better. The smartest man she'd ever met, outside of her former partner. In two prior murder investigations, Burke had shown an uncanny ability to combine logic and intuition. His insights had led to the arrest of the killer both times.

The waitress popped back into view and placed three plates on the table. "I'll be right back with your drinks," she said, twisting away.

"You said we needed to meet," said Jackie, ignoring her eclair for a second.

"Yeah, I thought we should," Burke said, biting his cheeseburger. "I wanted to see where you were with the Chapman situation."

Jackie shrugged, not sure how much she should tell. She glanced over at Debbi. "I want it clear that whatever I say is off the record."

"I'm not working this," insisted Debbi. "Nothing goes beyond this table."

"Good, then we can talk."

"So what's the latest?" asked Burke, obviously anxious. "Anything new about Stacy? What about Cleve? Have you talked with him yet? Do you think he—"

"Whoa, guy," said Jackie, throwing up her hand. "One question at a time."

"I'm just nervous, I guess," said Burke. "Worried about Stacy. It's been over four days now, and I can't help but think something terrible has happened to her. If it hasn't yet, it will soon. If somebody doesn't find something, do something soon . . . I don't know, I just don't see much hope." His voice almost breaking, he stopped and lowered his eyes.

Jackie leaned over to him. "I know," she soothed. "I feel the same way—scared, discouraged, almost hopeless. But I can't let it keep me from thinking clearly, can't let my emotions control what I'm doing. If I do, I don't have a snowball's chance in July of finding that little girl."

"So what have you found?" asked Debbi, breaking into the conversation.

The waitress interrupted them before Jackie could answer, plopping three soft drinks onto the table. "Anything else you need?" she asked. Jackie shook her head. The waitress moved away.

Jackie focused on Debbi again. "I wish I had something concrete to tell you, but I don't. We've come up with a couple of scraps, but nothing serious yet."

"What kind of scraps?"

Jackie took a sip of her drink. "Cigar butts, six of them. On the side of the road across from the trailer."

"Somebody sitting there watching her?" asked Burke.

"That's our conclusion. Three of the butts were squashed, like a car had run over them. The others were okay."

"Can you tell what kind of cigar they are?" asked Debbi. "Maybe a particular type?"

"We're checking that," said Jackie. "We'll see, but we don't expect it. That would make it too easy. Besides, kidnappers don't usually smoke designer cigars."

"But that's something," said Burke, his voice hopeful.

"Yeah, it's something, but it's not nearly enough."

"That all you got?" asked Debbi.

Jackie shrugged. "Not quite. We've got tire tracks too. From a truck. We're working to match the treads now."

"Good thing it rained," suggested Burke.

"Yeah, that softened the road, made the tracks for us," agreed Jackie.

"Anybody in the trailer park see anything unusual on Friday?"

Jackie took a bite out of her eclair, chewed on it for a second, then swallowed. "We've got two different people, a woman two trailers up and a thirteen-year-old boy on a bicycle, who say they saw a man in a green pickup drive by a couple of hours before the dog started barking. As they put it, almost identically by the way, the truck moved real slow, even stopped once or twice right in front of Bethany's place. They said the man drove like he was lost. They couldn't tell the model of the truck."

Burke took a deep breath. "They get a look at the driver?"

"Not much. But both said he had light hair."

For several seconds, the table fell silent. The three of them took bites of their food. To Jackie, the eclair tasted bland, like cardboard with whipped cream in it.

"What about Cleve?" asked Burke.

Jackie dropped her eclair onto her plate. "What about him?"

"You talk to him yet?"

She shook her head. "No, not yet. No time."

"Does he fit the description?" asked Debbi.

"He has blond hair," said Jackie.

"But you haven't talked to him yet? Why not?" asked Debbi, her tone indicating disbelief.

"About 30 percent of the population in Atlanta has blonde hair. Should I talk to all of them?" asked Jackie, half annoyed at her friends for insinuating she hadn't done her job correctly.

"No, no," said Burke waving his hand in apology. "We're not questioning what you've done. We know what kind of detective you are."

"I saved your bacon once," said Jackie, a smile on her face.

"Yep, and we're both mighty grateful," agreed Burke. "But you can understand why we would ask about Cleve."

"I understand. And I'll check him out. But you have to let me do it in my own way, in my own time."

Burke sucked in a deep breath. "I hope we have that much time," he said, his voice edgy. "I hope we have enough time to find Stacy, to save her and to . . . I don't know . . . to save Bethany too. I'm worried that she's about to slip away from us. Even if we find Stacy alive, I don't know if it'll happen in time for Bethany."

Jackie focused on him, her curiosity aroused. Something in his voice seemed tight. Staring at him, she noticed his eyes. They looked animated, brighter even than usual. Sipping from her drink, she suddenly remembered she'd seen that look on a couple of other occasions, times when Burke Anderson knew something she didn't know. She placed her glass on the table.

"Tell me about Bethany," she said, careful not to reveal her suspicions. "You're her counselor."

"I can't tell you much," said Burke. "A client's confidentiality, you know about that."

Jackie nodded. "I know," she said. "And I wouldn't want you to do anything to compromise that. But if you know something, something she's told you about any enemies she might have, anything about herself, about her problems—you know what I mean—then I need to hear it."

Burke took a bite of his burger. "I know what you mean," he said, "and I don't know anything to tell you."

"Have you seen Bethany today?"

Burke stayed quiet for a second, then rubbed his palms on his pants. "Why do you ask?" he said.

"Oh, you know, the mother is always under suspicion until something proves otherwise. We need to get her conscious again, that's all."

"That's all?"

Jackie looked at Burke, knowing she needed to tell him the rest. Not wanting to hold out on a friend, she decided to spill it all. "Well, we found a piece of paper in Lydia Spicer's hand. Two letters were written on it. *B* and *E*, then a scratch like she wanted to write more. Like she wanted to leave a message."

"*B* and *E* as in 'Bethany'?" asked Debbi.

"Yeah, as in 'Bethany.' Unfortunately, we don't know for sure that that's what she was trying to say. And we don't know what she meant even if she was trying to write Bethany's name. It might mean 'Bethany, I love you,' or 'Bethany, I saw the kidnapper,' or 'Bethany is the kidnapper,' or heaven knows what else. She might not even have been trying to write 'Bethany.' It might be she was writing down a grocery list and needed to remember to get some beets."

"No way to tell, is there?" said Burke, his palms momentarily still.

"Nope, none at all. That's why we need Bethany coherent."

"I saw her this morning," said Burke. "At the hospital."

"How'd she look?"

"Oh, you can imagine. Pale. Thin. Like a mother with a missing daughter, I guess."

Jackie leaned back in her seat, watching Burke all the while. "You tried to talk with her?"

"Sure, like everyone else."

"Any response?"

Burke rolled his shoulders and rubbed his hands on his pants.

The waitress stepped into the scene before Burke could speak. "You doing okay here?"

"Fine," said Jackie, waving her away. "Just fine." The waitress disappeared. Jackie looked back at Burke. He pointed down at the table. There in a Ziploc bag lay a gold earring.

Burke handed the bag to Jackie. She held it up to the light for examination. She considered going back to her question about Bethany, but Burke interrupted her before she could.

"I found—well, I should say Bethany's dog found it a couple of hours ago," he said. "In a hole under the doghouse. It's an earring."

"I can see that. Any idea whose it is?"

"Nope, not sure. It could be Bethany's or even her mother's. Who knows?"

Jackie rolled the bag around in her hands, holding it up to the light. "It's a big one," she said.

"Yep, and a bit showy too."

"Not like Bethany?"

"Nope, not like her at all. It's not particularly clean either."

"What do you mean?"

"Look closely, you'll see."

Jackie pulled the bag closer. She studied it, her mouth falling open. Her nose twitched as if it itched. "There's something on the clasp of the earring," she said.

"Yep."

"Any idea what it is?"

"You got me."

"Looks like stale gum."

"Or lint."

"You touch it?"

"No, I kept my hands off. Put it in a bag and brought it straight to you."

"So what's your guess?"

Burke cleared his throat. "I'd say it's skin."

"Skin?"

"Yeah, as in flesh, as in the stuff that gets scraped and cut and bruised and torn off."

For several long seconds, Jackie stared at the earring. Burke and Debbi nibbled at their sandwiches. "If it's skin it could be Bethany's," Jackie said.

"Could be," agree Burke. "But she's not injured that I know of."

Jackie nodded. "It has to be fairly fresh or it would have decomposed already."

"I expect so."

Jackie laid the bag down and took a long slow sip from her Dr. Pepper. She licked her lips. "I think I need to get this to the lab," she said. "You'll excuse me if I go now."

"I'd be surprised if you didn't."

With that Jackie stood, sucked down a final drink of Dr. Pepper, and walked out of Danny's.

CHAPTER SIXTEEN

8:55 P.M.

T he meeting was set for nine o'clock, right after dark. The place was a two-acre pond almost forty miles out of Atlanta, just off I-75 headed south toward Griffin. Rusty didn't mind the long drive. It got him out of Atlanta, away from the frantic search that he assumed had already started in and around his trailer park.

He flipped on the light and checked the time. Bingo. He glanced over at Taylor Bradford, strapped into the child's seat. The kid stared back at him, his brown eyes the size of poker chips. The eyes never strayed from Rusty's face.

For a second, Rusty felt the urge to reach over and push Taylor's eyes shut. He'd seen those eyes ever since he'd kidnapped the kid. The boy stared at him constantly because he never fell asleep. Not for one instant. In spite of the regular doses of cough medicine Rusty had poured into him, the kid never closed his eyes. Not even once.

The eyes stayed open, twin points of brown fixation, focused on his abductor. Rusty considered giving Taylor an even higher dose of the cough syrup. But not knowing when the dosage would become dangerous, he decided against it. No reason to endanger the kid's health. He didn't want that on his conscience.

Rusty stuck a cigar into his mouth and gnawed on the end. The kid's stare couldn't hurt him. At least he stayed quiet, didn't wail like Stacy Chapman. Her crying pounded in his memory for an instant. He quickly jerked his head to the side to throw it out. He flipped off the light in the truck and turned left onto a slender ribbon of a road just as he'd been told to do. He forced himself to think of something else, anything but the baby girl. Think of . . . Florida . . . Beautiful Florida . . . Florida, where he would soon lie on the beach and soak up the sun and drink cold beer through the afternoon. Florida, where he might run into Bernardo the Beast. He might even ask Bernardo for a job. Maybe as a bodyguard. A celebrity like Bernardo surely needed bodyguards. Rusty would make a good one.

A half mile up the road, just as his directions said, he passed an out-of-business restaurant. A sign, the paint peeling from it like dead skin from a body, pronounced proudly—"Best Food, Best Friends."

Rusty looked for a dirt road on the right. He spotted it and turned, his headlights catching the faces of a group of sad-faced cows gathered by a barbed wire fence near the edge of the road. The cattle stared back at him, their eyes huge and brown, their gaze fixed on him.

He shuddered—brown eyes in Taylor Bradford, brown eyes in mournful cows, brown eyes everywhere. Rusty fixed his attention straight ahead, not daring to look over at Taylor. A pain cut through his stomach. It felt like a sharp stone cutting at his intestines. For the fleetest of moments, he thought of stopping the truck and backing up, backing up and spinning away from the dirt road, of taking Taylor back to the trailer park and leaving him where the police could find him and take him back to Mom and Dad.

But then he knew he couldn't do that. Couldn't do that because the cops would be all over the place. They probably had roadblocks set up around the trailer park right now. No way could he get in and out without them catching him. Then they would know he had also taken Stacy. They would demand to know where she was. They wouldn't believe it when he said he didn't know. They would arrest him and try him for Stacy's murder and they would find him guilty and sentence him to death. No, he couldn't go back.

He had to go ahead with the plan. Deliver Taylor Bradford, collect his thirty thousand dollars, and get to Florida. No way out now.

To the left, he saw the barn his directions identified. A ramshackle structure sitting in the middle of the field, a silent dark building about fifty yards off the dirt road inside the barbed wire fence. No door on the barn. A black hole where the door had been. Quickly, he searched the side of the road for an open gate. He spotted it—ten feet ahead, just as he'd been told. Hitting the brakes, Rusty pulled his truck through the gate, switched off the ignition, and killed the lights. Quietly, he climbed out, eased the door shut, and circled around to the passenger side. He opened the door and eased Taylor out of the child's seat. Careful not to look at the boy, he held him as far as he could from his body, held him out like a smelly sack of garbage and stalked toward the barn.

Overhead, the moon glowed brightly, its face peeking down on him and Taylor. The smell of cow manure seeped through the hot summer air and to his left he heard mooing. Taylor hung heavy in his arms and sweat dropped off Rusty's forehead and into his eyes.

Under his breath, he cursed. He cursed the light from the moon and the heat of the night and the mooing of the brown-eyed cattle. He cursed the weight of the boy in his arms and the sound of crying in his head. But most of all, he cursed the life that had brought him to this deserted field forty miles out of Atlanta, the life that had left him no choice but to do what he now found himself doing—peddling little kids for cash.

He reached the barn.

He paused and, his arms weary, pulled Taylor closer to his chest. The child stayed quiet. Amazing. Not a peep since he had taken him from his mother. The medicine hadn't put the child to sleep but it had sure made him sluggish.

Swallowing, Rusty stepped through the gaping entrance of the barn. Instantly, the light from the moon disappeared and a wave of sweltering heat washed over him. He felt drowned in inky blackness, swallowed up by black fire. The sweat poured out through his arms, his back, his eyes. It felt like the heat of the whole summer had been captured and stored in this one place, this stifling spot in the middle of a cow pasture. He clutched Taylor tighter.

"You have the child." The words, spoken in a deep bass, came from the dark loft of the barn.

Rusty craned his neck, facing the voice. "I have . . . have the child," he said, his voice shaky.

"Is he as I demanded?"

"Yeah, sure, he's fine."

"Is he perfect?"

That question again. This time from the man. What did it mean? Perfect in what way? Physically? Emotionally? How could he know

that? He hadn't scrutinized him like a meat inspector checking out a piece of beef. "He's great, you know, like you wanted."

"Good. Anything less will not do."

For a brief second, Rusty wanted to ask, "Do for what?" but he dared not. He didn't want to stay a moment longer than necessary in this black furnace of a barn. Even more, he realized, he didn't really want to know. The less he knew the better. To know more meant he might never clear his head of the cries of Stacy Chapman and the eyes of Taylor—

"Leave the child," said the man in the loft.

Rusty shivered in spite of the heat. The same words as the first time. The time he'd received no payment. He grunted and clutched Taylor closer. The breath of the boy tickled his chin. Rusty swallowed hard. He had to do it.

"I need my money," he said.

A low chuckle rolled down from the loft. "You trust me not."

Rusty stayed quiet. The heat pounded down on him and his head started to throb. He thought he heard a rustling, a movement of feet above and to his left. He dropped into a squat, his eyes searching the blackness. He smelled straw beneath his feet. Sweat rolled off his chin now, rolled in heavy swirls down his neck and into his shirt collar. Something swished behind him, and he pivoted on the balls of his feet, his eyes wide and frantic, his head about to explode with pounding, his heart about to pop through his chest. He heard a whimper, then realized he was squeezing Taylor too tightly, crushing him in his fear.

The air stirred and, in a split second, he knew that the man had descended from the loft, that he had come at him from the rear, that he—

A touch of steel in the back of his neck froze Rusty in place. "It's a gun," said the bass voice. "And if you move, you will die."

Rusty didn't move.

"One more makes three," said the man.

Rusty didn't speak. He couldn't speak. His tongue stuck to the roof of his mouth. His heart felt as though it had stopped.

"I need three," said the man. "One more. You can do one more, can't you?"

Rusty tried to answer, but again found himself mute. The jab of the gun in his neck made his mouth unable to function.

"Come now," said the man behind him, a touch of exasperation in his tone. "I'm waiting, but not forever. I'll offer you a choice. You make the decision. You do one more. One more makes three—a human trinity. That's what I need."

Listening to the man, Rusty found himself gaining control of his nerves again. The man wanted one more child. Another business transaction. Rusty knew how to deal with that kind of situation. He'd done it for years. The only problem was the guy had already welshed twice. Two kids delivered, he'd done his part. But the man with the gun had failed to produce the cash.

A rush of anger poured through Rusty. The anger gave him courage. "What's to keep you from standing me up again if I grab another kid? You can promise all kinds of money now, but so far you've skimmed out two times already. I don't see much incentive for me to risk it. Pay me now for the first two, and maybe I'll consider the third one. If not—"

"Enough," roared the man. "You forget one thing. I said you had a choice. You do. You agree to the third one—under two again, a girl this time. You agree to the third one and collect sixty thousand dollars and live happily ever after or you say no and I deposit a bullet into the back of your less than fully developed brain. That is the choice you have, nothing more and nothing less." As if to make his point, the man pressed the barrel of the pistol harder into Rusty's head.

Feeling the gun, Rusty quickly calculated his chances for escape as slim to none. Given those odds, he really didn't have a choice. "Okay," he said, his voice shaky. "I'll . . . I'll try to get you a third kid."

"I need more than a try."

Rusty sighed. "Okay, I'll get you a third kid."

"Excellent. By Thursday. That's our deadline."

A sudden thought hit Rusty. "I can't go back to my trailer," he said. "Too many cops there. How will I contact you when it's done?"

"You won't. I'll contact you. Get a room at the Old South Hotel, a grand place in Gwinett County. I'll get in touch once you're in place, tell you who to take, where to make the delivery, and where to pick up your payment."

A pang of distrust swept through Rusty again. "You'll keep the deal this time?"

The man chuckled slowly.

"You trust me not."

"You'll keep the deal?"

Rusty felt the gun move and heard a rustle behind his back. Instantly, he knew that the man had slithered away in the darkness, a black snake who struck and then disappeared back into his hole. Rusty started to turn around but then thought better of it. The less he knew the better. If the man thought Rusty could identify him, he might shoot him on the spot. If not now, then later when he delivered the third child.

A shudder passed through Rusty, and he suddenly remembered that he still held Taylor. Taylor the boy with the big brown—

"Leave the child!" shouted the snake of a man, his voice a hiss in the darkness. "Leave the boy and go!"

Without glancing down, Rusty unhooked Taylor's fingers from his shirt and lowered him to the straw. Then, quietly but quickly, he raised himself and turned toward the gaping entrance to the barn. The moonlight outside the entry beckoned to him and he began to run. Within two steps he was in a dead sprint toward the light of the moon and away from the boy with the brown eyes and the snake in the black loft with a gun in his hands.

CHAPTER SEVENTEEN

9:32 P.M.

Within five minutes after he walked into his house, Burke's phone rang. Leaving his toothbrush by the sink, he hustled to the bedroom to get the call, hoping the ringing hadn't wakened Elizabeth Joy. He barely beat Debbi, grabbing the phone just as she threw herself across the bed to take it. To his surprise, he heard Jackie Broadus on the other end.

"You sitting down?" she asked, her voice agitated.

"No, but I can if I should," he said. "What's up?" He raised his eyebrows at Debbi and whispered to her. "It's Jackie." Debbi punched the speaker button on the phone.

"You won't believe it if I tell you," said Jackie, her voice echoing through the bedroom.

"Don't keep me in suspense."

He heard her take a deep breath. Then she spoke. "Several things. First Bethany Chapman is missing."

Burke almost dropped the phone. Debbi fell flat onto the bed. "What do you mean, she's missing?" asked Burke. "You had her under guard."

"Yeah, well, sometime between 5:30 and 6 P.M. she disappeared."

"Any chance someone kidnapped her? Like with Stacy?"

"No way. We had a guard there, remember?"

"So the guard could keep her from getting kidnapped, but not from escaping, is that it?"

Jackie didn't answer. For a long second, Burke waited.

"That wasn't very kind," said Jackie.

Burke shook his head. "Okay, I know, but it doesn't make sense. How did she get by the guard?"

"We're not sure, but she does work at that hospital, knows the routines and all. Anyway, just after five a custodian came by to clean her bathroom, change towels, bedclothes, you know the routine. Well, Bethany was in bed, but the custodian still changed her bed covers. He threw them into the clothes bin, then moved to the bathroom. When he finished, he never even looked back at the bed. We figure Bethany climbed into the clothes bin, pulled the dirty linens over her head, and rode out with the custodian. Simple as that."

Remembering his morning visit with Bethany, Burke closed his eyes and rubbed his forehead. Had she been faking the coma? Fooling them all since the beginning? Did she have Stacy now, hidden somewhere, the poor baby the victim of a deranged mother? Suddenly, he had a terrible headache.

"I need to tell you something, Jackie," he said.

"I thought you might."

"I never answered you at Danny's when you asked me if Bethany had responded when I saw her."

"I know. We got interrupted by that overzealous waitress and never came back to the question. That's why I called you. Thought you might want to answer now."

"Well, I'm not sure 'want to' is how I would put it, but given the turn of events, I think I don't have a choice."

"I agree. So what happened?"

Burke spilled it all out. His visit with Bethany. Her requests. His agreement not to tell that she was conscious.

"So you deliberately kept this information from me?"

"No, not deliberately. I was concerned for her welfare, thought she might harm herself if she faced arraignment and went to jail. As her analyst, I thought a couple of days at the hospital would give her time to get a grip. You don't know how close to the edge she's been during the last four months."

"But you lied to me at Danny's," said Jackie, the hurt obvious in her voice.

Burke grunted. Technically, he hadn't lied. He just hadn't answered the question. But he knew that wouldn't soothe Jackie's feelings. And if the shoe were on the other foot, it wouldn't soothe his either.

"I'm sorry," he said. "I did what I thought best for my patient."

"At the expense of your friend."

"I prefer not to put it that way."

Jackie didn't answer. Burke stayed quiet too. Debbi broke the silence for them both. "You said you had several things to tell us."

"Yeah, get this. Bethany's scrubs, the ones we took off her the first day. Well, they've disappeared."

"But she couldn't have gotten to those," said Burke, defending his client.

"I agree, but someone she knows at the police station could have. Remember, she's got friends here."

"Cleve could have taken them. You know, to keep the blood from verifying her story."

"That's true, and I'm going to check that. But that's not all. A little bit ago, we ran a check at her bank. Seems that on Friday afternoon after she left the hospital, she cashed out a ten-thousand-dollar CD. It was in her mother's name, but Bethany signed for it."

"But that doesn't prove anything," argued Burke, not willing to give up his defense. "She could have had a hundred reasons for needing that money."

"Any idea where Bethany is?" Debbi interrupted.

"I was hoping Burke could tell me," Jackie said.

Debbi looked at Burke. He shook his head.

"He's thinking," said Debbi.

Burke turned his palms to the ceiling.

"Well, while he's thinking, there's more to consider," said Jackie.

"What do you mean?" asked Debbi.

"Are you sitting down?"

Debbi pulled Burke down on the bed beside her. "We are now," she said.

"Good, let me make it quick and simple. Another kid is missing."

"What?" The two of them exploded the question simultaneously, Burke jumping from the bed like a pogo stick and Debbi wrapping herself into a ball beside him.

"A boy, Taylor Bradford, from the same trailer park as Stacy, is missing."

"Since when?"

 *Dark Road to Daylight*

"Since around seven. He disappeared from his front yard while his mother sat in the swimming pool. She says she climbed in for about fifteen minutes, climbed out, dried herself off, then realized she hadn't seen her son for a while. She searched the yard, the trailer, the road in front, the trailers adjacent to hers, the playground half a block down the street. But she found nothing, no sign of the kid. That's when she called 911. About eight o'clock."

"Any connection between the kids?" asked Debbi, gaining her voice a split second before Burke.

"Yeah, we checked that. They played together fairly frequently—three or four times a week. Taylor was one of the few children whose mother didn't work outside the home. So he was there all day. So was Stacy."

"And when did Bethany escape the hospital?"

"Between five and six."

"Enough time to make it to the trailer park before the boy disappeared," said Burke, stating the obvious before Jackie beat him to it.

"But why?" asked Debbi. "Why would Bethany take the boy?"

"That's assuming she did," said Jackie. "And that would assume she also took her own child, hid her somewhere or, worse yet, harmed her in some way."

"But that's crazy," said Burke. "She would have to be—"

"You're the doctor," interrupted Jackie. "You'd know better than me about that."

"What about clues?" asked Debbi, changing the direction of the conversation. "You find anything to tie the two together?"

"Not much yet. But we just got started."

"Any chance the two disappearances aren't connected?" asked Burke.

"Well, there's always that chance. It could be a copycat kind of thing. Or the boy could have just wandered off. They don't have a fenced yard and there's no sign of foul play this time."

"You think that's possible?" asked Burke, anxious to find some answer other than Bethany. "That he just wandered off?"

"You want an honest answer?" asked Jackie.

"Sure."

"Well, here it is. One, I don't think the boy wandered off. And two, I don't think it's a copycat. I don't have the evidence to support this yet, but I have a feeling that these two go hand in hand. Whoever took Stacy also took Taylor. The odds of anything else are remote."

Several seconds skipped by. Burke stared at Debbi. She reached out and took his hand. A sinking sensation fell into his stomach. He had talked to Bethany that morning. Had kept it a secret that she knew him and talked to him. Had not told Jackie, a close friend, that a suspected criminal was conscious and coherent.

Now, another child had disappeared. A baby boy. A boy with a mom and a dad who right now surely felt that someone had ripped out their hearts and cut them into tiny bits. Staring at Debbi, Burke slumped into her arms. By trying to help one person he had perhaps destroyed another three.

CHAPTER EIGHTEEN

1:12 A.M.

His eyes heavy, Rusty Redder yanked off his blue jeans, fell into the queen-sized bed of room 112 of the Old South Hotel, and tried to sleep. On the floor around the bed lay seventeen empty bottles—the evidence of the beer he had swilled down since his arrival just past eleven. He had needed the beer to numb his twittery nerves.

In all his years of crime, nothing like tonight had ever happened. Never before had he felt a gun jabbed into his neck. Never before had death been so close, right there behind him, ready to blow him away, blast his brains into the straw of an old barn in the middle of a pasture in the middle of nowhere.

One by one, he had sucked down the bottles of beer. As the beer went down, so, it seemed, did his anxiety. He could handle this, the beer told him. He could snatch one more kid, make one more delivery, pick up his sixty grand, and leave this life behind forever. Someone had left the directions for the drop in an envelope at the desk. Rusty had picked it up when he checked in.

Lying in the bed, he watched the room swirl about him, around and around—a merry-go-round powered by the beer he had poured into his body. For over an hour he watched the ceiling twist in circles. Finally, he fell asleep.

Outside a dog barked. By the window of 112, a streetlight hummed as thousands of moths fluttered and popped into it. Cars and trucks lumbered past, their engines breaking the quietness of the night. Through the early hours of the morning, Rusty tossed, rolled, and wrestled on the bed. Sweat seeped through the red hair on his chest and made a wet circle on the green bedspread. He muttered in his sleep, a dream suddenly upsetting his beer-induced rest.

Cows . . . a herd of cows, thirty or more, a herd pressing close upon him, a herd with heavy breath exhaling on his face. Big brown eyes staring into his soul. One cow bumped him, then another and another. The bumps knocked him side to side, like a bumper car at an amusement park. Everywhere he turned, a cow bumped him, turning him first one direction and then another.

The cows started to moo. The sound erupted quietly at first, a soft rumble from the bowels of one huge body. A second cow took up the chorus, then a third and a fourth. Within seconds, all the cows were mooing, their gentle sound becoming a thunderous roar that shook Rusty's body and sent shivers of fear through his spirit.

Pushing his hands against his ears to shut out the mooing, Rusty turned around and around, searching for a place to escape from the sound and the eyes. He saw none. He pressed his hands harder against his head.

The cows pressed in on him, their ponderous weight squeezing him tighter and tighter. He couldn't breathe! He became the center of a sandwich—squeezed tighter and tighter between the cows.

His eyes were level with theirs, which were wide and glassy with anger. The cows pressed him harder and harder. His body hurt from the squeezing. He knew he could die under the weight of the herd.

The mooing elevated in pitch. Higher and higher rose the sound, until it became a shrill wailing, like the cry of a baby in distress, a cry Rusty couldn't shut out no matter how hard he pressed his hands against his ears.

Rusty screamed. The cows shrieked. Their brown eyes shifted, twisted, changed.

A child appeared before Rusty. A boy with big brown eyes. Taylor Bradford. The boy lifted a hand and pointed. Dropping his hands from the sides of his head, Rusty turned to see the object of Taylor's interest.

Another child. Behind Rusty. A girl—Stacy Chapman. Tears the size of marbles cascaded down her cheeks. She opened her mouth and

wailed. The crying bit into Rusty's heart, taking a chunk out. His chest felt heavy, crushed by pounds of grief.

Stacy stepped toward him. He turned away from her, hoping to escape the sound of her crying. He saw Taylor edging toward him too, closer and closer, his big brown eyes wide. Stacy grabbed his leg from behind, her wailing causing him to lift his hands to his ears again. Taylor stared at him.

Stacy wailed.

Taylor stared.

Wailing.

Brown eyes.

Rusty jerked up out of bed, wildly kicking out his sweaty legs, rubbing his sleep-caked eyes. What the—?

A dream. That was it. He had a dream. A nightmare.

He sucked in his breath and threw his legs over the edge of the bed. His chest thumped heavily, and he cupped his hands together and placed them over his heart. Steady, now, calm down. Just a dream. Nothing more.

Rusty reached for the box of cigars lying on the lamp table by the bed. His heart slowed down. He pulled out a cigar and lit it.

Taylor Bradford and Stacy Chapman. In his dream. The two kids he'd kidnapped.

He took a drag off his cigar, drawing out the smoke, making sure it stayed lit.

He wondered about the two kids. What had happened to them? Who was this guy who wouldn't pay? And the woman with him? What kind of game were they playing?

Rusty blew a heavy cloud of smoke into the air. He hoped the kids were still alive. He was a lot of things, but he didn't cotton to the idea of murder. Especially the murder of innocent kids.

But why would the guy kill the kids? Was he some kind of serial killer? But Rusty thought those guys worked alone—they were psychotics who liked the control they gained over other people. That's why they did what they did.

But if not murder, then what? What would the guy do with the kids?

Rusty shuddered at his next thought, suddenly feeling chilled. He glanced around the room, saw his T-shirt lying on the chair across from the bed. With the toes of his right foot, he snatched the shirt, pulled it over, and slipped it on.

Did the guy want the children for some perverse pleasure? What a disgusting thought! Sad too. Sad for the kids and for the parents who waited and wondered what happened to them. What a tragedy—not knowing what happened to your kid.

A realization swept over Rusty. He didn't know about his own kid. His little boy, Shane. Did he still live with his mom in Perry?

How long since he'd seen his kid? Two years? A bit more? Yeah, that sounded about right. Christmas over two years ago. That would make Shane seven years old. A boy with wiry hair the color of radishes. Just like his dad. Freckles the size of tiny pebbles dotting his cheeks and running across his nose.

Rusty recalled the last time he saw Shane. He gave him a basketball hoop and ball for Christmas. Lowered the hoop so Shane could make his shots. Played with the boy for almost an hour. Shoot and chase the ball. Shoot and chase the ball.

What a great day. He hadn't felt that good since then.

He chewed on the end of his cigar for several seconds. Smoke billowed around his head. He spat out a bit of tobacco that had dribbled from the cigar into his mouth. He made a decision.

He would not take another child. Money or no money, it didn't matter. He had stepped past a line somewhere, stumbling into something that just didn't fit his conscience. Yeah, he was a criminal, but he wasn't a mean man. He didn't want to hurt kids.

He thought he could kidnap them and keep that part of the scheme separate from what happened to them later. He thought he could rationalize his actions, keep the questions about the children out of his head. But he couldn't do it.

Taylor Bradford's brown eyes appeared in Rusty's head again. He heard Stacy's wailing. He shook his head violently, pushing away the thoughts. For a split second, he considered trying to find the two children, going back to the drop-off points, searching the spots for clues so he could track them down and rescue them from whatever fate they faced.

But he knew he couldn't do that. The trail was too cold. His employer too careful.

Rusty stubbed his cigar out on the table by the bed. Switching on the lamp, he picked up his pants and slid into them.

He couldn't rescue Taylor and Stacy, but he could refuse to take anyone else. He could disappear into the Atlanta traffic, vanish like a fog burned off by the sun.

He tied the laces of his scuffed Nikes and sat up straight again. He took a deep breath, feeling better already. He wouldn't kidnap a third child. He would kiss the sixty grand good-bye and head to Florida. He would head to Florida and find honest work and go straight and make amends for the life he had chosen for the last six years.

He pulled his wallet and keys from the drawer of the lamp table and walked out of the room. Florida, look out. Rusty Redder was on the way. Just one thing to do before he got there. Rusty would stop in Perry to see his seven-year-old boy, Shane.

Wednesday
August 27

CHAPTER NINETEEN

7:30 A.M.

For the second time within twenty-four hours, Burke and Debbi took a seat in their favorite blue booth near the back left corner of Danny's Doughnut Shop and ordered breakfast. Across from them sat Jackie Broadus, her charcoal-colored hair dropping in odd places out of what had been a tight bun. Her khaki slacks were wrinkled, and her white blouse had a smudge on the collar. Even her navy blazer seemed tired and droopy. Jackie didn't order food. Only a diet Dr. Pepper for her, she said.

Burke sized Jackie up for a moment. Her eyes, normally so clear, looked like someone had stitched red strings into them. An oily sheen lay on her hair.

"I take it you didn't sleep much," said Burke.

"Try none at all. One missing kid frightens a family and a neighborhood. Two missing kids frightens a whole city."

"We saw the television this morning," said Burke.

"And the newspaper," added Debbi. "Seems like everyone is concentrating on Bethany Chapman."

Jackie nodded. "So far no one else comes to mind."

"But why would she take the boy?" asked Burke, eager to find a way to shift the suspicions. "That doesn't make sense."

Jackie shrugged. "Depends on how you look at it. Remember, the two kids knew each other."

"Is that enough to make Bethany a suspect in the second kidnapping?" he asked, unconvinced.

"No, by itself, that's probably not enough, but that's not all. It gets worse—or better, depending on how you see it."

"Well, tell me the worst of it."

"Bethany's diary. She talked about the Taylor kid in her diary."

Burke's eyes squinted in confusion. "Bethany talked about Taylor Bradford?"

"That's right, more than once. Wrote how glad she was that Stacy had a friend. Wondered if children felt as lonely as adults do. Said she hoped Taylor made Stacy less lonely, became Stacy's pal—something Bethany didn't have but wished she did."

Debbi piped in a question. "You think she took the boy so Stacy wouldn't be lonely?"

"It's a theory floating around at Longstreet. We don't know. Still guessing mostly."

"That assumes that Stacy is still alive," said Burke. "Bethany took her to keep her from Cleve but she's okay somewhere. She wouldn't care about a playmate for her if Stacy was already—"

A waitress, the same one from yesterday, appeared with their food, cutting Burke off. When the waitress left, Jackie took a sip of her Dr. Pepper and returned to Burke's statement. "Unless she thought a playmate would still be needed."

Burke leaned back. "I don't understand," he said.

Jackie licked her lips. "Well, you know, maybe she thought Stacy needed a playmate later. It's complicated, but . . ."

"You mean later as in after she died?" asked Debbi, hearing the implication.

"Something like that. Crazier things have happened."

"So, let me get this straight," said Burke, his skepticism evident. "Bethany—or someone Bethany hires—grabs Stacy, maybe to keep her from her father, who's threatening to take her away, maybe with a murder-suicide in mind. But Bethany doesn't go through with it. At least not yet. She keeps Stacy under wraps somewhere while the cops arrest her. Then, after coming out of a catatonic coma, she grabs a second kid so her daughter can have a little friend to keep her company—either for now or for eternity?"

"When you put it that way, it sounds rather implausible," agreed Jackie. "But believe me, I've heard of more unbelievable things than that. So have you. Jeffrey Dahmer, Son of Sam, Wayne Gacey . . . you name it, somebody is evil enough to do it."

Dark Road to Daylight

"But those people were crazy," argued Debbi, obviously wanting to support Burke's position. "Certifiably psychotic. Nutcases. Fruits. Guys a few croutons short of a salad."

Jackie smiled. Burke laughed outright. "It's not politically correct to speak of the criminally insane in such insensitive terms," he said.

"And this is no laughing matter," said Jackie.

"But those people were crazy, right?" said Debbi, not willing to concede her point. "They did crazy things because they were crazy!"

"And you're saying Bethany isn't?" Jackie addressed the question to Debbi, but she turned immediately to Burke for the answer.

He took a huge breath and stared down at his hands. His fingers wrapped around his root beer glass. For the first time in four years, he felt a lack of confidence sweeping over him. Before he met Debbi he almost always felt this way. People called him "Freon" back then because of his reticent approach to life, his cool detachment from other people. Not that he didn't know he had certain capabilities. Practically a straight A student in high school and college, the same in the seminary studies that followed.

But that hadn't kept him from feeling uncomfortable with himself, guilty about himself. Having gone through countless hours of group therapy, he knew the roots of his feelings. One, he suffered from epilepsy. He didn't have attacks often. In fact, he hadn't had a full seizure in almost four years. Medicine kept the condition in check. And even when an attack came, his type of epilepsy didn't throw him to the ground twitching and jerking and frothing at the mouth. A psychomotor epileptic, he simply blacked out, lost control of what he did. When he regained consciousness, he couldn't remember what happened.

Tragically, one of those episodes caused the other reason for his low self-esteem. It happened the year he turned sixteen. He was baby-sitting his little sister, Sarah. He gave her a hot dog. She took a bite, then began to choke. He ran to her, ready to reach down with his fingers and jerk the dangerous food from her throat.

But he never reached her. The smell of onions suddenly filled his nostrils—the weird warning sign of an imminent seizure. The seizure exploded from nowhere—a sledgehammer knocking him off his feet, down to the floor of the kitchen. On his knees he tried to rise, to reach Sarah, to save her.

Gary E. Parker   **129**

Blackness swept over him. He sagged to the floor. When he regained consciousness twenty minutes later, he found Sarah on the floor beside him—her blue eyes open in a glassy stare.

Guilt had slammed down like a manhole cover on his shoulders that day. Over the years it had gotten worse and worse. He blamed himself, hated himself, wished that he had died instead of Sarah. He believed himself unworthy of any lasting happiness.

Then he met Debbi. Fell in love with her. Debbi encouraged him to have faith in himself. Reminded him that he couldn't control his medical condition, told him over and over that he couldn't hold himself responsible for the terrible thing that had happened to his sister.

Gradually, in the years he had known her, he had come to believe what she said. He wasn't to blame. If she said it, then it had to be true. Like chaff burning off in a fire, his guilt burned away under the blaze of her steady love. His confidence in himself grew stronger, nurtured by her assurances. When they got married, she gave him a new nickname. "Star Trek" because he liked to explore new things, do what he hadn't done before.

But right now, staring full face at the possibility that one of his clients had perhaps kidnapped and harmed her own daughter, that confidence dissipated. As Bethany's therapist, he knew her better than anyone except her mother and maybe her ex-husband. He knew from the first time he met her that she had deep problems. Over the last four months, he had treated her. As he saw it, she had made steady, if unspectacular, progress.

At this moment, however, he wondered if he had misdiagnosed the depth of her troubles. Had he listened to her but not heard? Out of a need to believe that he was making a difference, had he convinced himself she had improved when she really hadn't?

Burke thought back to his sessions with Bethany. Was she disturbed enough to kidnap her own child, then take a second one too? Was she insane enough to kill first Stacy, then Taylor Bradford?

If so, he had blown it. And in doing so had contributed to the deaths of two children. His mistakes had done it. His screwups.

A pall of depression washed over him. First Sarah, now Stacy and Taylor Bradford. He slumped in his seat, and when he answered Jackie, his voice was soft, hesitant, weak.

"I don't know, Jackie," he said. "I don't know . . . if Bethany is psychotic or not."

 **130**

"But it's possible? She might be certifiably insane?"

Burke took a drink of his root beer, thinking about the question. "It's hard to quantify insanity," he said finally. "Which tests do you use? Are they completely reliable? When does a person actually go over the edge? Are we born that way or does it develop later? Why are we sane one moment, insane the next? Those questions are tough to answer."

"So you don't know," said Jackie, setting down her Dr. Pepper.

Burke shrugged. "That's basically it. I don't know."

"But it's possible." It was a statement of fact, not a question.

"It's possible," said Burke, resigned to Jackie's conclusion. She was right. Bethany might have stepped beyond what most people called sane. The call from Cleve might have taken a woman bordering on psychosis and shoved her right past the point of no return. Though it seemed illogical, Burke knew that logic held no grip on mental illness.

He suddenly felt sick to his stomach. His bowels clenched on him like a giant fist. A ball of bitterness climbed to the back of his throat. He pushed it back.

As if sensing his distress, Debbi reached over and took his hand.

"So where do we go from here?" she asked, obviously anxious to move them away from a dead end. "No matter who did this, we need to act. Whether Bethany is clinically psychotic or not doesn't solve the problem. If she's responsible for this mess, then let's find her. If she's not, then let's find the person who is."

"We're working on it," said Jackie, pulling a notepad from the inside pocket of her blazer.

"Anything new?" Debbi asked.

"A couple of things. We know from the lab that the material on the earring is human skin. And it's not more than a few days old. We hoped we'd find blood traces, but no luck. If it ever did have blood on it, it's gone now."

"Maybe the rain washed it off," suggested Burke, quickly taking to the possibility. "And if the skin's not too old, then someone could have lost the earring the day Stacy disappeared."

"Either that day or the day before," said Jackie. "That's what we think right now."

"But how did it get under the doghouse?" asked Debbi.

Jackie sipped her Dr. Pepper. "We don't know that. Maybe that's where the struggle took place. It got jerked off, fell on the ground, rolled under the doghouse."

"The ground is pretty dug up around there," suggested Burke. "The rain could have washed it under the house."

Jackie nodded her agreement. "But we don't know yet whose earring it is and when it got where you found it."

The three of them fell silent for several moments. Burke took a bite of toast. Debbi took out a paper and pad and began to jot down a few notes.

"If it's Bethany's then she should have a torn ear," said Burke, stating the obvious. "But she doesn't."

"So the earring isn't hers," said Debbi.

"Whoa," cautioned Jackie. "We don't know that for sure. The amount of skin doesn't tell us how bad the injury was. Use a touch of makeup and you might never even notice an injury to her ear."

"But didn't the doctors give her a good going over when she went to the hospital?" asked Debbi.

Jackie shook her head. "Never got around to it. She wasn't in for physical problems, remember. With mental patients, the physical exam isn't nearly so thorough."

Burke sighed. "So we really don't know what happened with Bethany, do we?"

"Exactly," said Jackie. "We have no clue."

"So what's next?" asked Burke.

"We continue the search. We go through the trailer park. With the second one missing, the court system is moving in a hurry. Within the day we should have permission to go into each trailer, search it, even if the occupant refuses to let us and even if no one is home."

"You don't have that yet?"

"Nope. Can't do a search without a warrant. And without probable cause, we can't get a warrant."

"A kid could die while you waited on a warrant," said Debbi.

"My point exactly," said Jackie. "I made it to a judge not more than an hour ago."

"How many trailers left to check?" asked Burke.

"More than I care to count," said Jackie.

Burke nodded. He could only imagine. He reached for the ticket and pulled out his wallet. Jackie didn't protest. With Debbi walking beside him and Jackie behind, he paid the bill and stepped out into the bright sunshine of another August Atlanta day.

 132

CHAPTER TWENTY

6:22 P.M.

The day had passed like a loaded freight train going up a mountain. Inch by inch, inch by inch the hours fell reluctantly off the clock. At the clinic, a steady stream of clients passed through Burke's office. A teenage girl with a drinking problem, an adult male struggling with sexual impotence, three couples with marriages on the rocks. One after another they came, a procession of strugglers for whom life had lost its luster, people with pain in their souls and depression in their strides.

Sitting in a flame-stitched winged chair in front of a sun-streaked window, Burke tried to concentrate on every one of them. He cared about his clients and wanted to help them. And now that they had admitted their inability to move forward without assistance and had come to him, he believed he could help them.

But maybe not today, he admitted to himself about 3:30. Today he seemed slow-minded and hard-hearted, unable to muster much compassion for their struggles or much patience with their chatter.

All day long, he had drifted from his focus, thought about Bethany and Stacy Chapman and Taylor Bradford. Over and over again he found himself staring through his clients, past them to the window that beckoned temptingly just over their shoulders as they sat on the brown leather sofa that dominated his office. The office felt confining today, a straitjacket of glass and steel, a tomb containing a mahogany desk, a wingback and a sofa, a computer on a credenza and a stack of papers in the corner by the five-foot-tall potted plant.

Time and time through the day, he experienced an almost panicky feeling—a feeling that he wanted to flee this hermetically sealed room, that he wanted to rush outside and take off his tie and his shoes and run through the grass. Rebelliousness tugged at his soul, and he wished more than anything else that he could drop everything on his calendar and hurry away from the responsibilities that weighed so heavily upon him.

Burke understood why this urge pressed in on him so powerfully. Though he tried mightily to avoid the notion, he couldn't. He had blown it with Bethany. Now, other people had to pay the price for his foul-up. He wanted to run from that reality, but he couldn't.

He glanced at his watch. Across from him sat a divorcee complaining about her husband's failure to pay his child support. Burke nodded his head and stared at her mouth, forcing himself to pay attention. He failed in his effort. His mind drifted.

It wasn't that he didn't feel for the woman. But her problem seemed minor when compared to the problems faced by so many.

He glanced at his watch again. Almost 6:30. Time for the session and, thankfully, the long day to end. Burke held up his hand. "I think we better stop here," he said as gently as he could. "If we start a new area of discussion, we won't have time to do it justice."

The woman smiled and nodded. She understood.

Standing, Burke ushered her from the office and told Molly to make her an appointment for the following week. The divorcee smiled again and left.

"Is that it?" he asked Molly.

Molly scanned her appointment calendar, her reading glasses perched smartly on her nose. "No more today, but tons of paperwork to clean up."

Burke groaned. Molly stayed on him constantly about the paperwork. "I'll get to it in the morning," he offered, hoping that would satisfy her.

"Until the paperwork is finished, the checks don't get written."

Burke smiled. She said that to him at least once a week. "I'll be here at eight in the morning," he said. "That'll give me an hour and a half before my first appointment."

Molly nodded. "You're the boss."

"Why is it I don't believe you really mean that?"

She smiled and turned back to her calendar. "See you in the morning."

Burke snapped off the light in his office and exited quickly through the back entrance. Hustling, he jumped into his Cavalier and spun onto the highway. Within fifteen minutes, he hit the interstate and headed south. Though traffic still stretched out as far as he could see, at least the worst of rush hour had passed.

Pressing the accelerator, he rolled down his window. Even if he couldn't take off his shoes and feel the grass between his toes, he still wanted to feel the wind on his face. To his left an eighteen-wheeler passed him. He checked his speedometer. Sixty-five. Fast enough.

Burke took a deep breath and settled into his seat. If all went well, he would reach the Lincoln Family Trailer Park within a few minutes. He didn't know yet what he hoped to find there. But all day long, as he sat through the sessions with his clients, something had nagged at the base of his brain. Something he had missed somewhere.

He thought of the clues Jackie had told him about since the beginning of this awful nightmare. The cigars—nothing unique about them— off-the-rack types anyone with a dollar could buy at the corner store.

The bit of skin from the earring. Not identifiable as to gender and not conducive to DNA testing.

Tire tracks, identified as those of a pickup. The green pickup truck seen driving slowly past Bethany's trailer prior to the kidnapping.

The letters *B-E* and the start of a third written on the note by Lydia Spicer. No clue as to what they meant.

Burke zipped past a Cadillac moving about fifty miles an hour. A sense of anxiety rushed through him, and he sat up straighter in his seat.

Seeking to clear his head so he could think better, he leaned closer to the window. Streams of hot wind swished by him. To his left, a road construction crew poured asphalt on a pothole. Traffic slowed to avoid the workers and Burke hit the brakes. A long line of cars stretched out in front of him. Great! Just what he needed—a traffic jam. The acrid smell of black tar seeped into his nostrils as he waited on the traffic.

The minutes ticked by—five, ten, twenty. Fighting his impatience, Burke thought back over the whole scenario. What was it he had failed to see? Was some clue connected to something Bethany had told him in a former session? Was it something he had seen on his trip to pick up Scooter's doghouse? Something connected to the earring? What was it?

The car in front of him moved and jarred him back to the present. At last, the traffic began to speed up. He moved ahead, eager to get to Bethany's. A few minutes later, he saw his exit sign and pulled off the interstate. A left over the bridge and a right at the light. A couple of moments later, he reached the road leading into Lincoln Family Trailer Park. For a couple of seconds, he stopped the car, put it in park, and closed his eyes. He slowed down his breathing, relaxing his mind. He wanted to go back to yesterday, to the exact moment when he turned down this road. He wanted to remember everything, every shadow, every second, every image, thought, smell, and sound.

Slowly, ever so slowly, he drifted back. He heard his heart pumping rhythmically. A second passed. Another second.

Okay, he had it under control. He could see clearly.

Easing the car into drive, he rolled past the entry sign and drove down the gravel road. His left arm braced on the window ledge, he peered out. The shadows today were almost identical to yesterday's. The afternoon almost as late. But the breeze was nonexistent. This time no shadowed trees danced on the hood of his car.

To his right, he heard laughter. He turned toward it. Saw a mass of children running in and out of a spray of water that gushed from a garden hose. A man with a gray beard but no shirt held the hose.

Burke faced the road again. Only about a hundred yards from Bethany's place. No traffic on the road. Quiet. Like—

That was it! That's what he had forgotten. Yesterday, two vehicles passed him on the opposite side of the road, throwing up a spray of white dust. The dust had practically blinded him to the second vehicle. But in the rearview mirror, Burke had caught a glimpse of the back of that vehicle.

It had a trailer hitch on the bumper and a busted left taillight. Even more significantly, it was a pickup and it was green.

Burke slammed on his brakes and threw his head into his hands, realizing the implication of what he had seen. At the same time he had arrived in the Lincoln Family Trailer Park yesterday, a pickup fitting the description of one seen just prior to the kidnapping of Stacy Chapman had sped out of the park.

Even more unsettling, that time frame fit almost exactly with the time frame for the disappearance of Taylor Bradford. Unless he was sadly mistaken, the green pickup that passed him on the gravel road in a cloud of dust probably carried the little boy away from his home.

Grunting his dismay, Burke punched the dial on his car phone. Jackie needed to know this. She needed to know it now.

CHAPTER TWENTY-ONE

8:15 P.M.

The dispatcher at Longstreet Station told Burke she couldn't reach Jackie Broadus. Lieutenant Broadus was currently at the scene of a homicide and couldn't be disturbed except on official business. She would, however, contact the lieutenant as soon as possible and tell her of the urgent nature of his call.

Disappointed and anxious to do something about this new information, Burke decided not to go home just yet. He would drive through the trailer park first, see what the rest of the place looked like.

Pulling off the side of the road, he slowly made his way to Bethany's trailer. There he parked and climbed out. As if trying to sneak past a sleeping parent after staying out past curfew, he tiptoed into the yard. For almost fifteen minutes, he walked around outside, examining the ground, trying to get a feel for what had happened in this tiny space of dirt.

At the place where Scooter's doghouse had been, he bent down and examined the ground, especially careful to inspect the holes the spaniel had dug. This time, however, he found no treasures.

Standing, Burke stretched his back and stared up at the sky. The shadows had lengthened until they now engulfed the yard, casting dark patterns across the azalea bushes.

Noting the fleeting daylight, Burke walked away from Bethany's yard and down the street. Overhead, a row of streetlights blinked on, and thousands of moths instantly flocked to them. From the woods across the street, the sounds of cicadas clicked and clacked through the air. Cars and trucks passed him on the road, casting gravel into the air with their spinning tires.

Burke turned a corner and walked through another street, then a third. All around him, lights came on in the trailers as night fell. One after another, cars and trucks pulled into their driveways and tired men and women rolled out of their vehicles and trudged into their houses. The smell of food—grilled beef of some kind from one yard, cabbage from another, fish from a third—wafted through the night air and filled Burke's nostrils.

He walked down another street, then another. On every road, he saw the lights. Trailer after trailer all lit up with people inside. Lights and people in trailers. In every trailer he passed.

He walked to the sixth street past Bethany's. One trailer, then a second, a third, and a fourth. Then a fifth, this one with no lights burning. Burke paused and stared at the dark trailer. It seemed so out of place in all the hustle and bustle of the rest. But it wasn't so unusual. Not every worker was home yet. And not every unit was occupied.

He started to walk past the dark yard. At his feet, a plastic soda bottle lay in the street. He kicked the bottle and it clattered along the road. He kicked it again, then a third time. The bottle lay directly under a street light. He drew back his foot for a fourth kick. His foot stopped in mid-swing. A cigar butt lay by the bottle. His heart pounding, Burke squatted and picked up the butt. For several seconds, he held it up in the light, studying it carefully. A chewed end, round, not crushed. Fairly fresh.

Carefully, he stuck it in the pocket of his shirt. Still squatting, he scanned the ground around his feet, wondering if he would find any more cigar remains. He didn't. He backed up a few steps. Still nothing more. Okay, only one. But one might be enough.

His breath in short gasps, Burke stood and stared at the dark trailer in front of him. For a moment, he thought about going back to his car to call Jackie. But he decided against it. In the time it would take to get to his car, make the call, and return to the scene, the occupant of the trailer might come home. Burke couldn't afford to wait for Jackie. He'd already let the green truck get past him. He wouldn't make the same mistake twice.

Dark Road to Daylight

Besides, Jackie hadn't been available when he called less than an hour ago. He had no reason to think she would be available now. Given the circumstances, Burke saw no choice but to handle the situation himself.

But what should he do? Wait and see if anyone came to the trailer? No, that might lead to disaster too. The occupant—he assumed it was a man because of the cigar—might return, then leave again. He might even pack his bags and leave Atlanta. And what could Burke do to stop him? He had no authority to question the man, and he certainly didn't want to get into a confrontation with some guy who might have kidnapped and killed two children.

Stuck with his dilemma, Burke took a step closer to the trailer. He had no choice but to do something now before the opportunity passed.

Burke tiptoed into the yard. The light from the streetlight overhead dropped off his shoulders. He stood now in almost total darkness. He inched farther toward the trailer. It loomed before him like a stationary train car, boxy and black.

He reached a stoop, climbed the steps, and came to the door. For a second, he paused, contemplating his next move. Down the street, a cat screeched and a car pulled out of a driveway.

Burke considered what would happen if someone saw him on the stoop, standing still in the dark. Given the events in the trailer park over the last couple of days, someone would surely call the cops immediately. He didn't need that kind of attention. If he planned to do anything, he had to act quickly.

He knocked on the door of the trailer but received no response. Just as he expected. He sucked in his breath and wiped his hands on his slacks. His heart notched up like a piston engine, and he braced himself for his next move. He grabbed the doorknob and twisted it. To his surprise, the knob turned in his hand. He pushed the door open, then paused.

Okay, no sound from inside. Quickly scanning the street behind him, Burke eased through the door and into the dark trailer. He quietly pushed the door closed and waited for his eyes to adjust. Gradually, the darkness gave way to patches of gray light, and within a minute or so he could see enough to move away from the door.

To his left he saw a television, to his right a sofa. Straight ahead sat a coffee table. Not wanting to risk a light, Burke pushed forward

Gary E. Parker

into the room. Nothing in it told him what he needed to know about the occupant—the person's gender, age, occupation—nothing.

Though he was getting more frightened by the moment, Burke refused to give up yet. The cigar butt outside was no coincidence. Whoever lived here knew something. Whoever lived here had sat at one point or another across from Stacy Chapman's place and smoked cigars, dropping the remains on the road when finished.

Driven by his suspicions, Burke stepped out of the living area and walked to his left, past the television against the wall. In the hallway, the glow of streetlights disappeared, and he had to steer himself by touching the paneled walls. Five steps, ten steps, twelve steps he took. Then his hand felt air to his right. A doorway. Burke stepped through it. Light flooded into the room from the streetlight outside.

Burke looked around. A mattress on the floor. A dresser under the window. A stack of newspapers in the corner.

Without hesitation, Burke hurried to the dresser and opened the top left drawer. Having come this far, he might as well make it worth the risk. He found nothing in the drawer. He opened a second drawer, the one on the top right. Nothing. Middle left and middle right. Nothing in either. Two drawers remaining.

He jerked open the bottom left and found nothing. His hands shaking, he grabbed the handle of the last one and ran his hands through the inside of the wood. Not a thing.

Frustrated, he stepped back from the dresser. In the narrow room, the back of his calves bumped into the mattress on the floor. The touch in the darkness startled him. Before he could catch himself, he lost his balance and tumbled backward. His right shoulder fell into the mattress. Though disoriented by the fall, he bounced up quickly. His adrenaline surging, he tumbled forward this time, off the mattress and into the stack of newspapers. He fell a second time, his knees banging the papers as he crashed over.

His knees hit the floor, and his forearms rested on the newspaper stack. Sweat poured off his face and dripped onto the papers. As he stared down at the papers, he spotted a picture lying in the corner.

Squinting in the gray light from the street lamp, Burke could barely make it out—a black-and-white picture of a man leaning against a pickup truck. Catching his breath, he grabbed the picture and pushed up from the corner. He eased toward the only window in the room and held the picture up to the light.

Dark Road to Daylight

Good heavens! An earring as round as a half-dollar dangled from the lobe of the man's left ear.

At that moment, he heard the sound of a vehicle pulling up outside. A beacon of headlights flashed into the room. A car door slammed.

Clutching the picture tightly, Burke rushed out of the room and down the hallway. In the living room again, he stopped for an instant to catch his breath. Who was outside? The person who lived here?

He stared across the room to the window on the back wall. On the wall, he noticed a poster of a vaguely familiar face.

Burke gasped.

Rushing, he crossed the room, jerked the poster off the wall, and skittered to the front door.

Suddenly the lights from the vehicle outside flickered off.

Not knowing what else to do, not daring to see if someone would now climb the stoop and enter the trailer, Burke yanked opened the door and ran. Without looking back to see if anyone followed, he plunged down the stoop and out into the street. He ran with all his might, using his well-exercised legs to carry him away from the trailer, away from the trailer where the poster of Bernardo the Beast had been stuck to the wall.

CHAPTER TWENTY-TWO

9:02 P.M.

Hitting the brakes and grinding to a sudden halt, Jackie Broadus popped open the car door and hit the ground running. About two hundred feet away, at the edge of a weedy yard, she saw a scene she had witnessed far more often than she cared to admit—a mob of onlookers, the curious who flocked to a murder site as if drawn by an invisible beam. Just past the crowd, she spotted an ambulance and two police cars—all three parked square to the curb. The lights of the vehicles flashed blue and red, marking the spot as surely as a swirl of vultures marked a meal. To the left of the squad cars, she noted the glaring white light of a television camera and a navy van with WATL printed on the side. The news media—flies swarming a roadkill.

Behind the ambulance, almost hidden from her view, she spotted a gurney covered top to bottom with a white sheet. In a few minutes the gurney would transport a bloody body, the latest victim of Atlanta's seemingly insatiable thirst for mayhem.

Though not eager for the task, Jackie nevertheless hustled over the sidewalk toward the ambulance. A police officer for fifteen years, she had about seen it all. The commonplace murders—the Saturday night shootings at the local bar and the gang-related drug hits. The weapons of choice, knives and guns.

But she had also bumped into another breed of murderer—the rarity that sprang up without warning, a human blip on the radar screen—a serial killer who tortured the victims and left behind a psychotic signature to mark the work. Through it all, she had managed to maintain a professional facade of cool composure. Living by the motto her now-retired former partner had given her, "Never let them see you hurl," she had struggled over the years to prove herself as tough as the men with whom she worked. Proving herself to them meant a lot to Jackie. No matter what the situation, she kept her cool.

As Jackie saw it, she had managed the pressures about as well as anyone—man or woman. She had seen scores of murder victims in her years on the force. She kept a record of them in a black ringed binder in her closet. Kept the names of the deceased, the dates of their deaths, the results of her investigations.

She kept these records because she didn't want to forget the people who employed her. That's the way she understood her work. She did her job for them—the dead ones, the murdered, the people who could no longer speak for themselves.

So long as she remembered them, she could live with the horrible images her job often brought. Their names and faces—always available in her black book—reminded her that no matter how gruesome her work, she did something important. She tried to bring the murderers of innocent people to justice.

Stepping past the yellow crime scene tape, Jackie took a deep breath and reminded herself why she did this job. More than once in the last couple of years, she had seriously considered giving it up. Long hours, dangerous conditions, loneliness—all of it made her consider flat out quitting.

But she couldn't do that. At least, not today. She sucked in her breath and nodded to the EMT standing by the gurney. "They said it's bad," she said, her voice a monotone.

"One of the worst I've seen," said the EMT. "Blood all over the place."

"Who's inside?" she asked, jerking her head toward the center of activity—a one-story brick house to their right.

"Two uniforms from Longstreet. Patrick and Chapman. You're the first shield to show up."

Jackie nodded. "How long since you got here?"

The EMT rubbed her forearm with a slender palm. "Oh, twenty minutes or so. Long enough to know this job would be transport and nothing else."

"A DOA?"

"As DOA as they get. By the time we got here, no hope, no way, nohow." The woman looked away from Jackie, her thin arms now wrapped around her chest.

Staring at the house, a square block with shattered windows and a crack in the concrete porch, Jackie grunted and clicked her teeth together. "You did what you could," she said.

The EMT nodded. "You got it. I did what I could. Now it's your turn."

Jackie paused for another moment, then knew it wouldn't help to put it off any longer. Inside, a body waited for her, another in the long line of those whose cause she had taken up, another entry in her book of black.

She stepped past the EMT and up the steps of the cracked porch. The door of the house hung open like a mouth agape. Jackie tiptoed through it, careful of her steps, not wanting to disturb any evidence. Past the door, she turned to the left and entered a living room. Stopping for a quick survey, her eyes came to rest on the blue-shirted backs of Patrick and Chapman. They stood in the center of the room, bent over at the waist, staring down at something on the gray floor. Instinctively, Jackie knew what held their attention, but she didn't let herself look at it just yet.

Instead, she scanned the room. It contained no furniture. Nothing. Not a chair, not a sofa, not a table, not a lamp—nothing. Nothing hung on the grimy beige walls either. The floor of the room was bare gray concrete. It looked as if someone had deliberately pulled out all the sensory distractions.

The only feature that disturbed the room's lack of adornment was a boxlike fireplace cut into the far wall past the two patrolmen. In front of the fireplace, balanced on what looked like a one-foot hearth, stood a stack of reddish stones. The stones, flat and round, made a mound about three feet high.

Intrigued by the stones, Jackie lowered her eyes and glanced past the black shoes of Patrick and Chapman. There—there it was. The telltale white sheet. The white sheet surrounded by a puddle of almost-dried crimson fluid that she identified immediately. The fluid led like a lava flow from the sheet to the edge of the reddish stones.

Realizing what that meant, Jackie's stomach gripped up on her and her throat clamped shut. She found it almost impossible to breathe. It seemed as if someone had pulled the air out of the room

 144

along with the furnishings. She doubled over at the waist, sucking in heavily, hoping against hope that the moment would pass quickly.

Patrick stood and swiveled around. Jackie jerked up, not wanting him to see her so upset. His face wrinkled up as he saw her, but he didn't speak. Patting her lips as if pushing back a burp, Jackie exhaled and nodded.

"It's not a pretty sight," Patrick said, shaking his head.

"None of them are," said Jackie, struggling to make her voice even.

"But this is worse."

Jackie nodded, knowing Patrick expected her to walk past him, pull back the sheet, and see for herself. But she didn't want to do it. For the first time she could remember, she wanted to skip that gruesome detail on this case.

Patrick stared at her, a quizzical expression on his wrinkled brow. Jackie gulped. She had no choice but to see the body, do her job, stand up to the horror of it all. She stepped past Patrick, over to Chapman, knowing she couldn't show him any weakness.

Careful not to disturb the blood, Jackie squatted down, the cold stone floor grinding under her feet. Her hands shook at her sides, but she steadied them as she reached for the sheet. She touched the sheet's corner, gripped it, then pulled it quickly down, exposing the body.

It took no more than a millisecond for the image to record itself on the memory chips in her brain. She dropped the sheet back over the victim and raised her hands to her face, palms pressed against her mouth. A wrench of bile pushed up from her stomach but she choked it back down.

As if fleeing from a burning building, she pushed up, turned from Patrick and Chapman and rushed out of the room and down the steps of the death house. In the trash-littered yard, she doubled over at the waist, closed her eyes, and retched into the patchy grass. Vaguely, from somewhere deep inside, she felt the bright glare of a camera light on her back. She didn't care. She threw up her heartache and cast it into the dirt.

Let them watch, she thought. *Let them watch. Anybody who can see what I just saw and not feel sick to their stomach has lost their soul.*

Her stomach still cramping upward, she retched again. As she did, she suddenly realized it felt good. After all these years of pretending it didn't affect her, now she could throw it out, she could spew out the pent-up grief of dozens of dead, the images forever etched on her mind, the names forever noted in her black book of death.

She retched and retched. Her body shook and her throat recoiled until nothing spewed out anymore. Her body collapsed onto the ground in weakness, her hands limp at her side, her eyes watery from pain and sadness. It was over. Finally, she could vomit no more. She wiped her mouth with the back of her hand and took a deep breath.

In a way she felt better. She wouldn't need to pretend anymore. Death hurt and she wasn't immune. So what if others thought her weak.

But the retching hadn't exorcised any of the pictures of the deceased from her mind, hadn't erased a single name from her black book. Worst of all, the retching hadn't made her forget the sight of that body under the sheet in the block stone house directly behind her.

In that second, her khaki slacks getting dirty in the grass, Jackie knew that sight would stay with her forever. That sight would haunt her as long as she lived. The sight of a child—with injuries too gruesome to enumerate—lying in a pool of crimson at the foot of a stone altar of horror.

CHAPTER TWENTY-THREE

11:30 P.M.

It was a girl," said Jackie, her voice a dead monotone, her eyes glassy from the sadness that had fallen over her in the two hours since she pulled back the sheet and saw the child. "A black-haired baby girl."

Sitting across from her at Longstreet Station, Burke rubbed his hands across his pants pockets. Jackie had asked him to meet her there. No time to go to Danny's.

He had the picture and the poster from the trailer with him, wrapped in a manila folder, but he hadn't had a chance to show them to Jackie yet. The instant he walked in the door and spotted her, he knew something had happened. She seemed altered somehow, as if a bomb had exploded inside her spirit, rearranging who she was. Maybe most people wouldn't see the difference. But he did. Even before she said a word.

So when she spoke it came as no surprise to him that her words fell so heavy from her lips. He nodded, sat up straight in his metal chair across from her desk, and let her pour it all out.

"We haven't identified the baby yet," the monotone continued. "That'll take some time. She's too young for a dental record, and her fingerprints certainly aren't on file anywhere."

For an instant, Jackie fell quiet. Burke waited. Jackie leaned forward and fiddled with an ink pen. Burke looked at a clock on the wall behind her desk. The second hand clipped past the three, then the four. He focused back on Jackie. Her eyes were glazed, open but unseeing.

Or maybe they do see, thought Burke. Maybe they saw something beyond the room, something drawing her into some part of her past. Maybe she saw too much.

He decided to break the silence. "And her injuries are too extensive for a visual identification."

Jackie blinked, stuck the pen into her mouth, and chewed on it. "Yeah, too extensive."

"But you do know it's not Stacy Chapman."

Jackie nodded. "Yes, we at least know that. This girl's dark-skinned, maybe an Afro-American child, maybe a mixed-race baby. We're not sure at this point. Lab work hasn't even started yet."

"Any missing child reports other than Stacy and the Bradford boy?"

Jackie shook her head. "Nope, not yet. Nothing in the local, state, or national computer that matches this description."

"Surely, somebody has to know their kid is missing?"

Jackie shrugged. "Not necessarily. Remember, child care is a mess out there these days. Suppose the parents work. Somebody else keeps the kid for them. That baby-sitter isn't going to report this until they're sure they can't find the child. Or it's possible the parents are the killers.

"Or maybe it's just that the parents don't look after their baby so well. Maybe they're doing drugs right now. Somebody took their kid but they're too stoned to know it. Any of this is possible. And other things I can't even imagine."

Burke leaned forward in his seat. "How much does the news media know?"

"Not much yet. Only that we've found a body. They don't know the age, gender, or degree of injury to this baby."

"How long can you keep it from them?"

Jackie bit the end of her pen. "We can't. We don't really have a choice. Not only do we need to find the parents of this baby, but we need to warn everyone else. Tell them to keep their children inside, to lock them away until we can catch whoever is doing this. We'll hold a press conference first thing in the morning."

Burke wanted to ask more, but he dared not. Jackie looked so frail right now. For the first time in their four-year friendship, she seemed vulnerable. Not weak exactly, but fragile, a piece of exquisite glass, molded and shaped beautifully but easily broken. He leaned back in his chair, not wanting to force Jackie to keep reliving the awful moment. He stayed quiet. The second hand trudged by the twelve.

Jackie rolled back too, laying her pen on her desk. Seeming happy to change the subject, she said, "You said you had something for me?"

Burke swallowed, trying to decide how to tell Jackie what he had done. After all, he had broken into someone's home and Jackie *was* an officer of the law.

"Well . . ." he started. "A couple of hours . . . well, just after dark I . . . I went back to Stacy Chapman's trailer park. I . . . walked . . ."

As he spoke, his confidence increased and the story flowed out of him. He told Jackie about the green truck he had seen, about his walk through the trailer park, about finding the cigar remains, about entering the trailer, searching through it. As he talked, Jackie picked her pen back up, and the pen's point disappeared into her teeth. She chewed on it, her teeth making tiny indentations around the middle. The indentations multiplied as Burke outlined the search, as he told her of the lights outside, of his frantic rush from the premises.

"So I found a couple of things I thought you should have. I brought them with me. I have them right here . . ." He reached to the floor beside his feet and lifted the manila envelope and laid it on Jackie's desk. "I think this has relevance to Stacy Chapman's disappearance." He pointed at the envelope.

Jackie stopped chewing her pen and stared at the package. For the second time since his arrival, Burke knew she had zoned herself out; she was somewhere else, somewhere he couldn't go.

The second hand on the clock behind her head moved five seconds, then ten. At the fifteenth second, Jackie spoke. Her voice sounded soft, a whisper floating across the room.

"She was lying on a stone altar, like a sacrifice or something. Blood flowed from the altar to the floor," she said, the pen in her fingers again. "Like one of those satanic cults you hear about. We've known of some of that happening around here, but until now, we've never seen any evidence of human torture. A few animals. You know, a cat with a throat cut, a dog maimed and blood sprinkled on a wall.

You expect a little of that in a city the size of Atlanta. But this, well, we haven't seen this . . . a stone altar . . . torture . . . a human sacrifice . . ." The pen dropped to the desk.

At first, Burke felt surprised that Jackie hadn't responded to what he had told her. She hadn't even seemed to hear him, to care that he had illegally entered the man's house. More amazing, she hadn't bothered to open the envelope.

For a second, Burke wondered if her inattention was a protective measure. After all, he had gathered the material illegally, and it was probably all inadmissible as evidence. But then he knew those details really weren't Jackie's concern. No, she hadn't opened the envelope because she wasn't really in the room with it. Sure, she had heard him describe it, but what she heard hadn't clicked. It hadn't dislodged the searing image stuck in her head, the image of the little girl, crimson red, lying on the stone altar.

Burke swallowed a lump the size of a tennis ball. Just as Jackie hadn't really heard him describe the contents of the envelope, he hadn't really heard her describe the awful possibility her suspicions suggested. The possibility of a cultic sacrifice and what that meant hadn't dawned on him until now. He knew those kinds of things happened, had read the stories about the lunatic fringe—the crazies who practiced their voodoo with their bloody chickens, the witches and warlocks casting their spells and incantations. But he'd never seen it. The idea that Stacy Chapman and Taylor Bradford had fallen into the hands of some evil coven had never occurred to him. His mouth went dry at the thought. It was a real possibility.

He licked his lips, working to figure it out. If these kidnappings and now this death had come at the hands of a satanic cult, then where did Bethany Chapman fit? Did this prove her innocence? If so, why had she run? And what about Cleve? Did this rule him out as a suspect? Or was one of them mixed up in some strange cultic religion that no one knew about?

And what about the man with the earring whose picture lay in the manila folder on Jackie's desk? What role did he play in all this?

Most puzzling of all was this latest child. No one had reported the little girl missing. Was this a part of the pattern like the first two? If so, did that mean that they were also dead somewhere, their blood flowing like red lava down the face of a stone altar?

Burke shuddered at his next thought.

Dark Road to Daylight

Three children.

A trinity.

A stone altar.

A satanic cult.

With all his heart, he prayed that he had jumped to a wrong conclusion.

Shaking himself like a wet dog casting off water, Burke pointed to the envelope again. "You'll want to see this," he said. Jackie blinked twice, and it seemed as if her motor clicked on for the first time since Burke entered the room. She laid down her pen and picked up the envelope.

"So you found this at the trailer park?" she asked, verifying that she had heard him correctly.

"Yeah, like I said, I, uh, found it in the trailer." He dropped his eyes, sheepish and chagrined.

Opening the envelope, Jackie smiled thinly. "Don't worry, Burke, I heard you clearly. You did a bit of police work without proper authority. I won't report it, at least not yet. If we can get enough personnel we'll search those trailers before midnight anyway. Got the court order about an hour ago. It'll disturb a few folks this late and all, but it can't be helped. We'll see if anything else comes up, anything to corroborate what you have."

Jackie pulled out the photo he had taken from the trailer. Silently, she studied it for several seconds. A man standing by a pickup truck. Wearing an earring that looked very much like the one they had at the lab.

She glanced back at Burke. "You said you saw a green pickup yesterday?"

"Yeah, just like the one described by the folks in the trailer park."

Jackie fingered the photo. "Did you know Cleve Chapman also has a green pickup?"

Burke jerked back in his seat. "You're kidding me?"

Jackie peered at him over the edge of the picture. "I think not."

"A coincidence?"

"Possibly. We don't know yet. I talked with Cleve last night. He's not a pleasant man, I must tell you. Seems to think himself quite the superior being. Though I've never met a Nazi, he'll do until the real thing turns up. He, of course, knew what the witnesses had said.

Said that didn't surprise him. He told me he drove by Bethany's place fairly often. To check on his daughter. Maybe the folks in the park saw him. But nothing sinister about it, he assured me."

Burke shrugged. It made sense. "But what about the truck I saw yesterday? At almost the same time the Bradford kid was taken?"

"Cleve said it wasn't him."

"Was he on duty then?"

"Nope, not at the time."

"Does he have an alibi?"

"Said he was painting his garage."

"You check?"

"Yeah, his garage has been recently painted. But whether it happened at the time he said, I have no way of knowing."

Jackie stared back at the photograph. "The earring seems to match," she said.

Burke nodded. "That's what I thought."

"But tons of people wear big gold earrings," cautioned Jackie. "Men and women."

"I know that," agreed Burke. "But with the cigar and the truck, it seemed pretty convincing to me."

Jackie tossed the picture onto her desk, then ran her hand across it, smoothing it down. "I'll run this picture through the system," she said. "See if his mug shows up anywhere. See if he's got a criminal record, anything like that."

Burke nodded. That's what he figured she would do. She continued to focus on the photo.

"A scraggly looking guy, isn't he?"

Burke grinned. "Yeah, beard, sleeveless tank top, bulging biceps, tattoo. Right out of *Esquire*."

Jackie opened the top drawer of her desk and fished through it for a few seconds. When her hand reappeared, it held a magnifying glass.

Leaning forward, she peered through the glass at the photo. "I think I can read the tattoo," she said. She studied it for several seconds, her eyes squinted. "B-E-A-S-T," she said.

"That's a strange one."

Burke jolted forward in his seat. *BEAST!* The note left by Bethany's mom!

BEAST.

 152

Like on the poster.

Bernardo the Beast.

He pointed to the folder on Jackie's desk.

"You need to check the rest of what's in there," he said, working hard to keep his excitement down.

Shrugging, Jackie laid down the picture and picked the folder back up. She reached inside and pulled out the poster Burke had folded there. She flipped open the poster. The savage face of Bernardo the Beast stared back at her.

For a second, her face wrinkled up and she tilted her head to the left. Then, as if making a decision, she threw the magnifying glass onto the desk and popped up out of her chair.

"I think we need to find this guy," she said, her eyes gleaming. "Find this guy and see just what kind of beast he is."

CHAPTER TWENTY-FOUR

12:59 A.M.

Hoping not to wake Debbi, Burke quietly brushed his teeth, dropped his clothes to the floor, and flipped off the lamp. He nudged Debbi gently from his side of the queen-sized mattress, climbed into bed, and closed his eyes.

"What time is it?" Debbi asked, raising up, her elbows propped under her back.

"Shush," coaxed Burke. "It's late, no reason for you to wake up."

"I just got to bed about thirty minutes ago," she said. "Elizabeth's eleven-to-twelve feeding. You could set your watch by it."

Burke laughed quietly. "She is a machine when it comes to food."

"You've had a long day," said Debbi, her tone suggesting she wanted to hear about it. "You get to see Jackie?"

"Yeah, like I said when I called you earlier, she wanted me to come to Longstreet. I met her there."

"You gave her the picture and the poster?"

"Just like I said I would."

Debbi dropped back onto the bed, her elbows collapsing. She threw a leg over Burke and snuggled her chin onto his chest.

"Then that should do it for you," she said. "It's as far as you can go. Jackie's got it now, you're clear of it."

Burke stroked Debbi's blonde hair and inhaled a thick drink of air. He didn't know exactly how to tell her this, but Jackie had asked him to stay in touch on this one. Reminded him that she didn't have a partner yet at Longstreet. Said she wanted him to help her sort through the stack of facts she had gathered so far.

Burke knew that Jackie didn't really do that well with details. She saw big pictures, but she often needed someone else to pick up on the minutiae of a case. Too many details confused the intuitive senses that she used so well.

When she had the right kind of partner—a bean counter—to drop the pieces of the puzzle on the table, she could see the scene and arrange the picture. That's the way she worked best, through the right side of the brain, the side that made the leap from facts to solutions.

She wanted Burke to help with the analytical, the bit-by-bit computation of the circumstances, the cutting out of the pieces so she could piece them together. After all, she had reminded him, he had worked with her two times in the past and had done pretty well. Maybe he had a knack for this sort of thing.

Burke didn't know for sure about that, but he did know that he wanted to assist Jackie if he could. If a friend asked for a favor, he tried to grant it. That's the way he was. Always had been. Always would be.

But he didn't know if Debbi would go for it. Since Elizabeth Joy's birth, she had seemed more anxious about him, more demanding of his time, more protective about what he did.

In the past she had been the one who took the most chances. But suddenly, in the past six days, her patterns seemed to change. She wanted him home more and more and had seemed irritated the couple of times when he didn't quite make it according to schedule.

Burke knew her behavior shouldn't surprise him. It was pretty typical of new mothers. They tended to feel overwhelmed when the first child came into the house. It made sense that they would want their husband around to give them support and assistance.

And, Burke complimented himself, he had done his part. Besides, after his mom left at the end of this week, he had promised to take two weeks off from work to stay home with Debbi. That was their agreement. His mom the first week, he the next two. He kissed Debbi on the head, then jumped right into it.

"Jackie wants me to stay in the loop on this. Act as a sounding board. Give her an objective look at what she finds."

Burke felt Debbi's body stiffen slightly, as if enlivened with a gentle electric current. "Isn't there someone else who can do that?"

Burke thought carefully for a second, then stated his case. "I would think so, but right now, apparently not. As you know, she's new at Longstreet and doesn't have a full-time partner yet. She's worked with two or three other detectives, but they've been slow assigning anyone permanent to work with her. Plus, she's not made any friends yet either. No one she can trust."

He paused to give Debbi a chance to respond, but she didn't. He continued with his explanation. "More than that, maybe because of it, Jackie seems vulnerable right now, different . . . as if she might collapse, like she's got a ton of sadness on her shoulders. And Aaron's out of the country—working with some European conglomerate, putting in a computer system for them. He's not scheduled to return for almost two weeks. Jackie needs someone to lean on."

"And you're the only candidate?"

Burke squeezed Debbi tighter. "As far as I can see."

"I could get jealous."

Burke dropped his chin and stared at her lovely face. She had her lips pouted out. He recognized the mock anger. He kissed her on the head again. "You know you're the only girl for me. Besides, she's an older woman."

Debbi pinched him on the side. "Older women can be the most dangerous."

Squirming away from her fingers, Burke disagreed. "No one can be more dangerous than you," he laughed. "You're the most dangerous woman alive."

Debbi suddenly stopped her pinching, and Burke felt her body stiffen again.

"This could get dangerous," she said, her voice shifting into a serious tone.

"I doubt it. All I'm going to do is listen. Give Jackie an opinion about what she tells me."

"You said it wouldn't be dangerous the last time."

Burke nodded. Debbi was right. The last time, almost two years ago, what seemed safe didn't stay that way. He had a scar on his right wrist to show just how dangerous "listening" could get.

"I'll take care of myself," he said.

Debbi didn't say anything. Instead, she slipped away from him and climbed out of the bed. He twisted toward her, saw her walking toward the closet on her side of the room. She disappeared into the walk-in. A light flipped on in the closet, and he heard her rustling through the shelves. Thirty seconds later, she stepped back into the bedroom, her hands behind her back.

At the foot of the bed, she drew her hands to her stomach. Burke took a deep breath. Debbi held a gun in her hands.

He knew about her gun. A four-and-one-half-inch, eight-bullet-clip, .25-caliber Beretta. Debbi's father, an ex-Marine, had given it to her when she moved to Atlanta. Had given it to her, taken her to a pistol range and taught her how to use it.

Sweat beads the size of peas broke out on Burke's forehead, and a very unpleasant memory flooded back to him. He had shot a man with that gun. To save his own life and Debbi's.

In the dead of a Halloween night, Burke had pulled the trigger and blown away a human being.

"I don't want your gun," he said, his voice firm.

"I want you to take it," said Debbi, her voice equally determined.

"Guns kill people," said Burke.

"Guns keep people from getting killed," said Debbi.

"Not if the person holding the gun won't use it," said Burke.

Debbi paused at that. Burke studied her face. He noticed the corners of her mouth pointed down. But she wasn't faking this time. No playfulness in that frown. Burke swallowed.

He didn't want to make Debbi think he didn't want to please her. And, God surely knew, he didn't want anything to happen to himself. He had too many reasons to live. But killing one person was enough.

"I don't know if I can bring myself to use it again," he said. "Even if it should come to that, which I don't expect it will."

Debbi nodded, then extended the gun. "Maybe you won't use it for yourself," she said. "But use it for me. If it comes to that, use it for me . . . use it for me and for Elizabeth Joy."

Burke saw he had no choice. If it would ease her mind for him to take it, then okay. He took the gun. "For you and Elizabeth Joy," he said. "If it comes to that, I'll use it for you two."

Gary E. Parker **157** &~

Thursday
August 28

CHAPTER TWENTY-FIVE

6:30 A.M.

After only two hours of sleep, Jackie arrived at Longstreet before the Atlanta traffic had a chance to back up on the loop. It wasn't that she particularly wanted to face the gruesome details of her latest investigation, but she knew that the sooner she sorted them out, the sooner she found the killer and closed this case, the sooner she could put this episode behind her and move on with her life. That's what she really wanted to do. Solve this and move past it.

She had stayed up most of the night trying to do just that. But she hadn't had much luck. Though she and a crack team of lab technicians had worked over Rusty Redder's trailer from stem to stern, getting his name from the supervisor of the trailer park, nothing else had turned up. The picture of Redder wearing his earring and leaning against his truck. The remains of the cigar. A tattoo with letters that matched the two left behind by a woman in a coma. That's what she had. All of it was circumstantial. Enough to question Redder for sure, but maybe not enough to hold him.

Pushing through the door and heading to her desk, Jackie realized that she had pretty much given up on the possibility of finding either Stacy Chapman or Taylor Bradford still alive. Given the death of this third child, it didn't seem likely that the first two had escaped a similar fate.

At her desk now, she threw off her shoes and switched on her computer and punched through the keyboard. She knew she shouldn't reach those kinds of conclusions. Nothing specifically tied the three children together—nothing but the fact that all three had disappeared within a week of each other. It just made sense to Jackie. The fate of the third was almost certainly the fate of the first two.

Wanting to see if any new information had come in while she was gone, Jackie pulled up the file on the third child—Baby Doe. A whir and a click or two and the punch of several keystrokes and the information popped onto her screen.

Reading through it, she picked up a blue pen from her desktop and shoved it into her teeth. Chewing on the pen had replaced her former smoking habit. Cleaner and better for her body.

She leaned up in her seat. According to the file, they'd learned more in the wee hours of the morning.

They had found the identity of Baby Doe. A mother had called in. A woman named Wilma Williams. Said her baby was missing.

A team of uniformed cops had gone out to her project, a sprawling ten blocks of brick apartments called King Village. Within an hour, they brought Wilma Williams to the station.

Jackie punched the keyboard again. A picture of the woman popped onto the screen. Jackie studied the picture. The woman's hair squiggled out in all directions. Her skin was the color of concrete, but it didn't look firm. Instead it looked saggy as soggy bread. Her teeth were bad too. The one on the top right appeared to be chipped off about halfway down.

Dropping her eyes from the picture, Jackie read the information printed underneath. The report called Wilma Williams a drunk, a chronic and sloppy drunk.

According to her story, she had left her daughter in the care of her seven-year-old son while she watched television and drank beer. No problem with that, she said. With no man at home to help her, she did it all the time. A woman needed some space to herself, as she put it, and the boy could handle his baby sister okay.

Since the air conditioner in their tiny apartment was broken, the boy had taken the baby into the parking lot to play at about ten. Figured it would be cooler out there. Then, amazingly, the boy forgot his little sister.

Visiting with his friends, the kid lost track of the baby. When he went to bed about midnight, he simply assumed she had gone back into the apartment. After all, she could walk. Did it all the time. Toddled about everywhere. In and out of the apartment, up and down the concrete sidewalk in front of the place. Pretty independent child.

But this time, the baby girl hadn't gone back inside. She had wandered off. Or been taken, snatched from the street. No one knew which.

It wasn't until almost 3 A.M. that Wilma, asleep in front of the television, had wakened from her stupor and staggered past her baby's room. At that point, she noticed the baby wasn't there. She woke up her son and the two of them searched the apartment. When she didn't find the baby, she called the cops.

That was it. The police had responded instantly. Gotten a description of the little girl. Matched it with their Baby Doe.

Wilma confirmed their suspicions, tearfully going to the morgue and identifying the little girl by the birthmark on the inside of the child's left ankle, a birthmark that looked like the head of a cat. Toshua was the baby girl's name.

Chewing furiously on the pen, Jackie kept reading. Wilma, though broken up over the death of her daughter, had a thought or two about who might have taken her.

A gang in the projects, she suggested. The BloodHunters. A racially mixed gang from King Village, where they roamed—boys and girls, blacks and whites mostly, a couple of Hispanics.

According to Wilma, the BloodHunters had at least a few members who practiced some strange rituals—stuff from Haiti and the Caribbean, she said. More than one family in the project had complained about missing pets. And a man she knew who worked with the sanitation department had told her about finding a headless chicken in the garbage Dumpster one morning a few weeks back.

Jackie took a big breath and added all this to what she already knew about the BloodHunters. They pretty much controlled the drug trade in that part of town. People didn't cross them. They were known for their cruelty. They shook down small children for the change in their pockets, attacked strangers in the neighborhood with knives and razors, occasionally even guns. A couple of drive-by shootings a couple of blocks away from King Village were supposedly their handiwork, and they were proud of it.

Chewing on her pen, Jackie continued reading Wilma's statement. As Wilma described it, the residents of King Village pretty much obeyed the BloodHunters. Chalked up their actions as one of the prices of living in such a dangerous place.

But, thought Jackie, maybe this time the gang had gone too far. A robbery here and there was one thing. Even a turf war could be understood. But killing a child? Well, that was another matter all together.

Jackie finished the report, threw her pen down, leaned back, and interlocked her fingers behind her head. If what Wilma Williams said was true, then maybe the answer lay right here. As simple and as horrible as that. A gang in a project. Playing around with voodoo, maybe satanic worship. Graduating from cruelty to animals to the worst crime of all. Scouting the city for vulnerable babies. Babies to use for their own hideous purposes.

Jackie calculated the distance from Stacy Chapman's trailer park to King Village. About thirty minutes depending on traffic.

Maybe the gang started in the trailer park. Away from their home base. Safer out there. Sent someone out to bring back a victim for their first offering.

They found Stacy.

A couple of days later, they went for another. Why not? Their first effort turned out so well. So Taylor disappeared.

Then came Toshua. An offering from right near home. Again, why not? They couldn't go back to the trailer park again. Too many people on guard there. So snatch a girl close to home. Piece of cake.

Jackie unlocked her fingers and raised back to the computer keyboard. But what about the man in the picture Burke had given her? If the gang did it, where did he fit? Was he part of the gang?

He didn't live in King Village. Maybe he was a former member, now out on his own.

She stroked the keyboard again, her fingers flying through the prompts, bringing up what they had found overnight about the man with the tattoo. Before she had left last evening, she had scanned his picture into the computer, started the search program.

Her fingers stopped. The computer blinked. Three pictures popped onto the screen—the one she had scanned in about midnight and two others—a front view and a side view of a man with mutton-chop sideburns and a prisoner number on a card under his chin.

Redder had a number of minor violations charted under his picture. None of them were big-time. Currently, he had no warrants pending against him, and he wasn't on parole.

Jackie checked his previous address: 202 Garden Terrace Dr.,

Dark Road to Daylight

Perry, Georgia. According to the file, a wife and a son lived there, Reba Dawn and Shane Johnston. The boy was seven.

The report ended. Jackie shifted in her seat, pushing the back of her chair against the wall. For several seconds, she stared up at the ceiling, watching the fan whir around and around. Where to start first, she wondered? King Village? Or back out at Rusty Redder's trailer?

She knew a crew had stayed after she left to finish the work at Redder's place. But the report gave no indication that they had found anything new. And Redder hadn't come back. If so, someone would have called her last night.

From all indications, Rusty Redder had flown the coop. Whether or not his disappearance had anything to do with these children, she didn't know. But he was gone now.

She punched a button on her phone. The duty dispatcher answered her page. "I'm going out to King Village," Jackie said. "Anybody on the scene?"

"Not right now," said the dispatcher. "A crew of uniforms worked most of the night, but nothing happened. No action, no sign of the BloodHunters. You'll need backup."

"Yeah, who's in the area?"

The speaker fell silent for a moment. Jackie slipped her shoes back on.

"Hey, you're in luck," said the dispatcher. "Patrick and Chapman. On duty at seven and in the area. I'll tell them to meet you there."

Leaving her computer running, Jackie walked from Longstreet Station, climbed into her squad car, pulled onto the highway and turned toward King Village. Patrick and Chapman. Wouldn't you know it? Lately, every time she turned around, they showed up.

Wheeling onto the city loop, she pulled her navy blazer closer to her neck.

CHAPTER TWENTY-SIX

7:15 A.M.

The phone jarred Burke out of a heavy sleep. Never one to like waking up, he tried to ignore it. *Let it be a dream,* he thought, shoving his head deeper into his pillow. *Let it be a loud, shrill, awful dream.* The phone rang again. He nudged Debbi with his hip. "You going to get the phone?" he whispered.

"It's on your side," she said, not moving. "And it's time to get up anyway. Aren't you supposed to be in the office by eight?"

The phone rang a third time. Not wanting it to wake Elizabeth Joy, he grudgingly slid over from Debbi and picked it up.

"Yeah," he grunted, gruff and displeased, still more than half asleep.

"Burke, Jackie Broadus here. You awake?"

"Yeah, I had to get up to answer the phone," he said, wiping sleep from his eyes and squinting at the clock on the nightstand.

"You're a funny man, Burke," she said. "If you don't make it as a psychologist, you can do stand-up comedy."

"Yeah, but I'm only good before 7:18 A.M." he said, noting the time on the clock. "And there's not much traffic in the nightclubs that early."

"Then stick with the counseling gig."

"That's my plan."

Beside him, Debbi raised up, puzzled by the conversation. He shrugged at her, wondering himself why Jackie had called. Had she learned something new? Maybe she knew more about Rusty Redder.

"Look, Burke," said Jackie, "I'd love to continue this sterling banter with you, but I don't have time for it. We've identified the Baby Doe—her name is Toshua. Her mom came in a couple of hours ago. It's a long story, but the end result is that I'm in the car, headed to a place called King Village—an apartment complex a couple of miles from downtown. I'm going to check out a gang that runs over there. A group called BloodHunters. The mother of the missing girl thinks they might know something. She says they're into some of everything—maybe even a bit of voodoo, satanic rituals, you name it and they try it. It's possible they had something to do with this last baby."

"What about Redder?" asked Burke, his mind beginning to click now. "You find anything on him?"

"That's why I'm calling you. Wanted your thoughts on this before I get to the Village. Don't know if I'll get much of a chance later today to talk with you. The computer says Redder is a small-time con man. His parents are deceased. He's got an ex-wife and a son in Perry. Wife's name is Dawn Johnston, boy is named Shane. Redder has several priors on his sheet. Nothing major, nickel-and-dime stuff. Never served any serious time. But there's enough here to know he's no angel."

"Enough to make him a suspect?" Burke asked, pausing to assess this latest information. "Is he connected with this gang, the . . ."

"BloodHunters," said Jackie. "I have no idea if he runs with the Hunters or not. And even if he does, I don't have any idea if they have anything to do with this killing. Or if this killing has anything to do with the other two missing kids. They could be completely separate."

"You don't think they're connected?" he asked, his tone contradicting that possibility.

"No, I didn't say they weren't. Just that we can't say they definitely are. We're still trying to find out. Right now, I have nothing to officially connect them, other than the fact that each of the kids is under two."

Burke rubbed his hands through his hair. Jackie was right. Maybe the first two were connected but not the third one. But what were the chances of that? It didn't seem reasonable that three kids, all of them under two, would disappear over a one-week period within a fifteen-mile radius of each other without some tie between them.

A feeling of nausea rushed through him. If the three incidents were the work of one person, it meant that the first two had probably suffered the same fate as the third.

"Do you think Redder is involved with all of this?" he asked, forcing himself away from the morbid possibilities dancing in his mind.

"I want your opinion on that. Do guys like him move up, shift toward meaner and meaner crimes? Can a small-time hood become a baby killer?"

Burke sighed heavily and tucked his pillow behind his back. "Isn't that your area of expertise?"

"Sure, but I've seen it go both ways. One guy drops lower and lower on the scale, like garbage down a drain, until he hurts someone. Maybe when he does, he finds out he likes the power it gives to him. So, he moves on, moves from hurting someone until there's only one thing left on the scale—murder. But another guy, well . . . some seem to catch themselves right before they bottom out. They grab hold to some sliver of human decency and they stop. They hear a voice or something saying enough is enough, and they turn their lives around. They straighten up, you know. . . ."

"Sure, Jackie," he said. "I know what you're saying. And you're trying to figure out which way Redder is headed."

"Exactly."

"Well, somebody sure killed this last child."

"And in the worst possible way."

"And it could have been Redder."

"I'm afraid so."

"It's a scary world out there," Burke said, thinking of the gun Debbi had given him last night and suddenly becoming worried about Jackie. "You got good backup with you this morning?"

"Yeah, no problem. Besides, I don't expect the BloodHunters will be too rambunctious this early in the morning. All I'm doing right now is asking questions. Don't know enough to do anything else."

"Just stay safe," said Burke. "I don't want anything to happen to you."

Jackie laughed thinly. "My sentiments exactly," she said. "I don't want anything to happen to me either. I've got plans."

"You and Aaron?"

Jackie laughed again, this time more freely. "Don't get nosey, there, Doctor."

"But that's my job. I get paid for it."

"When I know something, you'll know too," said Jackie. "After all, you have to do the ceremony."

"I can't wait," said Burke.

"See you soon."

"Take care of yourself."

Burke hung up and slid back down into bed. Debbi snuggled close to him, her blonde hair tickling his nose.

"Jackie okay?" she asked.

Burke nodded.

"It's dangerous work she does," said Debbi.

Burke nodded again, then breathed a silent prayer. Next to Debbi, Jackie was the best friend he had. He didn't want anything bad to happen to her.

CHAPTER TWENTY-SEVEN

7:30 A.M.

King Village was stirring as Jackie drove up. A stream of cars met her as she pulled into the asphalt parking lot and stepped out. Twenty yards to her right, under a stand of pink crepe myrtles, a group of women in cutoff shorts stood talking, their voices ringing out in the early morning air. To Jackie's left, the *whap, whap, whap* of a ball took her attention from the women. Three boys, in their early teens Jackie surmised, had already started a basketball game. Behind the basketball court, Jackie spotted a line of men and women walking like a stream of ants toward a set of steps that led from the complex to a street overpass. Beyond that overpass was the Marta station.

Jackie took a deep breath. Most of them were headed to work, she figured. The masses of Atlanta—the bustling, striving, working class of the great city.

Beside her, Patrick and Chapman also stepped out of their cars.

"A busy place," said Patrick, his eyes warily sliding side to side. "A bunch of people."

Jackie nodded. "And most of them don't like cops."

"So I've been told."

Chapman said nothing. His silence didn't surprise Jackie. After their recent conversation, the two weren't on the best of terms.

With Chapman and Patrick flanking her, their hands tense at their sides, Jackie walked across the cracked asphalt that spread out before her like a giant black football field. She stayed as vigilant as the two men, her eyes scanning the apartment complex.

It was one of the last of the government housing projects, built near the end of the "Great Society" experiment, the belief that free housing, food, and education would lift the people out of their poverty and carry them into the middle class. Twenty-six buildings made up the complex, one for each letter of the alphabet, each exactly ten stories high, each containing exactly ten apartments on each story. A total of 2,600 apartments, each averaging just over four people per unit. About ten thousand residents in the sprawling village.

Jackie wasn't fooled by the line of traffic leaving the parking lot and walking over to the Marta line. She knew that almost 50 percent of the men in this complex didn't have a job. She knew that same statistic held true in several other apartment complexes in Atlanta.

She didn't know if it was because the men didn't really want jobs or the jobs simply weren't there. She figured it wasn't her place to answer that question. All she knew was that men out of work led to men with too much time on their hands. As she put it, "Time minus dollars equals trouble."

She'd been dealing with that equation for years. And it hadn't changed in that whole time. Jackie wondered if it ever would. Probably not anytime soon. Regardless of the politicians' revamping of welfare programs, some things didn't seem to have solutions.

Shoving the issue aside, Jackie stepped past the concrete stoop and through the door of building F. According to Wilma Williams, a man named Hector, the leader of the BloodHunters, lived here.

A smell akin to that of a wet cat rolling around in a litter box smacked Jackie in the face as she entered the building. The sunshine that burned so brightly on the pavement outside suddenly disappeared. She found herself in a shadowed hallway—a place not pitch-black, but plenty dark.

On either side of the hallway, a row of doors ran down the wall. One door, two doors, three doors, then darkness.

Jackie let her eyes drift through the shadows to the other end of the hall. A single light, a round white bulb without a cover, stared back at her from the center of the wall about a hundred feet away. Between her and the bulb, she saw nothing but darkness. Not a single light burning overhead.

Gary E. Parker   **171** 𝕏

For a short instant, Jackie wondered what happened to the other lights that should be burning on the walls. Had they burned out or had someone deliberately knocked them out so whatever took place in this dark hall would go unseen?

She swallowed hard and told herself to calm down. She'd faced situations like this more times than she could remember and she knew how to handle them.

"Look for 1143," she said, squinting and turning to Patrick and Chapman. "That's this Hector guy's number."

For several moments, she stood in the dark hallway and examined the doors nearest to her. No numbers on the two on the right. One number—1120—on the nearest one on the left. No number on the second one on that side. The third one, the last one in her vision, read 1002.

The door from 1120 opened and light flooded the hallway from the apartment inside. For a second, the light blinded Jackie. Then the door closed and the light disappeared and a man as wide as a refrigerator pushed silently by her, the smell of coffee strong on his breath.

"Looks like we'll need to knock on a few doors," said Patrick, his voice just a bit more than a whisper.

"1143," said Jackie. "That's the one we want. I thought the numbers would be in order but I guess not."

"Kids change the numbers," said Chapman. "They think it's funny."

"Not at 7:30 in the morning," said Jackie.

Chapman grunted. "I'll start at the other end of the hall. Work my way back to you two." He moved away into the shadows, his wide back disappearing in the inky blackness.

"I'll do the right side of the hall," said Patrick.

"That leaves me the left."

Patrick moved away.

Jackie turned to knock on the door to her left. She heard the sound of a rap beat from inside the walls, but no one answered. She smacked on the door again. Nothing.

From the next apartment, a black woman stuck her face through the door. Her hair, almost completely gray, was wrapped tightly in little curls around her ears and eyebrows.

"Nobody be home there," she shouted, her high-pitched voice squeaking through the hallway. "They be at work by seven."

 *Dark Road to Daylight*

"What about the music?" asked Jackie.

"You a cop?"

"Yeah." Jackie pulled her badge from her pocket and showed it to the elderly lady.

The woman nodded, then scratched her right hand through her hair. "My name is Inez," she said. "They leave that music on. Leave it on all the time. You come by here at three in the morning, that music be on. All the time I hear that music. After a while, a body gets used to it. Who you looking for anyway?"

Jackie took a step toward the lady, noted her worn pink housecoat and fluffy blue shoes. She kept her voice low when she spoke. "I'm looking for a man named Hector," she said. "You know him?"

Inez grabbed the throat of her housecoat and pulled it tight around her neck. She darted her eyes to her left, down the hallway where Chapman had gone.

"How many menfolks you got with you?"

"Two," said Jackie, reacting to the woman's sudden unease, edging herself to the side of the hallway.

"And you looking for Hector?" she asked in disbelief.

"Yeah, you know him?"

Inez shook her head vigorously. "No, no, no, honey. You need more men than that. That man be trouble, that's what I'm saying to you. You get more men here with you and I tell you where to find him. But Hector, he be trouble, he be—"

A crash from the opposite end of the hallway interrupted Inez. Jackie jerked back tighter against the wall. "Shut the door!" she shouted.

Inez's gray head disappeared as the door slammed. The hall became even darker as the light from her apartment was shut out. Jackie heard feet slapping against the floor down the hallway, then the place became quiet.

"Patrick?" she called.

"Over here," he said. Through the shadows, she saw him three doors down, his back against the wall, his gun drawn.

Looking toward the light at the other end of the hall, she searched for Chapman, but she didn't see him.

"Cleve!" shouted Patrick. "Hold your position."

Chapman didn't respond.

"Back me up," yelled Jackie.

Gary E. Parker   **173**

Patrick flipped her a thumbs-up sign.

Her gun drawn, Jackie edged forward against the wall of the hallway. Patrick followed fifteen feet behind, watching their backs.

"Chapman," Jackie yelled again. Still no answer.

Her mouth dried up on her, and she found it hard to breath. She didn't like this, the shadows of the hallway, the mystery of a man named Hector, a baby at the bottom of a stone altar, the crimson of the child's blood flowing from the base of the altar. She had been doing this too long she decided, so long she couldn't take it any more—the familiarity with danger, with death, the moments when time froze and life hung as tenuous as a spider web over a fire.

"Chapman!" she shouted, the sound of her voice breaking the tension in her throat.

Nothing.

She was almost at the end of the hall now, and the light from the bulb beckoned her. Seeing the glow of the light, Jackie suddenly felt better. If she could make it to the light, she would get through this.

She focused on the light. It seemed to spread out before her, a safe place in the shadowed hallway.

Her gun led the way as she took bigger and bigger steps, her feet rushing through the darkness, her hands reaching for the light. Only a couple of more strides and she would reach it, the light at the end of the—

She heard a creak. She slowed her steps, then heard a longer squeak, the unmistakable sound of a door opening. The sound came from her left. She slowed to a walk, her eyes piercing the darkness. She saw a door to her left, slightly ajar.

Jackie froze and turned toward the dark apartment. Her eyes landed on the number in the center of the door. 1143.

The hair on the back of her neck stood up, and the gun in her hands trembled.

"Chapman," she called.

Nothing.

She stepped to the door. A hand emerged in the darkness.

The hand held a gun.

Jackie tried to twist away, but she knew even as she did that it wouldn't do her any good. A brief flash erupted in the dark hallway, and a jagged edge of pain sliced through her left side. Then the roar

hit her—the roar of a furious ocean, an ocean driven by hurricane winds, roaring onto the beach crushing everything in its path.

Jackie fell to the floor of the dark hallway. Above her, she saw the figure of a grinning man. Behind him glowed the one light, the light hanging in the center of the hall, the white light that now illuminated the grinning man's face.

Jackie raised her right hand from her side. Her hand felt wet. She stared at her hand and saw blood on her fingers. She arched the hand upward, reaching for the light behind the grinning man.

She heard a thump, then a crash. The light at the end of the hallway went out. Jackie dropped her hand back to her side, and the roar in her ears ceased.

CHAPTER TWENTY-EIGHT

11:14 A.M.

Burke canceled his appointments for the rest of the day and left the clinic the moment Debbi called him. She had gotten the news from a coworker at the *Independent*. A story about a cop being shot earlier that morning, now in critical condition at Murphy Memorial. The identity of the detective wasn't public yet, pending notification of the family, but a source at Longstreet had given the name to the paper. It was Jackie Broadus, the lead investigator in the missing baby cases. Shot in the upper torso on the left side, nicked in the heart. Not dead, but not far from it.

Leaving Molly to make his excuses to his clients, Burke jetted from the clinic to the hospital, making it in less than thirty minutes. Rushing from the parking lot, he took the elevator to the fifth floor and climbed off. To his surprise, Debbi met him as he stepped into the waiting room outside ICU.

Grateful she had come, he reached for her and pulled her close. He wanted to cry, but knew he didn't have that luxury right now. If Jackie died, he would cry later. He could lament his inability to help her, share his part of the blame for the death of his good friend, a woman he cared for like a sister.

For now his grief would have to wait. Right now, Jackie needed his strength, or at least what strength he had. With no family close by, he and Debbi were all she could count on. He would not let her down.

"Mom got Elizabeth Joy?"

"Yeah, figured you needed me here."

Burke nodded his agreement. "Jackie conscious yet?"

"Nope, not yet, according to our reports. The doctor said she's lucky, an inch higher and the bullet would have hit her in the center of the heart. Anybody call her family?"

"Don't know, but I expect the people at Longstreet will take care of that. But her mom lives in a nursing home in Charlotte and her dad is deceased. She's got some brothers and sisters, but they're scattered all over the Southeast."

"So, we don't expect anybody to get here too quickly."

"Nope, we're it."

Sliding his hands across the front of his trouser pockets, Burke led Debbi toward a cream-colored metal desk in the right corner of the room. A woman in a pink smock, a volunteer who kept the coffee hot and helped monitor the comings and goings of the waiting room, sat at the desk.

Burke knew the scene well. As a former pastor, he had visited waiting rooms time and time again. Different groups of people gathered in separate huddles—each huddle dealing in its own way with the uncertainty of the intensive care unit, an uncertainty that hung in the air like a cloud of smoke.

To his left sat a woman in a lime green sweatsuit, a magazine in her hand. Two younger men waited beside her. A mother and her boys waiting to hear word on her husband, Burke figured. Maybe the man had suffered a heart attack, or had just gone through cancer surgery. From the woman's semi-relaxed state, Burke guessed the emergency had passed. Or had not yet happened.

Beside them, a man who looked to be about forty held on to a woman of equal years, their eyes wet with tears. A man in a tie and sport coat stood with them, his hands on their shoulders. The threesome made a little circle and closed their eyes, and the man in the tie began to speak. A death, thought Burke. Or close to it. And a pastor trying to comfort with a prayer.

Feeling like an intruder upon the sacred moment, Burke averted his eyes and smiled at the woman in the pink smock.

"I'm here to see Jackie Broadus," he said.

The woman, smiling back at him, clicked the keyboard of the computer on her desk.

"Are you family?" she asked, still smiling.

Gary E. Parker   **177**   ༄

Burke shook his head. "No, but she doesn't have any here. I'm a friend."

The woman's smile dried up. "I'm afraid she can't have visitors," she said. "Orders of the police department."

Burke turned to Debbi, shaking his head. She shrugged, obviously not sure what else to do.

Burke faced the woman again. "I'm a minister," he said.

The woman's smile returned, but she didn't give in. "I wish I could say that helps," she said. "But I'm bound by the instructions from the police. Ms. Broadus is a 'no visitors' patient."

A flush rolled through Burke's cheeks. He needed to see Jackie! Needed to tell her she wasn't alone, that she had someone here who cared for her. He felt Debbi tugging his elbow. She turned him to his left. He spotted a policeman walking toward the desk. A slender black man, a man whose bulky holster and pistol looked out of place on his hip.

Burke walked toward the cop and extended his hand. "I'm Burke Anderson," he said. "This is my wife. We're Jackie Broadus's best friends."

"I'm Simon Patrick," said the cop, shaking his hand. "I was with her this morning, when . . . when she was shot." Patrick dropped his eyes. His shoulders sagged.

"What happened?" Burke asked. "Who did it?"

Patrick shook his head, his eyes still focused on his shoes. "Don't exactly know," he said. "Cleve Chapman and I were with her, checking out a guy named Hector. At King Village. We were in a hallway, it was dark. The numbers on the doors were all mixed up. We were looking for 1143. Chapman went on ahead, me and Jackie working toward him. I was protecting our backs, looking in the other direction. We were almost at the end of the hall. I heard a door open, turned around, heard a shot, saw Jackie hit the floor, heard a crash— glass breaking—saw Chapman run from 1143. Cleve shouted at me, told me to stay with Jackie, he was going after the shooter. That's what I did. I stayed with her until the ambulance came and we brought her here. That's all I know . . ." Patrick's voice broke.

"Did Chapman catch the guy he was chasing?"

Patrick swung his head side to side. "No . . . no, he didn't. The man got away."

Burke rubbed his hands on his pants. "Did you see the other guy?"

 **178**

Patrick shook his head. "It was too dark in there."

"But you saw Chapman running after him?"

"Yeah, I was at the door of 1143 by then."

Burke paused, considering the possibilities. How did the shooter disappear so quickly? Was it possible that Chapman had done the shooting, then pretended to chase someone? He stared at Patrick, wondering if the gentle cop had any suspicions. Probably not. No reason for him to distrust Chapman.

Patrick raised his eyes from his shoes. "You seen Jackie yet?" he asked Burke, his eyes red.

Burke shook his head. "They won't let anyone but her family or the police in."

"But she's got no family here," Debbi added quickly. "We're the closest thing to it."

Patrick sighed heavily. "I never saw a shooting before this," he said, his tone weary. "Never in my four years as a cop. I keep thinking I could have done something, should have done something, thinking that if I had just been quicker, more alert, maybe I could have protected her, I don't know, something . . ."

Burke touched Patrick's left shoulder. "Blaming yourself won't help," he said. "What you've got to do is find the person who shot her. That's what she would want, don't you think?"

Patrick looked at him, relief written on his thin face. "Will you folks stay with her?"

Burke glanced at Debbi. "Every hour that we can," she said. "Between the two of us, one of us will be here."

"It would help if we could see her," said Burke, hopeful that Patrick could get them into Jackie's room.

Patrick brightened and he stood up straighter. "I can do something about that," he suggested. Without hesitation, Patrick stepped past him and smiled at the woman in the pink smock.

"I'm from Longstreet," he said. "And these are friends of ours at the station. They're friends of Lieutenant Broadus." He indicated Burke and Debbi. They smiled at the lady. Patrick kept talking. "You can let them see Detective Broadus."

The woman frowned slightly. Patrick kept talking. "Treat them like her family," he said. "She needs them." Patrick eyed the woman carefully, then spoke with authority. "Give them access just as you would the next of kin."

The woman gave up her frown, apparently resigned to Patrick's orders. "Okay," she said. "You're the police." She smiled at Debbi and Burke. "Patients in the intensive care unit can have visitors for ten-minute periods each hour unless a doctor or nurse is working with them." She glanced at her watch. "So, in about . . . twenty-two minutes you can go right through those doors . . ."

Burke smiled at her and Debbi nodded, but Burke didn't hear the rest of what she said. He knew the routine from here. In twenty-two minutes, he would get to see Jackie. He would get to explain to her his desire to help in any way he could, to try and make up for his failure with Bethany Chapman. Grateful for the chance, he stepped away from the smiling woman in the pink smock and offered his thanksgiving to God. Like the pastor in the tie, Burke closed his eyes and mumbled his words of prayer.

CHAPTER TWENTY-NINE

12:45 P.M.

Bethany Chapman stepped off at the Marta station at Lenox Square and headed to the mall. Wearing a pair of jeans with holes in the knees, a black sleeveless blouse, a straw hat, and a pair of high-top tennis shoes, she tucked her chin to her chest and walked briskly down the street. Within minutes, she stepped inside the air-conditioned commercial center and spotted a phone. Warily, she glanced up and down the walkways of the busy building. No cops in sight.

Grateful for her good fortune, she hustled to the phone and turned her back to the passing crowd. In spite of the yellowish circles under her eyes and sunken skin around her high cheekbones, she figured the police would still recognize her. A picture taken from her trailer and plastered over every television screen and newspaper in the city would do that for a person. Give them their fifteen minutes of fame and then some. That's why she wore the hat, why she had snipped her hair off up to her ears. She looked like anybody—nothing distinguishing about her. No purse, no makeup, no jewelry. It wasn't much of a disguise, but so far it had been enough. So long as a cop didn't get a direct look at her face, it would probably work a few more days.

Slipping a quarter from her pocket, she dropped it into the phone and punched the number. Waiting, she reviewed what she wanted to say. No reason to go through where she had been the past two days. No reason to say she had slept in her mom's car, a beat-up, ten-year-old Sunbird that had been in the shop before Bethany picked it up the day she ran from the hospital. No reason to say she had spent the last two days dodging the authorities, that she had broken into Janette Wilmer's apartment looking for something, anything that would tie Cleve to all of this. No reason to say she had walked into Murphy Memorial last night at 2 A.M. logged onto the computer, tapped into the files at Longstreet Station, and pulled up a psychological profile on Cleve. No reason yet to tell anyone that his profile showed that he might have the emotional makeup to hurt his own daughter.

No, she thought as the phone rang, no reason to tell all of that. She didn't expect anyone to believe her anyway.

The phone rang a second time.

At this point, it didn't matter if anyone believed her or not. She had to depend on herself. She was all she had.

The phone rang a third time.

Bethany chewed on the end of her index finger. In spite of the tragic turn her life had taken in the past week, one good thing had happened. She had learned that she could handle herself. She was a survivor.

If anyone had tried to convince her beforehand that she could make it through what she had faced since Cleve called, she would have laughed in their face. No way, nohow.

But, amazingly, she had made it. She didn't know exactly how, but she had endured it. Somehow between the time of Cleve's call and the day she walked out of the hospital, she had experienced a transformation. She had taken matters into her own hands and made things happen. She had faced the worst of her fears and had decided that she wanted to live. Right now, suicide was the farthest thing from her thoughts. She felt alive. Alive because she had overcome the victim's role. She had become a doer, rather than the done-unto. She felt good about that. Not because she had done everything right—she didn't know about that, not yet anyway. And not because everything had happened the way she wanted it to happen. Far from it. Still, she had acted. And no matter what happened from this moment on, she would never again let another person control her life the way Cleve had.

A female voice answered the phone. "Hello, this is the Personal Care Clinic, Molly Bratcher speaking. How can I help you?"

Bethany glanced quickly over her shoulder, then cupped the

phone to her chin. "Molly, this is Bethany Chapman. Is Dr. Anderson there?"

Bethany heard a sharp intake of breath. For an instant, Molly didn't speak.

"Molly?"

"Uh, yeah, you just surprised me, that's all. Uh, Dr. Anderson is . . . um . . . out of the office right now. But I know he wants to talk with you. Tell me where you are and I'll . . . I'll have him call you."

Bethany grunted. "No can do, Molly. Too easy for you to call the police instead of Burke. When do you expect him?"

"Not until tomorrow morning."

Bethany leaned against the back of the phone stall, her chin still down, the hat low over her eyes. "Can you give me his pager number?"

"I thought you already had it."

"Well, I did, but I'm not where I can get to it, if you catch my drift."

Molly laughed, but only briefly. "Yeah, sure, I guess not." She paused and Bethany could almost hear her considering what to do.

Molly cleared her throat. "Well, I know Dr. Anderson wants to talk with you . . . so I don't think there's anything wrong with giving you the number. It's 818-7753."

Bethany repeated the number to Molly.

"Yeah, that's it. I know he wants to talk—"

Bethany hung up the phone, cutting her off.

For almost ten seconds, she leaned back and breathed deeply. If anyone would believe her, Burke would. But he was the only one. And he needed to know what she had found. He needed to know it so he could pass it on. If she was going to survive this, Burke would have to help her. He was the only one who would.

She pulled another quarter from her pocket.

818-7753.

She dialed the number. Relayed to the pager the number of the pay phone where she stood. She hung up, pulled her hat lower, and waited for him to call back.

CHAPTER THIRTY

1 P.M.

Burke stood over Jackie, his right hand on her forehead, his left one around Debbi's waist. They had been in this position almost an hour, alternating between prayer, silence, and quietly speaking to Jackie. To his surprise, the hospital staff left them alone.

As Burke expected, Jackie seemed more dead than alive. Tubes extended from her nose and throat down the side of the bed, attached to the machinery that ringed her like an electronic family keeping watch over a loved one. A monitor behind her head rhythmically noted her pulse—*beep, beep, beep*—and the light overhead hummed gently.

Except for the offending tubes, Jackie's face appeared serene, as if she had fallen asleep and someone had jammed the intruders into her body without her noticing.

Burke rubbed his hand over her forehead and tried once more to talk to her. "It's Burke, Jackie. Burke Anderson. I'm here with Debbi." The monitor beeped.

Debbi squeezed Burke's hand, then leaned past him. "We're praying for you, Jackie," she said. "We've called the church too, asked them to pray." *Beep. Beep.*

A sigh escaped Burke. It seemed so hopeless. A missing baby, her grandmother the victim of a stroke. A mother running from the cops. Another child abducted, a third horribly murdered.

Now this. Jackie, shot—close to death.

Prayer seemed like the only hope. Not that he believed prayer solved every problem. If it did, everyone would pray. If all a person had to do to guarantee success every day was squeeze off a few words to the Almighty, then prayer would certainly be a growth industry. If that's all it took to make Jackie well again, she would rise up right now and walk out of the hospital, her wound nonexistent, her body fully recovered.

But Burke knew that wasn't all it took. That would make prayer a mechanical transaction and God a cosmic candy dispenser. Prayer meant more than that. It meant faith, faith in spite of tough times, faith in spite of cancer and crime, faith in spite of failed businesses and faltering fortunes.

Genuine prayer meant listening to God and for God, listening when nothing but empty silence rolled back into your ears, listening when nothing you asked for ever came to you.

Burke squeezed Debbi's hand, then brushed Jackie's blonde hair off her forehead. He had prayed ever since he heard about the shooting. And his prayers had seen him through his guilt and self-blame, through his grief and fears about Jackie's recovery. He hoped and prayed all the prayers offered on Jackie's behalf would see her through as well.

He closed his eyes for a second to gather his wits. It seemed no matter how far away from tragedy he tried to run, he always ended up in the middle of it. Maybe some people, he thought, attracted tragedy like bright flowers attracted bees for pollination. Maybe it came with his job. He wanted to make a difference for people, to make a difference for the God whom he knew was real, for the God he knew cared about people. He knew that defined his makeup as both pastor and psychologist. Maybe it was what landed him in these awful situations time after time.

Well, he didn't know if he had made a difference for Jackie to this point or not, but he did know he would do all he could to make a difference from this moment. Whatever it took to find the person who shot Jackie, that's what he would do.

He moved his hand from her forehead, laid it on her left hand, rubbed her hand with his. Bent lower over her face. Whispered into her ear.

"I don't know if you can hear me or not Jackie," he began. *Beep.* The monitor marked the break in his statement. "But if you can hear me, I want you to know this—" *Beep.* "I'm going to find out who did this to you—" *Beep.* "I'm going to follow up on what you told me about Rusty Redder." *Beep.* "I believe he's the key to all this, he's the one who can lead us to whoever shot you." *Beep.* "When I leave here, I'm going to Perry, see if I can find him, see if his wife knows where he might be—" *Beep.*

"Can you hear me, Jackie, can—?"

Beep, beep, beep.

Debbi tugged at his elbow. He turned to her.

"It's your beeper," she said. "Your beeper."

Surprised, Burke pulled the pager from his belt. "I told Molly not to call," he said, checking the number.

It wasn't Molly's number. Instead, the note said: "Call Bethany. 921-3367."

His mouth fell open. He showed the note to Debbi. "Bethany," he said. "Bethany called me."

Debbi nodded. "Then I suggest you call her back."

Working to get a handle on his thoughts, Burke nodded too.

"I'll stay with Jackie," said Debbi.

"I'll be right back," said Burke.

He squeezed Jackie's hand one more time. "We'll get the guy who shot you," he said.

CHAPTER THIRTY-ONE

1:15 P.M.

About two hours away from Atlanta, in Perry, Georgia, Rusty Redder tossed a basketball to his boy, Shane. Rusty's red hair, wet from sweat, lay flat on his head. He and Shane had been hard at it since about eleven that morning. Toss and dribble and shoot. Run and get the ball and toss and dribble and shoot.

Daddy did most of the running, Shane did most of the dribbling and shooting. Though Rusty was tired, he could see the boy had no intention of stopping any time soon.

Shane dribbled the ball to the left, nearer the basket, then shot it through. He was amazingly good for a seven-year-old, thought Rusty. Better than he ever imagined. He grabbed the ball as it fell through the basket and tossed it to his son again.

Man, it felt good to be here. Here in this tiny Georgia town. It felt good to stand in this driveway and feel the heat of the sun on your back and see the clear blue sky overhead. It felt . . . well, it felt like home, like the days when he was a kid growing up outside Valdosta. Boy, what he would give to go back to those days.

Dawn had kindly let him spend the night at the house. He figured she would. She tended to do that—forgive easily and believe the best about people. She had a personality as gentle as a naive dog.

So when he drove in last night and told her he wanted to spend a couple of days with her and Shane, she quickly agreed. She wanted her son to know his father, she said, wanted him to know his daddy loved him.

The basketball bounced past Rusty and lodged under a hedge of honeysuckle that hung on the wood fence running the length of the driveway by the white-framed house. Shane, his freckles vivid in the early afternoon sun, stood ten feet away, his little hands on his hips, his red hair falling into his eyes. Shane pointed to the ball. "Get the ball, Daddy," he yelled. "You're the rebounder."

Smiling, Rusty obeyed the order. Get the ball, let his boy shoot it. He dropped to his knees and reached for the ball. The grass felt warm to his touch and the smell of the honeysuckle filled his nostrils.

Rusty couldn't believe how good it felt to be here. Here with his boy. Dawn hadn't taken Shane to her mother's today like she usually did. She had left him here with Rusty while she went to work at her dad's place—a small but fairly profitable peanut farm. She was such a trusting person. She deserved better than what he had given her.

He pulled the ball from under the honeysuckle and stood up.

"Throw me the ball," yelled Shane.

Rusty stared at his son—so perfect in his boy-sized high-top basketball shoes, baggy black shorts, and Hawks T-shirt. He tossed Shane the ball.

Why not stay, he wondered? *Why not ask Dawn to take him back?* She might do it. If he convinced her that he had changed his ways. If he promised her that he would settle down, get a job, maybe work for her dad like she did, like she had begged him to do in the past. He could go back to school, she had urged, go back to school and get an education. Then if he wanted to leave Perry, they could. She would help him do it, she had always said. But he hadn't listened back then. Could he do it now?

He moved to the basket, waiting for the ball to fall through the net.

He could, he decided suddenly! He could settle down. He could put the past behind him, keep a regular job, do right by his boy and his wife. Heck, even if Dawn wouldn't take him back he could stay in Perry. Stay close to his kid. Play ball with him everyday. Prove himself to Dawn, make her want to take him back. Shoot, if worse came to worst and she wouldn't have him, he could find himself another good woman.

"You shoot one, Daddy," yelled Shane, throwing the ball across the driveway to him. "It's your turn."

Rusty caught the ball and rolled it around in his fingers for a

moment. It would be so easy, he thought. So easy to settle down and put it all behind him. Except for one thing.

He raised the ball over his head and flicked it toward the basket.

The kidnappings. Stacy and Taylor. The cry of the precious little girl. The eyes of the handsome boy.

The basketball arched through the air.

Rusty didn't know what had happened to those two babies.

The ball dropped toward the rim.

Were they dead like the one the cops found in that project, the one he read about in the paper this morning? He suspected so. Apparently, the man who hired him had taken the third child himself when Rusty failed to do the job. That man had taken the third child and—well, Rusty didn't even want to think about what had happened to that baby. Though the newspaper hadn't given too many details, he could guess.

The ball hit the rim and bounced up in the air. It seemed to hang there, suspended, trying to decide which way to fall.

If those kids were dead, Rusty thought, then he was a murderer as surely as if he had killed them himself. He was a beast. A beast worse than Bernardo, who claimed the name for fun and fame. He was a beast who had let the lure of cash pull him down into the garbage, into the cesspool from which nothing good could come.

He hadn't meant for his life to turn out that way. It had happened gradually, slowly, without warning. No alarms had sounded to warn him he had fallen. But he had, one rung down the ladder at a time.

He supposed that's the way it always happened. One bad choice after another. After a while the bad choices piled up so high they became a ton of weight and a person couldn't climb out from under them. A dark road down. Yeah, that's what had happened to him.

Now he was a beast and he was guilty and he deserved nothing but death like that poor baby, death and damnation forever and forever.

The basketball clanged onto the rim again, then dropped to the left, no good.

"You missed, Daddy," yelled Shane, a toothless grin punctuating his glee. "You missed your chance. Throw me the ball."

Rusty grabbed the ball and whipped it to his boy. Weird, he thought, reaching into the pocket of his cotton T-shirt for a cigar. The boy had nailed it right on the head. He had missed his chance. If those kids were dead, then no way could he put that behind him. He would forever remember Stacy's wailing, would forever see Taylor's eyes in his dreams. If those babies were dead, no matter how much good he did from now on he could never make up for the awful things he had done. The scale would be tipped too heavy against him. He would never be able to do enough good to tip them back right and he would die under their weight.

Sighing, Rusty lit the cigar and grabbed the basketball as it dropped again off the rim. Throwing the ball to his boy, he took a suck of the cigar and made a definite decision. If, by some miracle, those babies weren't dead, if by some wonderful twist of luck another chance ever rolled his way, he would try to shoot it straighter.

CHAPTER THIRTY-TWO

1:30 P.M.

Using a phone in the waiting room, Burke reached Bethany Chapman after one ring."Where are you, Bethany?" he started. "I've been worried sick about you, you need to tell me where you are so I can come get you—"

"Whoa," interrupted Bethany, her voice sounding amazingly strong to Burke. "Just hold on a second and I'll tell you what I can."

Burke took a deep breath and switched the phone to his left ear. "Okay, Bethany, okay. You tell me where you are and I'll come get you."

"No go on that, Burke. Just listen to me. There's a couple of things you need to know, but where I am isn't one of them."

"But you need help."

He heard her sigh. "No, not this time, Burke. This time I don't need help. This time, I'm taking care of myself. For the first time in my life, I'm standing up, doing unto others instead of waiting for them to do unto me."

"That's not quite the Golden Rule there, Bethany."

"Nope, but my life is living proof that following the Golden Rule doesn't always work out. All my life I've tried to do the right thing by other people. But every time I do, it seems that somebody kicks sand in my face, takes advantage of me, uses me, hurts me. . . . I'm tired of that. When Cleve threatened to take Stacy last week, I don't know, something snapped, I said enough is enough. . . . Since then I've been looking out for myself."

"You've got friends who can help you, Bethany. You're not alone, you know."

For a moment, she didn't respond. Burke wiped his hands on his pants.

"I know you're a friend, Burke, but there comes a time when a person has to take control of her own life, you know what I mean?"

Burke hesitated, not knowing whether to say what he wanted or not. He had never used his position as a counselor to push his individual faith on any one. Didn't think that quite right. But, he mused, this wasn't exactly a normal counseling situation. In fact, it had long since moved beyond that. No counselor would do what he had already done for Bethany. So why not let her know his personal beliefs?

"That kind of attitude leaves any notion of God out of the equation, doesn't it?"

"I suppose so, but I left God out of the equation long before any of this."

"Could that be part of the problem?"

"How so?"

"Well, you know, if you had known God all along, tried to find some divine direction for your life, maybe everything would have turned out differently. Maybe you wouldn't have married Cleve. And if you'd never married Cleve, maybe you wouldn't have ended up in the mess you're in now."

"That's too many ifs for me. You know the old saying, 'If ifs and buts were candy and nuts, what a wonderful world this would be.' No, Burke, I can't go back. What is, is what is."

"But you can do something different now. You can let me come get you, we can go to the police, get all this straight. I know you didn't do any of this, I'll help you prove—"

"NO, BURKE!" shouted Bethany, cutting him off. "That's not the way it's going to happen. It's too late. I've got to do this my way. If all this turns out okay, then later we can talk about this God of yours. It's not that I'm against what you're saying, but I called you for one reason, and it wasn't to get talked into giving myself up. I can't do that, don't you understand? If I come in, I'll end up in jail, even if for only a little while. And while I'm there, I'll disappear, I know I will. It'll kill me. . . . Don't you understand?"

Listening to her, Burke suddenly did understand. Yes, it would kill her, he realized. Maybe she wouldn't literally die, but she would very likely collapse in on herself, into complete insanity.

"What do you need from me?" he said, resigned.

"Just this. I need you to know about Cleve. I searched Janette Wilmer's apartment. I—"

"How did you—?"

"I had a key. Cleve wasn't too circumspect about his adultery. Left one at home months ago. I picked it up then, not knowing what it fit. Tried it out a couple of nights ago. Presto, instant entry."

"So you searched the place," said Burke, eager to know what she found.

"Yeah. And there's a couple of things you should know. My scrubs from the hospital, the ones that disappeared from the police station, they were in a trunk in his closet, washed clean. I left them there, figured it better if someone from Internal Affairs at Longstreet found them after you tip them off."

"You saying he took them from the evidence room?"

"How else did they get there?"

"But he can say they're not the same ones, he can—"

"Are you on my side or not?" grunted Bethany, her words clipped as if speaking through clenched teeth.

Burke switched the phone to his right ear. "Well, sure, Bethany, it's just that . . . I know what he might say, that's all."

She calmed down. "I know, Burke, I know how good he is. He's always been good at covering his tracks. And I've helped him do it. Just like Janette's doing now."

"You think she's involved in this?"

"I don't know for sure that she actually did anything with Stacy. But never doubt that she will cover for him if necessary."

"Why do you say that?"

"Because she already is."

"How so?"

"Well, she's not telling anyone about a couple of things."

"Like what?"

"Well, the abuse for one."

"Abuse?"

"Yeah. Does that surprise you?"

"What are we talking about here? Verbal, physical, what?"

"I'm sure it's both. But the physical is the worst. He's beating her."

"How do you know that?"

"Because of the pictures."

"Pictures?"

"Yeah, he takes pictures when he finishes."

Burke almost dropped the phone. His knees felt rubbery. "When he finishes?"

"Yeah, when he finishes his 'discipline' as he calls it. He takes pictures of the bruises. I found a stack of them. Right where I expected. In the bottom drawer of his desk. Where he always keeps them."

"Where he always keeps them?"

Bethany grunted. "Sure, you don't think Janette is the first one to suffer Cleve's wrath, do you?"

"He hit you too?"

Bethany laughed. "From the first week of our marriage."

"But you never told me."

"I was too ashamed of being so weak that I let him do it and get away with it."

"But I should have known," said Burke, his face flushing, his guilt sensors warming up quickly. "I saw you for months, but never knew."

"Don't blame yourself. No way for you to know. I never told you, and by the time I started seeing you Cleve and I had been separated for months. No evidence left. Besides, he was real careful not to hit me in visible places. He kept his punishment confined to my back, my buttocks, my legs. He's a real pro at this. Stays real calm while he's clubbing you. Never out of control. Never a blow where anyone will see it. He's doing the same with Janette."

Burke hesitated for an instant, not sure where to go from here. He leaned against the wall. "Will you bring me the pictures, Bethany? Bring them to me, let me help you?"

Bethany laughed again, more softly this time. "You don't give up do you?"

"No. I'm a runner, remember. Runners are tenacious."

"I'm finding out nurses can be too. I'm mailing you the pictures."

Burke nodded, understanding for the first time that Bethany wouldn't yield. Whatever she had in mind, she would do by herself. She would continue to run until they found her or until they found whoever had taken the three babies. No matter what he said, she was calling the shots. His only choice was to do what she asked.

 194   *Dark Road to Daylight*

"You said you knew a couple of things Janette's not telling. What's the second?"

Burke heard Bethany swallow. When she spoke, her voice faltered slightly. "Well, this is the strangest thing of all. And I don't know how it connects to Cleve or even if it does. But it's just something I found . . . found it on a shelf over Cleve's trunk in the closet. It's a book . . ." She stopped for a second, suddenly sounding tired, unsure of herself again.

"What kind of book?" coaxed Burke.

"Well, it's an old book for one thing. The pages are all yellow and crinkly. And it smells dusty, like it's been in an attic for a long time."

"Is it Cleve's?" he asked, trying not to sound too anxious.

"I don't know. If it is, he got it after he left me. I know he didn't have it before then. Cleve's not exactly a reader, you know what I mean?"

His patience overcome by curiosity, Burke pulled his back from against the wall and switched the phone one more time. "What's the name of the book?" he asked.

Bethany paused before answering. Burke squeezed the phone tighter and gritted his teeth.

"*A Beginner's Guide to the Dark Side.*"

Burke stood up straighter. "What kind of book is that?"

"From what I could tell, and I didn't have long to read it, it's a primer of sorts, a kind of spiritual guide for people who want to know more about the power within themselves."

"That sounds like a million other books out there," said Burke, not certain how this information fit the puzzle. "Psychology from A to Z. How to uncover the power in me."

Bethany laughed again. "Yeah, at first I thought so too. But this one juices up that notion a bit. Says that real power comes from the selfish nature within all of us, says this selfishness is the snake coiled up in our soul. If we'll let the snake go, we'll gain power beyond our imaginations, we'll gain the power of the dark side."

"The 'dark side'?"

"Yeah, and here's the scariest part of all."

"I'm listening."

"The last chapter of the book suggests additional reading for those interested in going farther."

"And?"

"And the list is a whole bunch of books on Satanism."

Gary E. Parker   **195**

CHAPTER THIRTY-THREE

3:00 P.M.

With Debbi's warning to be careful still ringing in his ears and her .25-caliber Beretta tucked under the seat of his car, Burke pulled out of his driveway and turned left. Not confident in his old Cavalier on a road trip, he drove Debbi's car, a 1994 Jeep Cherokee he had bought last year after he went to work full-time at the clinic. Headed down I-75, he pondered the whole confusing mess. Stacy Chapman and Taylor Bradford missing. Toshua Williams dead. Bethany the suspect in the first two disappearances. The murder apparently connected to the kidnappings. But was it? Somehow, it seemed different. After all, the bodies of Chapman and Bradford hadn't turned up anywhere. Maybe someone still had Stacy and Taylor, keeping them for some reason he didn't understand. But who had them? And where and why?

He scooted south out of Atlanta. Bethany could have taken all three of the kids. Taylor and Toshua as well as Stacy. She had fled the hospital before they were abducted. She had the opportunity. But what about motive? Especially for the third one?

Headed toward Macon now, Burke turned his thoughts to Cleve. What part did he play in all of this? His violent nature and the book Bethany had described could certainly lead a reasonable person to think him involved. Had he twisted his soul to Satanism?

Cleve hadn't caught the man who shot Jackie. Burke wondered if another man had even been there. The only person Patrick had seen come out of that apartment was Cleve. Had he shot Jackie, then pretended to chase someone else? The miles flashed by as Burke rolled the possibilities through his head.

He drove past the Macon exit. He knew the depths to which people could sink. Evil recognized no boundaries. It seduced people by its promise of power and then manipulated them to its ends. Evil held humans in its paws and played with them like a cat with a ball of string. No matter how much a person wanted to believe differently, evil did exist. It was a part of the fabric of life.

Passing a tractor, Burke wished it weren't so. But his wishes didn't change reality. Though not everyone would agree with him, he believed what his faith taught him about evil. It bubbled up from the human heart like hot lava from a volcano. And just like a volcano had a source deep in the bowels of the earth, so evil had a source deep in the bowels of the universe. Evil was born from the father of evil, the master of horror—the tempter, the diabolos, Satan, the Deceiver, Lucifer, the serpent of a thousand disguises, the evil of a thousand names. No matter what you called it or him, evil existed. As surely as God and goodness called every human being toward life, so sin and evil called every human being toward death.

Burke wondered about Cleve Chapman. Had Cleve sold himself to the dark side, given himself over as a pawn in the hands of the Master of Horror?

With the suspicions raised by the information Bethany had given him, Burke had considered going to the Internal Affairs Division of the police. But he didn't have the book or the pictures yet. Besides, even if he did show those to the authorities, what would they do? A book on the power within the self didn't prove anything. And of course, Cleve shouldn't beat his girlfriend, but since she hadn't filed a complaint, the police could do little about it.

Burke knew he had made the right decision. No reason to go to the police. After all, he could be wrong. Bethany could be wrong. No hard evidence pointed to Cleve Chapman.

Then who? The highway stripes underneath the Jeep zipped past as he wondered. The sun shifted to the west as the afternoon rolled on. Suddenly hungry, he flipped open the glove compartment and searched through it for one of the power bars Debbi often kept there. He found one, ripped off the paper, and took a big bite. Only a short way to go to reach Perry.

Who could have done these horrible things? Rusty Redder. The Beast. The cigar smoking mystery man in the green pickup. It all trailed back to him. Find the man who took Stacy and move ahead from there.

Seeing the Perry exit, Burke swallowed the last of the food bar and turned off the interstate. A couple of minutes later, he crossed over the bridge leading into Perry, Georgia, a small town like so many others in the South, a town of few people but many values.

Burke stopped at a red light and pulled a card from his shirt pocket. On the card he had written the address of Dawn Johnston. Telephone information had given it to him before he left Atlanta.

The card in hand, he stopped at a convenience store, gassed up the Jeep, and visited the bathroom. While paying for his gas and a Baby Ruth, he asked for directions to Dawn Johnston's street. The attendant pulled out a pencil and a piece of yellow paper and drew him a crude map. About five minutes away, said the clerk. Thanking the attendant, Burke bit into the candy bar and climbed back into the Jeep.

Turning left, he mentally ran down what he would say when he met Dawn Johnston. He would introduce himself as a friend of her husband. Would say he wanted to see Rusty for personal reasons and hope she wouldn't get too nosey about the details. He would ask her if she knew where Rusty might be.

At a red light, Burke took a deep breath. It wasn't much of a plan, but it was all he had. If she didn't know where Rusty was, then he would have to go back to Atlanta and leave the case in the hands of the police.

He passed a car wash and turned right. Two blocks down, he saw the place—a white-framed one-story house with a wraparound porch. Number 202. Just like he had written on the card.

Burke braked the Jeep to a crawl and slowly edged toward the house. A dog bounded across the road and he swerved to miss it. He thought of Scooter.

He stopped the Jeep in the middle of the road. What if Rusty Redder was here? It was a possibility. Slim, maybe, but real. He might have left Atlanta and come here to see his wife and son. If so, what would Burke say to him? How would he convince him to tell him what he knew?

For a split second, Burke considered turning around and driving away. He thought of leaving this dangerous business to people trained

 **198**   *Dark Road to Daylight*

for it. But then he knew he couldn't do that. He had made a promise to Jackie. He couldn't let her down.

Touching the gas pedal lightly, he leaned forward and felt for the Beretta on the floorboard. He didn't plan to use it, but he had promised Debbi to have it handy just in case. If it came down to it, he would. For her and for Elizabeth Joy, he would.

He pulled the gun from under the seat, lifted his cotton pullover, and wedged it into the back of his pants. Tucking the shirt back in, he eased his Jeep to the curb.

CHAPTER THIRTY-FOUR

5:25 P.M.

Sitting at a round table in the kitchen, an almost-empty bottle of beer in his hand, Rusty Redder leaned back in his chair and wiped his sweaty forehead with a paper towel. Playing with Shane all day had worn him out.

He slugged down the last swallow of the beer and stood up, throwing the beer bottle and the towel into the trash can under the sink. He heard the sound of the television three doors down the hall. Shane was watching cartoons.

Grabbing a bucket, a handful of rags, and some cleaning detergent from the pantry, Rusty left the kitchen and walked out the back door, planning to wash his truck. When he went to ask Dawn's dad for a job, he wanted to make a decent appearance. His truck might be old and a little rusty, but it didn't have to be dirty.

He turned the corner at the back of the house and looked for the hose he knew Dawn kept outside in the summer. From a pine tree to his left, he heard a bird chirp. Spotting the hose curled up by the faucet, he bent to pick it up. A car door slammed a couple of houses up from him. He raised his head and saw a dark-headed man of medium height move away from a chocolate brown Cherokee and walk down the street toward Dawn's house.

As Burke headed up the sidewalk that led to Dawn Johnston's house, he heard a door creak from the direction of the backyard. His muscles bunched up in his neck and he suddenly found himself almost on tiptoe. His breath coming in quick gasps, he stepped onto the front porch and looked for a doorbell, but he didn't see one. He rapped on the screen door, then stepped back. To his left sat a rocking chair and to his right hung a porch swing. A bird chirped from the oak tree that shaded the house from the rocking chair side. Burke felt himself relax a little.

Leaning back toward the door, he heard a television playing. At least someone was home. He knocked again, harder this time.

The bird chirped again, and just the hint of a breeze blew across the porch. Burke's shoulders dropped and his neck muscles sagged down. Okay, just a visit with a woman about her ex-husband. He knew how to talk to people. No problem.

The door opened and a boy in baggy black shorts, a Hawks basketball jersey, and hair the color of a Halloween pumpkin stared out at him through the screen door. Burke leaned down so the boy could see his face without straining.

"Hello there," he said, looking straight into the boy's hazel eyes. "Are you Shane?"

"Yeah, that's my name." The boy scratched his nose.

"Is your mommy home?"

"Nope," said the kid, his face scrunched up in puzzlement. "She's at work." His tone indicated that Burke should have known that all along.

"Do you know when she'll get home?"

"Nope, she gets home in the afternoon, I'm not sure about times yet. They didn't teach us that in first grade. But I'll be in the second this year."

Burke smiled at the youngster. "Can you tell me how to drive to the place where your mom works?"

The boy shook his head, and his colorful hair dropped into his eyes. "Nope, she works on the farm. With my granddaddy. I don't know how to get there. But if you'll ask for where the peanuts are, anybody in town can tell you."

Nodding, Burke stretched up straight again. He should be able to find the mother easily enough. Just go back to town and ask for Dawn Johnston. But he would need to be careful. It wouldn't do for a strange man to ask too many questions about a single woman in a small Southern town. Someone might take offense. He didn't want that. Not in a place where no one knew him.

He focused on the boy again. "Is there an adult here with you?"

The boy nodded, then scratched the end of his nose. Burke noted his freckles. Cute kid.

"Could I speak with them?"

Quick as a top, Shane spun away from Burke and shouted at the top of his lungs. "Daddy, there's a man here wants to talk to you!"

At the side of the house, just past the corner of the front porch, Rusty Redder crouched and listened to the exchange between the dark-haired man and his son. Though he couldn't hear everything Shane said, he could plainly hear the man. Nothing in his questions seemed threatening. He wanted to see Dawn. Simple as that.

But who was he? A salesman? That didn't make sense. He didn't have on a tie and he carried no product to sell. He wasn't a cop either. That was obvious. So who was he?

When Shane yelled, his big voice rolling through the open windows of the small house, Rusty started to move, to go through the back door, to take Shane by the hand and go talk to the man. But he decided against it. He would wait a bit, try to determine the man's identity.

A boyfriend of Dawn's? Rusty bristled at the thought. But then he relaxed. A boyfriend would know where Dawn worked.

Shane yelled again, this time from the interior of the house as he searched for his daddy.

Careful not to be seen, Rusty eased the top of his head around the corner so he could see the man better. The porch swing helped conceal him as he checked out the stranger. Not too big, but his arms and chest had some definition to them, as if he lifted weights. He was dressed casually, a peach-colored golf shirt and a pair of navy slacks, like those Docker things. Expensive shoes, but not dress shoes. Cross trainers, that's what they were. The dark-haired man was an athlete of some kind. Or at least he saw himself that way.

Shane yelled a third time, his voice echoing from near the back of the house, from the kitchen area. Apparently, he had walked through the whole place looking for Rusty. He would step out into the yard next.

The man on the front porch leaned closer to the screen door, his back to Rusty. Rusty noticed a bulge in the back of the man's shirt, a bulge that could only mean one thing. The man carried a gun.

Rusty yanked his head away from the house and dropped into a squatting position. Skittering like a chipmunk, he crossed the ground between himself and his truck parked in the backyard and cautiously opened the door. Still crouching, he reached under the seat and pulled out his .38. The guy at the door carried a gun. It didn't fit with his appearance, but Rusty decided he wouldn't get caught unprepared. If the guy wanted to play it that way, okay.

He pulled his T-shirt out, stuck the gun under the front of his belt, and stood up. In that moment, Shane opened the back door of the house and spotted him. "Dad," he called, excitement in his voice, "a man's here to see you."

Nodding, Rusty walked to the back door and into the house. In the living room, he took Shane by the shoulders and crouched down beside him.

"You go watch TV," he said. "Me and the man on the porch need to talk adultlike. It'll only bore you. You understand?"

Shane nodded and scratched the end of his nose.

"Now run on."

Rusty patted him playfully on the rump and the youngster hustled away.

The instant the boy yelled for his daddy, Burke's heart jumped into overdrive and he thought about the gun stuck in the small of his back. His courage shaky, he considered pulling out the Beretta, holding it in both hands, and facing Rusty Redder down with it. But then he knew he couldn't do that. Redder might have no connection to anything. Burke had no right to point a gun at him. Besides, he realized with even more fear, if he pulled a gun, Rusty Redder might do the same thing. And if he were a wagering man, he would bet that Redder knew how to handle one better than he did.

Burke heard Shane shout a second time. Burke weighed his other options. If he couldn't pull his gun, then what? Leave? Give up the whole silly notion, leave all this with the authorities? No, he had made a promise to Jackie. Just as important, he wanted to do everything he could to find the missing kids. With the cops giving all their attention to Bethany Chapman—and he still didn't believe that she was responsible—he might be their only hope.

From the back of the house, Shane called a third time, and Burke reconsidered his decision not to go to the police. Maybe he should let them question Redder. But it was too late for that now. If he left, that would give Redder time to run and he couldn't allow that to happen.

His breath short and his palms sweaty, Burke told himself to calm down. He had driven to Perry for this one purpose—to talk with Rusty Redder. Now he had the chance. Just don't blow it.

He heard footsteps. A man with red hair stepped to the door. He wore blue jeans with holes in the knees and a T-shirt the color of a lemon. His feet were shoeless. Burke glanced at the man's left ear. The shadows of the house kept him from seeing it clearly. His glance fell to the man's forearm. To the tattoo. There it was—*BEAST*.

Burke was face-to-face with Rusty Redder.

"Maybe we ought to talk out here," said Rusty, opening the door and stepping onto the porch. "So we won't bother the boy's cartoons."

Burke nodded and stepped back to make room. Rusty stepped onto the porch and pointed to the porch swing.

"Have a seat," he said, his nerves tight as the skin on a trampoline. "I prefer the rocker." He grabbed it and dragged it toward the swing.

Burke seated himself in the swing and Rusty eased down across from him and began to rock. The steel from the .38 in his waistband cut into his stomach.

"Now, what can I do for you?" asked Rusty, his voice calmer than he felt.

"I'm Burke Anderson," said Burke, leaning forward in the swing. "And . . . I . . . have a friend you might know."

Rusty took a cigar out of his shirt pocket, licked on the end of it for several moments, then lit it. A curl of smoke wrapped around his head.

"I'm listening," he said.

 204

"Her name is Bethany Chapman."

Rusty stopped rocking. The air on the porch suddenly seemed electrified. A squirrel chattered on the ground by the oak tree. Rusty thought of his gun and moved his hand toward it. But then a sudden hope struck him. Maybe the man didn't know enough to do him any harm. Maybe he just knew a little bit, enough to make him suspicious, but not enough to prove anything. After all, the guy wasn't a cop. If what he had was thin, the cops wouldn't be able to do a thing. Rusty raised his eyes, feeling a bit better. He still had a chance.

"Who's Bethany Chapman?" he asked, starting to rock again.

"A woman whose daughter disappeared last Friday. Somebody took the baby right out of her front yard."

"I don't know who you're talking about."

For a moment, Burke stayed quiet. But when he spoke again, his voice had an edge in it. "I don't think I believe you," he said.

"You got cause to say that?"

Burke shrugged and pushed off in the swing, his feet light on the gray porch, controlling the movement of the swing. "I've got cause."

"I'd like to hear it."

"You live in her trailer park."

"So do over three hundred other people."

"The police found cigars in front of her place."

Rusty shrugged and clamped down on the cigar in his mouth. "Lots of people smoke cigars."

"I saw a green pickup leave the park about the same time Taylor Bradford disappeared."

"Who's Taylor Bradford?"

"A boy kidnapped on Tuesday."

Rusty glanced to the house, toward the room where Shane watched his cartoons. "That's too bad."

"Yeah, it is, it's too bad—now we got two kids missing. Two kids missing and their parents scared to death that their kids have been harmed, that maybe their kids won't ever come home again."

"It's a tough world out there."

"Yes, and like I said, I saw a green pickup the day Bradford disappeared. You drive a pickup. My guess is, it's green."

"So do lots of other people."

"How many people have a tattoo like yours? The Beast. Right there on your left arm."

Rusty stopped rocking for the briefest of seconds, then gently pushed off again. "So?"

"So, Bethany Chapman's grandmother left us a note."

He worked to stay calm. "How'd the grandmother get mixed into this?"

"She tried to protect the child. Before she passed out with a stroke, she managed to write a note with one word on it."

Rusty's rocking stopped completely. "This grandmother—you say she left you a note?"

"Yeah, that's how I found you. Found a picture in your trailer. Showed your tattoo real well. The Beast, right there on your arm."

"You been in my place?"

"Yeah, I have." Burke offered no further explanation.

Rusty took a draw off his cigar and rocked again, a touch faster. From the oak tree, a bird chirped. A car passed on the street, the first one since Burke Anderson had arrived.

Without warning, Rusty jerked himself up from the rocker, whipped the .38 out, and pointed it at Anderson.

Anderson popped forward in the swing, poised as if to jump. But he held his position.

Rusty, his shoeless feet gripping the wood floors of the porch, kept the gun trained on Anderson. Sweat burst out on his forehead, wetting the red bangs that fell into his eyes. He took a big suck off his cigar. It had come to this—his worst nightmare. This guy Anderson had tied him to Bethany Chapman. For a split second, he thought he heard Stacy Chapman's woeful wail cutting through his ears. He shook it off.

He took another drag off his cigar, trying to decide what to do. Shoot this guy and haul his backside out of here? Disappear? That was a possibility.

His finger twitched on the trigger.

But he suspected running wouldn't work. The cops would eventually find him. They always did. Even if by some chance they didn't, he couldn't outrun those two kids. The girl's crying. The boy's eyes.

He thought of Shane. If he ran, he would never see his son again. If he stayed and they convicted him of kidnapping, he would spend his life in prison. But at least his boy could visit him there. It wouldn't be much of a life, but it would be better than his other choice.

He relaxed his finger on the trigger. His heart just wasn't in it. He didn't want to shoot this guy. That simply added murder on top of murder. Worse still, his boy Shane was inside watching cartoons. What kind of daddy would he be if he shot a man right here on the boy's front porch? No, he couldn't do anything with his gun.

Rusty hung his head. The gig was up and he knew it. Unless he shot Anderson, the end of the road had come.

Suddenly a sense of relief washed over him. It was over. He could admit his terrible actions, tell them to someone else, get them off his conscience. Ever since he took Stacy, he had fought with his guilt, wrestled with it at night, tried to drown it in his beer. But he couldn't. It stuck to him like gum on the bottom of a shoe. The sound of Stacy Chapman's crying. The stare of Taylor Bradford's eyes. What a nightmare!

He sighed hugely. Now he could turn that over to someone else. Yes, he would have to go to prison, but even prison would be better than the sound of that voice and the stare of those eyes.

He dropped the gun to his side and collapsed into the rocking chair. "I didn't mean to hurt the old woman," he said, his voice gentle, his eyes watering. "I just wanted to get the baby and get out of there. But when she come at me, I didn't know what else to do. Is she gonna be all right?"

Burke's blood pressure dropped and the pounding of his heart slowed to a manageable drumbeat the second Rusty lowered his gun. Like a ricocheting bullet, his mind moved instantly from concerns about his own safety to the whereabouts of the two children.

If Rusty had taken Stacy, surely he had also taken Taylor and the poor dead child. What had he done with Stacy and Taylor? Burke jumped out of the swing and stood over Rusty.

"Where's Stacy Chapman and Taylor Bradford?" he demanded, his voice gruff, suddenly angry with the man in front of him, angry that he had threatened him with a gun and that he had kidnapped innocent children.

Rusty shook his head and kept rocking. "I don't know," he said, his voice breaking.

"What do you mean you don't know? You just said you took

her. I assume you took Bradford too. And the one already dead. Don't try to—"

"I don't know, I tell you," cried Rusty, dropping his head into his hands, his sobs audible on the quiet street. "I took the girl and the boy, yeah, just like I was told to do, but then . . . then I delivered them to someone else. I haven't seen them since, that's all I did . . . snatch the kids and . . . and deliver them. They promised to pay me. That's all I wanted, a chance to . . . to start over, to put my miserable life behind me and try to do better . . . better the next time. . . ." His cries trailed off, his head still buried in his hands. His rocking ceased.

Burke stood over him, a frenzy of emotions coursing through his system. He didn't know whether to believe Rusty or not. He didn't want to believe him. If what Rusty said was true, someone else had the children and he didn't have a clue where they were. Another dead end.

He focused on Rusty Redder again. The man remained in the rocker, his head bent forward, his shoulders hunched. He seemed genuinely repentant.

To his left, a bird chirped. A car passed on the street. Burke racked his brain trying to figure where to go from here.

"Who were you working for?" asked Burke, his tone loud and insistent.

Redder raised his eyes from his hands. "I . . . I don't know exactly."

"You don't know? What do you mean you don't know?"

Rusty shrugged. "Well, that's the way it works with me. I get phone calls. People ask me to handle jobs for them. I do it. Then they pay me. It's the way it works."

Burke paced across the front of the porch, wiping his palms on his trousers. "You're telling me you don't even know who you work for?"

"Yeah, that's it. I almost never do. People prefer to stay anonymous. It makes sense, you know? The less I know, the better for me and them. I'm ignorant and can't squeal on them, and if I can't hurt them, they've got no incentive to hurt me. I just get phone calls. The less I know, the better."

Burke stopped his pacing and stared at Redder. "So," he said, "let me get this straight. You got a phone call asking you to kidnap Stacy Chapman."

"Yeah, that's it. A woman called me, told me what she wanted.

 **208**

Dark Road to Daylight

Then a man took the phone, told me where to deliver and what he would pay."

"A woman and a man?" Burke thought instantly of Janette Wilmer and Cleve Chapman. "And you agreed to do it."

"Yeah, for ten thousand dollars. I grab the kid, deliver her to a drop-off point, collect my money, and get lost."

"So you did that last Friday."

"Yeah, Friday."

"Then you get another assignment, the boy, Taylor Bradford."

"Yeah, Bradford was next. They held up my pay on the girl. Said I would get thirty for the two of them together."

"So you took the boy?"

Rusty didn't answer this time. He stayed in the rocker, his shoulders hunched over, his eyes down at his feet.

Burke put his hand on Redder's shoulder and squeezed it, his impatience running out through his fingers. "So, you took the boy, picked up your money. Is that when you got your next assignment?" His tone betrayed his anger at Redder's actions.

Redder shook his head, not fighting against Burke's grip. "I didn't do the third kid," he said, his voice low and soft. "I didn't do the one that's dead. I didn't do her, you got to believe me on that. Somebody else did that one."

Burke let go of Redder's shoulder and stepped back from him. "I don't get it," he said. "You're telling me that you suddenly decided enough was enough? You do two but three is too many?"

Redder shrugged. "Yeah, that's what I'm saying."

"Then who did the third one?"

"Don't ask me. Maybe they got impatient. Maybe they found out that I had left Atlanta, saw that they couldn't count on me no more, even for the money."

"Or maybe it's another person altogether," suggested Burke, remembering the differences between the three situations.

"That's possible, I guess. All I know is, it wasn't me. They told me to do the third one, but I didn't. Even though they never paid me for the first two, I decided I had done too much already. I couldn't . . . well, my conscience, you know, my insides told me to stop. I have a kid too, you know, you saw him. I started thinking about him, about starting over, about putting all my bad days behind me and coming

Gary E. Parker   **209** ᘓᕲ

home to my boy and my wife and trying again. I believe in that, don't you? That a body can change, turn over a new leaf as they say?"

Burke sighed and found his anger dripping out through his hands. An admitted criminal, a kidnapper no less, asking him, a former minister, about the possibility of change. For a moment, he wondered about the possibility. Could a person so far gone as Rusty Redder change? Could he decide that he had sunk low enough and choose to pull out of it? Could the love of a son or a wife make that much difference in a human heart? Could God convict and transform even the worst of us?

Burke leaned back against the railing of the porch. To his left a squirrel chittered. A car passed on the street. Rusty Redder sat still in his rocker, his body tense as if waiting on a verdict from a judge. Burke suddenly realized that he really did want an answer from him.

Burke rubbed his hands on his pants. When he spoke, his words fell gently. "If anyone is in Christ he is a new creation. Old things are passed away. All things become new."

"That's from the Bible," said Rusty, raising his head.

Burke nodded. "That it is. And I absolutely believe a person can change," he said. "If they sincerely feel sorrow for what they've done and if they do everything they can do to make amends for their actions, anyone can get a second chance. It's not always easy. Fact is, it's usually pretty tough. Takes a lot of work, carries a person down a long road. Some say a dark road. But eventually, if you stick with it, if you stay with faith, it happens—you turn the corner, you reach the daylight, you become what God wants to make you. If I didn't believe that, I don't know that anything else would be worth believing."

Rusty Redder swallowed. "A dark road, huh?"

"Yeah, a dark road to daylight."

Rusty nodded. "Okay," he said. "That's what I want to do."

Burke stepped to him and put his hands on his shoulders. This time he didn't squeeze Redder in anger. Instead, he patted him with compassion.

Dark Road to Daylight

CHAPTER THIRTY-FIVE

7:30 P.M.

It took almost two hours for Burke and Rusty to get out of Perry. First, Rusty had to explain things to his boy, tell him why he had to leave so suddenly. Next, they delivered Rusty's truck to a garage several miles out of town. A man in brown overalls agreed to watch out for it. Finally, they took Shane to his mother. Almost as if she expected it, she asked no questions when Rusty handed the boy over. Rusty explained that he had to go, but that he hoped he could come back soon, that he wanted to have a long talk with her, that he was doing something he should have done a long time ago. Dawn listened quietly, her arms wrapped around Shane, her eyes watery.

Finished at the peanut farm, Burke and Rusty headed back to Atlanta in Burke's Jeep. Burke wasn't headed to the police though. Not yet. At this point, he didn't think that the wise course of action. His suspicions told him Cleve Chapman and Janette Wilmer might be mixed up in this. But without some evidence to support his suspicions, he couldn't make any accusations. Besides, if he went to the cops, chances were someone would tip Chapman off. If he and Wilmer were the kidnappers, they would just lay low, cover their tracks. Worse still, going to the police would take time. They would process the situation to death. By some miracle, if Stacy Chapman and Taylor Bradford were still alive, that process would decrease the chances of saving them.

With going to the authorities ruled out, he and Rusty came up with another idea—simple to be sure—but feasible. He had tried to call Debbi to give her the details, but he hadn't been able to reach her. Maybe that was best, he decided. She might not like what he planned to do and try to talk him out of it. He didn't want that. He was scared enough as it was, and Debbi's anxiety would only add to his fear. He left a message with his mom that he would call back later.

A roll of thunder rumbled in the distance, and Burke glanced out the window. To the west, he saw a storm brewing. Staring at the black clouds on the horizon, he wondered if his plan had any chance of success. He didn't know what else to do. This way, at least he would have done all he could.

Trying to calm his fears, he turned to Redder and went over their plan. Rusty would meet his employers at the drop-off point just as he'd been instructed. But he and Burke would have a surprise for them.

"We'll get to the drop-off point about 11:15," he said. "About forty-five minutes before the delivery time. I'll find a place to hide."

"I'll have a bassinet with a doll in it," said Rusty, confirming his understanding of the scheme.

"That we'll get from my house."

"When my contact gets there, I'll pretend to deliver the baby."

"I'll call the cops on the cellular." Burke pointed to the phone in the console.

"I'll keep the man and woman there."

Burke thought of the Beretta he had put back under the seat of the Jeep and the .38 Redder had. "We'll do whatever it takes to hold them until the cops arrive."

For several moments, the two men fell silent. A bolt of lightning ripped through the air. A whirl of wind grabbed the grill of the Jeep and tilted it sideways. Burke fought to hold the vehicle on the road.

"What happens to me after?" asked Redder, breaking the quiet.

"That's not for me to say," Burke said sadly. "The authorities will arrest you, try you for kidnapping."

"I didn't have anything to do with the murder," said Redder, his head hanging to his chin. "I took those two, the boy and the girl, but I ain't no killer." His eyes desperate, he turned to Burke and grabbed him by the elbow. "Will you tell them that for me, will you please? Will you tell them I did all I could to help you find the two I took?"

A dog darted across the road, and Burke swerved to miss it. His

eyes straight ahead, he spoke gently. "I'll tell them," he said. "And I'll stand by you through the trial."

Thunder rumbled again. A swirl of leaves blew across the highway. "Looks like a bad storm," Burke said, glancing to his left.

Redder stayed quiet.

Burke looked over at him. Redder had his arms wrapped around his waist, and his head lay against the window. His skin had turned white, and his eyes threatened to crawl out of his head.

"You okay?" Burke asked.

"I don't like storms," Rusty said. "Saw a man hit by lightning once."

"It'll probably be over by the time we get to the drop-off point," Burke said.

"Hope so," said Redder. "Storms scare me."

Burke concentrated on his driving. Within a couple of hours they would arrive in Atlanta. He would go by his house, pick up the things they needed, drive himself and Redder to the delivery point. When the kidnappers arrived, it didn't matter to him what kind of storm raged. He would make them tell him where to find those two kids.

CHAPTER THIRTY-SIX

10:16 P.M.

Debbi still wasn't home when Burke pulled into his driveway, flipped off the lights of the Jeep, and ran through the wind into his house. His mom, one day away from going back to Birmingham, met him at the kitchen door as he came in through the garage. Hurriedly, he kissed her on the cheek, introduced her to Rusty, and asked what she had heard from Debbi.

"She came home about six. Fed Elizabeth Joy, then left again for the hospital. Said she'd get back about eleven."

Burke glanced at his watch. Almost 10:30. He and Rusty had over an hour to get situated before the drop-off at midnight. But the weather was getting more threatening by the minute. He expected the rain to start any second. Add that to the thunder, lightning, and gusty winds that had been swirling ever since they left Perry, and driving conditions would deteriorate in a hurry. They didn't have time to waste.

"Mom," he said, moving away, leaving her standing by the kitchen table, "when Debbi gets here, tell her I'll be late. Tell her I'm on to something and I'll contact her as soon as I can. Tell her not to worry, I'll be okay."

Without giving her time to ask questions, he left his mom in the kitchen with Redder and rushed into the nursery. Elizabeth Joy lay sleeping in her crib, the night lamp casting a soft glow across her face. For several long seconds, he stood over her, listening to her breathing. A flash of lightning lit up the sky outside and, for a split second, the night lamp flickered off, then back on. A frightening thought suddenly gripped Burke, and he felt as if an evil presence had joined him in the room. He rolled his shoulders, shaking off the sensation. Nothing could happen to Elizabeth Joy. He wouldn't let it.

Quickly grabbing a baby carrier, a blue blanket with a strip of pink ribbon around it, and a flesh-colored doll the size of a newborn baby, he paused and scanned the room to see if he could think of anything else he needed. Nothing came to mind. He hustled out of the nursery and back into the kitchen.

Redder sat at the dining room table by the back window. He had a fork in his mouth and a half-eaten piece of apple pie sat on a plate in front of him.

"You eat any supper yet?" Burke's mom asked him.

Burke smiled, but only for a second. "No, Mom, not yet. But I promise you I'll get something soon." He looked at Redder. "You ready to go?" A crash of thunder shook the floor.

Redder jerked his head away from the window and almost choked on the pie in his jaw. "Sure," he said, his teeth clenched. "I'm ready. Your mom offered me some pie."

Burke kissed his mom again. "My mom believes a person should eat all day long, one continuous meal from the time you get up until the time you go to bed."

She beamed at him.

"I'll be back as soon as I can," he said as he headed to the door. "And, Mom—"

"Yes?"

"Thank you for all your help this week."

With Redder crouching low to the ground behind him, he left the house, threw his supplies into the back of the Jeep, and headed back into traffic. A light rain began to fall. The highway took on a slick, shiny look, and Burke found it tough to see.

"Your mom said there was a tornado watch until 1 A.M.," Rusty said. "I got to tell you I don't like the notion of being out in this weather."

Burke, with both hands on the wheel, nodded his agreement. "I'm with you. But we don't have a choice. We have to find those two kids. I may be wrong, but I think this is our last chance. I don't know if they're still alive or not, but if they are, we've got to get them tonight. So storm or no storm, we've got a job to do. You with me?"

Redder pulled a cigar out of his T-shirt pocket, but he didn't light it. Instead, he stuck it between his teeth and chewed on it. "I got no other option," he said. "It's the only way I can hope to make up for what I've already done."

Glancing quickly at Redder, Burke suddenly felt good. The man really did want to change his ways. With that kind of attitude and God's grace, he might actually do it. Warmed by that thought, Burke fell quiet. Outside, the rain started to drum heavier on the Jeep. Winds hammered the vehicle from all sides, pushing it first one way and then the other. Streaks of silver slashed through the sky, giving it the appearance of a black eggshell just starting to crack. The thunder rumbled so loudly Burke and Redder couldn't have heard each other even if they had wanted to talk. They passed out of Atlanta in silence. The rain pounded on the Jeep. Burke focused on the road, thinking about the danger ahead. The minutes passed. Five, fifteen, thirty, fifty . . .

The trip took almost thirty minutes longer than he anticipated. By the time he left city traffic and turned off State Highway 400 onto a thread of a road headed northwest—the directions given to Redder at the hotel—the clock in his Jeep read 11:35. He tried to calm himself. Surely the weather had also slowed down the people who had hired Redder.

"You think we're okay on time?" he asked Redder, his heart racing.

"Don't know. But we're almost there. Turn right just past that barn." He pointed to a gray building just ahead on the right.

Squinting through the downpour, Burke followed his directions. The wheels of the Jeep spun through a big puddle as he turned onto an unpaved road. Trees lined the dirt road on both sides, their tops tilted hard left under the influence of a strong wind, which was pressing them down. Thirty yards down the path, dead ahead in the glare of the headlights, he spotted an old building, its outer facade a faded white. Instantly, he stopped the Jeep, killed the lights, and stared at the building. Flashes of lightning illuminated it in eery splashes of visibility. The roar of thunder stayed constant, and the quaking air felt like it would rattle the Jeep right off its tires.

Trying to ignore the storm, Burke focused on the building ahead, looking for a place to hide. The building wasn't big, but it was obviously old. Years of summer heat and storms had chewed away at the paint. The only two windows in the front of the building, rectangular ones that ran almost from the bottom to the top, were shattered. A piece of a tree limb had lodged in those front windows. Above the windows, the roof sagged inward, like a rotting corpse. In the center of the roof, at an angle on its side, lay a steeple, its pointed end jabbing at the ground.

"It's an abandoned church," said Burke, his mind wandering for a second, his voice soft, not speaking to anyone but himself. "I wonder how long it's been here."

A gust of wind grabbed the Jeep and rocked it to the left, yanking Burke's thoughts back to business. The rain cracked down on the Jeep, sounding like a thousand carpenters hammering all at once.

"You see anybody?" he asked Redder, his neck tense, his hands wiping the front of his trousers.

Redder shook his head. Lightning split the sky behind them, and a piece of a tree limb scratched along the side of the Jeep for an instant, then scurried away in the wind. Burke pulled his watch close to his face. A streak of lightning lit up the dial. 11:48. They didn't have much time. He eased off the brakes, switched on his parking lights, and edged closer to the church, searching through the blustery rain for signs of company. Not seeing any, he pulled to the back of the building and killed the lights again.

He turned to Redder. "You think they'll even show?"

Redder shrugged. "Maybe not, who knows?"

"We've got to be ready either way."

Redder nodded his head, but not enthusiastically.

"You okay?" asked Burke, concerned that Redder might not want to go through with the plan.

Redder chewed on the end of his cigar. "Like I told you, lightning scares me. Saw a man struck by it one day. It killed him. Ever since then, I don't know, it seems personal with me, like it's determined to get me or something. . . ." His shoulders slumped, and he curled his arms around his stomach.

Burke leaned back against the seat, measuring the situation. He knew he couldn't wait long. Any minute now he expected to see the lights of another vehicle whip through the rain down the muddy path behind him. If he and Redder weren't in place by then, the whole scheme would fall apart. It would fall apart and the children would die if they weren't already dead. He didn't think he could deal with that.

He twisted to the right, his whole body facing Redder. "I can't do this without you," he yelled, his voice rising above the storm, the urgency in it making it audible through the roar of the thunder.

For several moments, Redder didn't speak. The intensity of the rain increased, and Burke heard a crack behind the Jeep, down the path leading away from the abandoned church. He wondered if a tree had fallen. Suddenly, he smelled the distinct odor of onions. Onions?

Oh no! Not now. Over four years since the last seizure. He had stayed on his medication since then. But intense emotion could trigger the seizures. He bit his lip, deliberately hurting himself, trying to force his body to stay conscious.

He tasted blood on his tongue. He gritted his teeth. His eyes flickered and the aroma of onions passed.

Not knowing if the threat of a seizure had passed for good or if it would come again within seconds, he knew he needed to act immediately. Feeling more and more panicked, he suddenly reached over and grabbed Redder by the shoulders. He jerked his face around to his, held it inches away, stared into the man's frightened eyes.

"What's it going to be?" he yelled at Redder, his own eyes wide and frantic, not liking the storm any more than his unlikely ally but determined to do whatever it took to finish what he had started. "Either you do what you can to make amends for what you've done, or you live with this on your conscience the rest of your life. Here's your chance. Most people never get one like this. It's risky, sure, but starting over always is. It takes guts to put your own fears aside, to act in spite of those fears, to do what's got to be done. Can you do that? Can you do what you said you would do?" His gaze still on Redder's face, Burke waited for an answer, waited for what seemed like forever, waited as the roar of the storm deepened its intensity, as the lightning bit through the night again and again, as the wind rocked them back and forth, back and forth. Time seemed to stop. Redder gulped and the cigar in his lips dropped onto his lap.

"Yeah," he said, his voice somber. "I can do it. If I want to start over, I got to do it."

Burke let go of his shoulders and reached to the backseat. "Okay," he said, "We need to move fast. It's almost midnight. Here's the doll. . . ."

CHAPTER THIRTY-SEVEN

11:55 P.M.

It didn't take more than five minutes to get in place, but it seemed like forever. The rain pelted down like wet rocks, and the wind blew so strong Burke had to bend forward to walk through it as he scooted out of the Jeep and led Redder through the back door of the abandoned church. Inside, Burke flipped on a flashlight he had brought from the Jeep. Immediately, he saw that he was standing in a hallway. The hallway led straight ahead. Cautiously, he inched forward, Redder close behind. They passed through a second door and stepped into a more spacious room. Burke knew instantly that this had once been the sanctuary. With Redder so close he could feel his breath on his neck, he paused and raked his light over the dark room. Compared to the noise of the storm, the place seemed quiet, as if a congregation had gathered for worship.

He and Redder stood just to the side of what had obviously been the platform area. He directed the light to the rostrum. Two wooden steps led up to where the pulpit had once stood. Behind the pulpit area, running across the back of the platform, a rail that looked to be about three feet high marked where the choir used to sit.

Burke shifted his attention from the rostrum to the rectangular sanctuary in front of it. The sanctuary was completely empty. Not a stick of furniture in sight. Not a pew, not a table. At the back of the sanctuary, he saw two double doors. Beyond the doors, he knew what he would see if he had time to inspect it. A vestibule. The place where the people had once taken off their coats, spoken their greetings to one another, and picked up their bulletins.

Burke heard a crescendo of *drip, drip, drip,* and directed the light to the roof. Rain seeped through the ceiling in scores of openings, creating a drumbeat of water hitting the floor. He stared down at his feet. Carpeting the color of a rusty pipe squished as he lifted a heel and put it down again.

"I can hide behind the door," he said, indicating the one directly behind them. "From there I can hear everything. You stay here, in front of the platform. The minute your contacts arrive, I'll get to the Jeep and call the cops. You keep the kidnappers here. I'll come straight back. Does that sound okay?"

Redder touched his shoulder. "It's good," he said.

"Okay. Remember—I'll be right here."

"Get moving," said Redder. "So long as I'm out of the lightning, I'm happy."

Burke almost grinned but didn't quite make it. Too much could go wrong for him to smile.

The instant Burke left, Rusty got ready. First, he laid the doll— a life-sized girl in a diaper and a gown—in the baby carrier. Next, he tucked the blanket Burke had given him around her legs, arms, and chin. Finally, he set the baby carrier in the center of the rostrum. His preparations complete, he took a seat beside the child, his body in front of hers facing the empty sanctuary, his legs folded Native American–style under his backside.

As comfortable as he could get, he reached into his T-shirt pocket and pulled out a cigar. Lighting the cigar, he leaned back slightly and took a big draw of smoke. The edge of his gun jabbed him in the side, and he shifted his position. He blew out the smoke of the cigar. A drip of water landed near his left leg.

He sucked on the cigar again. The glowing embers of the tobacco provided the only light in the room. The tiny heat felt good on his face. In spite of the danger, an odd feeling of calm rolled over him. Outside, the storm seemed to have let up a bit. Thunder still rumbled, but it sounded more distant and the lightning flashes came less

   *Dark Road to Daylight*

frequently. Exhaling, Redder relaxed a bit and pondered the twists of fate that brought him to this spot.

Hard to believe. In an abandoned church with a man of the cloth, a preacher—or at least a former preacher—named Burke Anderson. About to take a stab at rescuing two kids he had snatched from their parents. About to do a good thing instead of a bad one.

A splat of water hit him on the forehead, and he moved slightly to the right. Anderson had said he could start over. That God could make a man a new creature. He wondered if it could really be true. He hoped so. When all this was over, he would find out. He knew he would spend some time in prison, but if the two kids were okay and he could help rescue them, at least it wouldn't be for murder. He would use the prison time to investigate this new birth, to sort it all out. He would—

A beam of light cut through the front of the church, interrupting his thoughts. Rusty jammed his cigar out in the wet carpet and jumped to his feet. Pulling the gun from the waistband of his jeans, he held it in both hands behind his back. Though quivering inside, he stood still, watching a light swish side to side across the old building, its beam probing the darkness, probing like a dog's nose sniffing the air, searching for prey.

Redder crouched as if to hide, then knew hiding wouldn't cut it. He had to face these people if he wanted his chance to start over. He stood up straight again, the baby carrier right behind him, his finger tight on the trigger of his .38.

The light beam hit him in the face, moved for a split second to the left, then shifted back. It stopped directly in his eyes, blinding him. Redder suddenly felt chilled. He wanted to wrap his arms around his waist, but he was too scared to move.

"You brought the package?"

Redder swallowed. It was the same man who had taken Stacy and Taylor. For a split second, he heard Stacy cry again and saw Taylor's big brown eyes. A drip of water hit him on the shoulder and rolled down his arm. He forgot the two kids.

"I brought the package," he said, fighting to keep himself calm. "She's mighty quiet."

"She's asleep. I drugged her, just like the last two."

"Is she perfect?"

"I think so. She's beautiful. Now where's my money?"

The man laughed, and it sounded like the thunder of the storm. "It's behind you," he said. "Right behind the baby. Behind the rail, in the choir loft. Sixty big ones, just like we agreed."

Rusty relaxed just a touch. His hands loosened their squeeze on his gun for a half beat. He thought of the money behind him, the sixty grand he could take to Florida. He thought of giving up his dream of starting over, his plan to find out about the God who promised to make him completely new.

The money. He could still get the money!

He twisted a half turn away from the light still shining in his face. He could go to Florida and look up Bernardo the Beast. That's where Bernardo lived—in Daytona. He could take the money and run to Florida. Him and the Beast. He could grab his son from his mother in Perry and take his boy with him to meet the Beast. That's what he could do.

Wait a second, thought Rusty. *I'm not a beast. I don't want to live like an animal, always running, always hiding, with never a home and a family to call my own. I want something different than that, I can do something different than that. I can—.*

"Hand me the child," called the man behind the light, interrupting Rusty's thoughts. "Hand me the child, then take your money and go."

"The money first," said Rusty, knowing the man expected him to say that. "The money first, then the baby."

"Move away from the child," said the man. "Move toward the railing."

Rusty obeyed, sliding his feet across the wet carpet, easing past the doll in the baby carrier, nearer the old choir loft. The light moved closer to him, step by step up the aisle of the church. Rusty took a step closer to the choir. Twenty feet away, the man with the flashlight dropped it from Rusty's face and directed it toward the doll.

Behind the door just off the sanctuary, Burke heard the stranger's voice the second he spoke. Instantly, he turned away and headed through the hallway of the church to his Jeep. A quick call to 911 and then hold the kidnappers in place. That's all he had to do. He touched the Beretta in his waistband.

Moving rapidly, but careful not to bump into anything, he

reached the door and stepped onto the muddy gravel outside the church. By the Jeep, he reached for the door handle.

But then, from out of nowhere, another person materialized. Burke sensed it before he actually saw anyone. Before he could grab the Beretta in his waistband, a woman was beside him, a gun in her hand, the barrel jammed into the back of his neck. He knew it was a woman because a perfume the smell of roses engulfed him.

"Going somewhere?" she asked, pushing the gun deeper into his flesh.

His hand frozen on the door, Burke stared straight ahead into the window of his Jeep, trying to see the woman's reflection in the glass. The pressure of the gun kept him from turning around. He thought immediately of Janette Wilmer—Cleve Chapman's girlfriend. He couldn't see anything in the dark window.

As if waiting for this exact moment, the rain that had slackened for a few minutes now dropped down heavy again. It fell in sheets, instantly drenching his head and shoulders. The wind seemed to redouble its efforts too, and from far away he heard a howling noise, a noise like that of a high-speed engine about to reach its limits.

The instant the flashlight dropped to the doll, Rusty made a decision. He wouldn't just wait until the man figured out it was a doll instead of a baby. He would move now, move before the man made the discovery and shifted the light back to him.

Pivoting away from the railing, Rusty jumped to the left, off the rostrum. He jerked open the door leading out the back of the sanctuary, back toward the hallway he had come through with Burke. Rushing through the hallway, he heard the man behind him move, then saw the beam of light flicker at his feet. The man was following him.

Pushed by his fear, Rusty banged through the narrow hall, his feet slipping and sliding on the wet floor. He heard a weapon fire and realized the man had shot at him. A second shot ripped through the hallway, and Rusty threw himself against the wall, hoping to dodge the bullet.

A hot pain bit into the back of his right knee as the bullet ripped into his flesh. Rusty staggered and almost fell. Then he saw the flicker of the flashlight again, and he gritted his teeth and forced himself to keep moving. Only a couple of more steps to the door. If he could get to the door, Burke could help him. He reached out to push the door open. A shot popped through the dark hallway. He fell through the door and into the raging storm.

For a brief instant, Burke thought the cracking sounds from the church were lightning bolts hitting the ground. But then he recognized them for what they were—gunfire.

Redder!

Something had gone wrong with Redder.

Without thinking about consequences, Burke reacted, jerking his hand away from the door handle of the Jeep, reaching for the Beretta jammed into his stomach. He had hoped and prayed it wouldn't come to this, but he had no choice. For Rusty and for Debbi and Elizabeth Joy, he would do what he had to do.

In that split second, a slash of lightning, a slash sharper than any that had hit anywhere in Georgia all night, smacked through the sky. The finger of lightning reached from the upper corner of the night all the way to the ground. It splintered into a million shards of electric current and all of them dropped like sizzling heat into the woods around the church where Burke and the woman stood.

For a millisecond the night became as bright as a new morning. Burke yanked his head to the right and faced the woman, his hand almost to his gun. She wore a baseball cap, pulled low over her face, obscuring her eyes and cheekbones. Behind her he spotted a dark van parked by the church.

As if in slow motion, Burke saw the woman pull her weapon over her head. She slammed it down against his skull. He heard another crack. It sounded like another gunshot. But Burke knew it wasn't that. Instead, it was his head cracking under the weight of a vicious blow. He fell forward under the blow, his face splashed into the water, and his nostrils filled with mud and water.

Rusty spotted Burke the second he fell through the church door into the yard. He spotted the woman, too, and his spirits sank. She had her gun lifted into the air. But Rusty didn't give up.

Dragging his wounded leg, he grabbed for the gun tucked under his shirt. It wasn't there. Somehow, he had dropped it when he fell.

Enraged by his helplessness, he lunged for the woman. If he could only reach her before she shot Burke!

Halfway through his lunge, the lightning struck. Rusty froze in mid-leap and raised his face toward the sky. A shard of the lightning sizzled downward from the clouds, its radar focused right at his head.

He recognized it immediately. He saw it zip closer and closer, a heat-seeking missile honing in on its target. Instead of closing his eyes, he opened them wider. A flood of rain washed over his forehead and down onto his body. Suddenly thirsty, he opened his mouth and licked the rain into his throat. It tasted good, refreshing, life-giving.

The bolt of lightning was only inches away now, almost there, almost on him. He opened his arms toward the lightning and leaned back his head.

The rain poured over his body. It felt cleansing to him. He bathed in the water. *Wash me, O God,* he thought. *Wash me and make me clean.*

The lightning hit him, and his body shuddered and sizzled in the heat. But somehow, deep inside his head, Rusty didn't mind. The rain had already washed him clean. As he closed his eyes, his last thoughts were of Shane and Dawn. Shane and Dawn. They were clean, and now, so was he.

Kneeling over Burke, the woman searched through his pockets, pulling out his keys and tossing them into the mud, reaching for his wallet, taking it out of his back pocket, flipping it open. Standing beside her, a man in a clear rain slicker pointed his flashlight at Burke.

"Get the gun in his belt," he said. "He doesn't need it anymore."

The woman pulled the gun out and handed it to her companion.

"Who is he?" called the man, wiping rain out of his eyes, his voice cutting through the howling wind.

"Driver's license says 'Burke Anderson,'" shouted the woman. "That ring any bells?"

"None."

"So what's he doing here?"

"I have no clue. But I'd wager my last dollar that he's the guy who had the bright idea to bring a doll instead of a baby. See what else is in his wallet."

Pulling her baseball cap even farther over her face, the woman flipped quickly through the wallet. She dropped Burke's credit cards on the ground, his health club card beside them. Working rapidly, she opened his pictures, ran her fingers through them. Saw an elderly man and woman in one, a woman in a wedding gown in a second, and Burke holding a baby in a third.

The woman raised from her crouch. "Well, would you look here," she yelled over the wind. "Looks like Mr. Anderson has a baby girl himself." She clutched the picture close to her face, out of the rain.

The flashlight zeroed in on the photograph—Burke holding a little girl dressed in a white sleeping gown, her thick dark hair snug in a pink ribbon.

"Bring the picture and the driver's license," said the man, lowering the flashlight. "If we can get to her, this little baby will do just fine."

Tossing the wallet into the water, the woman turned and followed her companion to their vehicle—a van as black as the stormy night. In the van, she pushed back her baseball cap and ran her hands through her soaked hair.

"So good of Mr. Anderson to provide us a substitute," she said, her voice pleased.

"If we can get her, we can still meet our deadline," said the man. "Check Anderson's address."

The woman grabbed a map from the glove compartment of the van and flipped on the overhead light. "Looks like northeast Atlanta. Not far from the loop. If the storm lets up a little, shouldn't take more than just over an hour or so."

The man peered through the windshield at the swirling rain. "We'll get her," he said. "No matter about the storm."

CHAPTER THIRTY-EIGHT

12:20 A.M.

Debbi Anderson stood over Elizabeth Joy and watched her sleep. She had never known a child quite so scheduled in her eating and sleeping. Eat at eleven, asleep at twelve. You could plan your life by it and never miss an appointment.

Yawning, Debbi left the night lamp burning and walked from the room. In the kitchen, she joined Burke's mom at the dinette table for a cup of hot tea.

"You look tired," said Mrs. Anderson. "Did you eat anything at the hospital?"

Debbi smiled and drank from her cup. "Not really, but I haven't been hungry. I've been too worried. It's been a long day."

"How's Detective Broadus?"

"She's better. The doctor said it was a close call, but that everything was going to be okay. The bullet barely nicked the lower part of her heart. You said Burke came by with some guy?"

"Yeah," said Mrs. Anderson, standing from the table and walking to the refrigerator. "The man's name was Redder. Rusty, I think." She opened the refrigerator. "Burke also said to tell you he'd be late." She rummaged in the refrigerator for several moments, then pulled out the remains of an apple pie. "Said he had something he needed to check out."

"You didn't know the man with him?"

"Nope, but he seemed nice enough. Liked my apple pie."

"Burke said he would call?"

"Yeah, as soon as he could." Mrs. Anderson cut two slices of the pie, placed one in front of Debbi, then sat back down and started to eat the other.

"Did he say what time he'd get home? I don't like him out so late in this storm."

"Nope, nothing specific. And the storm wasn't so bad then."

Mrs. Anderson pointed to the pie with her fork. "Eat up," she said. "Then get on to bed. It's my last night with you. Tomorrow you've got that baby by yourself. Believe me, you'll need the rest."

Debbi nodded, then jabbed her fork at the pie. Shoving a mouthful into her cheeks, she chewed slowly, admitting to herself that Burke's mom was right. She already needed the rest. In spite of Mrs. Anderson's help, she felt exhausted. She closed her eyes as she ate. In a few minutes she would go to bed. But in spite of her weariness, she didn't think she would sleep too well. Until she heard from Burke, she might not sleep at all.

Lying facedown in the muddy water, Burke suddenly gagged and came to consciousness. Coughing up a mouthful of rainwater, he turned his head sideways so he could breath better. Not really sure where he was or how he had gotten there, he fought to raise up. Gradually, he raised his head and pulled his legs under him. His head ached incredibly. He felt a knot the size of a golf ball on the back of his skull.

For almost five minutes he sat there, his body fighting to regain some equilibrium, his mind confused and cloudy. The rain, though slacker than before, continued to pour down. For the moment at least, the lightning and thunder had moved away.

Slowly, the images filtered back to him. The church. The baby doll. The woman in the baseball cap. The terrible crack of lightning. The pistol whip across the back of his head. Rusty.

Rusty!

Burke jerked his head to the left and right, searching through the church yard for Rusty Redder. All about him the wind still whipped and swayed in the trees and the rain continued to fall. The cloud cover obscured the moon and almost no light escaped the sky. Burke squinted into the rain.

There! About fifteen feet away. A body. Almost half-submerged in water.

Gritting his teeth against his headache, Burke crawled across the squishy mud to the still form lying on the ground. It was Rusty. He lay with his face turned up to the sky. His eyes were open. From above, the rain soaked down on him, gushing through his red hair, falling in swirling streams off his ears.

Burke knew instantly that Rusty was dead. For a split second, he wondered what had killed him, but then noticed a charred slash across his right cheek. The slash ran down his chin and through his neck, then disappeared in the collar of his T-shirt.

Gently, Burke lifted Rusty's right hand and saw a black zigzag in his palm, like he had grabbed a hot poker.

Burke remembered the incredible flash of lightning that had struck just as the woman knocked him out. The lightning had hit Rusty Redder. Struck him down where he stood. Just as Rusty had feared. The lightning seemed to have picked him out—a human target for a deadly laser of electricity.

Burke closed Rusty's eyes. He had hoped to know the man better, to introduce him to the God who loved all people, no matter their crimes. Now he wouldn't get the chance.

Grieved over the lost opportunity, Burke placed his hand on Rusty's forehead. "O God of mercy," he whispered. "Be merciful to this man. I leave him in your care. Amen."

Still struggling against his aching head, Burke pushed up and sloshed back toward his Jeep. By the door, he reached for his keys but didn't find them. He checked all his pockets, front and back. They weren't there. Apparently, the woman in the baseball cap had taken them. He patted his back pocket. She had taken his wallet too.

He could live without his wallet. But what would he do without his keys?

Burke suddenly remembered—the key by the battery. He kept a key there all the time, magnetized to the frame, for the occasion when he or Debbi locked themselves out of the vehicle.

Thankful for his foresight, he pulled up the hood of the Jeep, grabbed the key, and slammed the hood back down. Inside the vehicle, he started the engine and flipped on the lights. In the twin beams of the headlights, he saw his wallet.

Stepping hurriedly out, he jerked the wallet off the ground, then saw the scattered credit cards beside it. Picking up the credit cards, he saw that his driver's license was missing. Curious as to what else the woman had taken, he flipped through the wallet, searched through its pockets, thumbed through the pictures.

Burke stopped and became dead still. Only one picture was missing—the picture of him holding Elizabeth Joy.

Instinctively, he knew what that meant. The man and woman wanted his daughter. He and Rusty had brought them a fake. Now they were after the real thing.

CHAPTER THIRTY-NINE

12:45 A.M.

The first tornado touched down almost thirty miles west of Atlanta, its black tail snaking through a deserted high school, its furious winds splintering the roof of the building into a billion bits and pieces. By the time that tornado had passed over the football field of the high school, a whole line of funnel clouds had formed and begun to drop in random locations in and around the greater metropolitan area.

Though she was unaware of the approaching tornadoes, Debbi Anderson knew the weather had taken a turn for the worse. Disturbed by the increasing wind, she rolled over in bed and dropped her feet to the floor. Over the last five minutes the house had shaken and quivered time and time again in response to the thunder outside. A noise that sounded like wood splitting made her wonder if the pines that surrounded her house might any moment come crashing down through the windows of her home. She switched on a lamp, pulled a red-and-black bathrobe around her shoulders, and stepped into the hallway. One door down, she stuck her head into Elizabeth Joy's room. The night-light glowed warmly across the crib, and Debbi smiled at the sight of her baby.

Amazing. The child slept like a rock. Momentarily comforted by her child's peaceful rest, Debbi padded to the kitchen, grabbed a pitcher from the refrigerator, and poured herself a cup of tea. Sitting the cup in the microwave, she heard a noise and turned around. Mrs. Anderson stood in the doorway to the kitchen, a housecoat pulled up to her throat.

"You couldn't sleep either, huh?" Debbi asked, grabbing another cup and pouring tea into it.

"Worst storm I've seen in a while. Radio said we were under a tornado warning. I'm surprised we've still got power."

"Underground lines in this area," said Debbi. "Not likely to lose power here."

Debbi sat the second cup of tea into the microwave, punched on the timer, then joined Mrs. Anderson at the dining room table. "The baby's still asleep," she said, pushing her hair out of her eyes.

"Takes after the Anderson clan," said Burke's mom.

Debbi smiled again, but the thought of Burke out in this storm made her feel less than happy. She bit her lip for a second, then twisted to face the window. Shadows danced across the glass, making the trees outside seem alive.

"Burke didn't say what time he'd get home?" she asked, though she knew the answer.

"Nope, just that he would call later."

The microwave beeped, and Debbi moved to get the hot tea. "He didn't say where he was going?"

Mrs. Anderson shook her head.

Debbi placed the two cups on the table, then took her place across from Mrs. Anderson again. "Wish he'd call," she said, taking a sip of tea.

"He's a grown man," said Mrs. Anderson. "He's got sense enough to come in out of the rain."

Debbi nodded. She knew Mrs. Anderson was right. Burke could take care of himself. He'd proven that more than once.

Sipping her tea, Debbi pulled her robe closer around her neck and stared out the window. Her thoughts didn't really make much sense. She knew Burke was smart enough to find shelter from the storm, but she couldn't get away from the notion that Burke hadn't come in out of this particular rain. For some reason, deep in her soul, she sensed that he was out there somewhere, in trouble and needing her help. She had nothing on which to base her suspicions—she just felt it, that's all.

Placing her tea cup gingerly on the table and standing up, Debbi touched Mrs. Anderson's shoulder. "I'm worried about Burke," she said. Her hands trembled.

Mrs. Anderson nodded and stood too. "I know child," she

agreed. "I know. But it's out of our hands. Best we can do is go to bed and say our prayers."

Debbi nodded, then turned away and headed to her bedroom. There, she tossed off her robe and flipped off the light. Falling into bed, she turned away from the window. Beyond it, the night suddenly became calm. The wind dropped to nothing. The thunder stopped. The lightning relented. The quiet soothed Debbi, and she closed her eyes.

Within an hour after Debbi flipped off the light, a black van pulled to the curb two doors down from her house. Instantly, the man behind the wheel turned off the ignition, doused the lights and leaned back in his seat. Then, as if suddenly weary, he hung his head forward and rubbed his palms over his forehead.

"We're almost done, Doug," said the woman beside him, her baseball cap low over her eyes. "One more kid and it's finished. We make close to half a million dollars and make three families incredibly happy at the same time. Not a bad week's work."

Doug nodded and raised his bald head, focusing his eyes straight ahead. Through the rain, he spotted a dim glow of light in a room on the right front, just past the covered porch. Either someone was up or the Andersons used a night-light. If it was a night-light, then the room was probably a nursery. Most likely, under the glow of that light lay the last of the three kids he and his wife needed to meet their deadline.

Three kids. A hundred and fifty grand a pop. To three different couples. Couples who couldn't have their own children. Couples his wife, Vera, knew about from her job with a private adoption agency. Couples who had plenty of money but who had reasons for not going through normal adoption procedures.

The husband of one of the couples had a criminal record. A little matter of a manslaughter charge from his early twenties. That made him and his new wife ineligible to adopt. A wife with cancer meant a second couple had no time for the usual process to work, even if the authorities would allow a sick woman to have a child. Which they wouldn't. So, if she was to experience motherhood, it had to happen now. A third couple wanted to choose what the kid looked like. Didn't get that much say through traditional agencies.

Doug grinned to himself. The couples didn't know about the kidnappings. No reason for them to know. They lived in three different small towns in Georgia. All of them at least four hours from Atlanta. They might know about the missing children—he wasn't sure—but even if they did, they had no reason to connect the children he would deliver on Saturday and Sunday to those unfortunate tragedies. So far as they knew, their kids came from a private adoption agency. His wife had all the papers ready. No sweat at all to make it happen. People knew so little about the adoption process and were so intimidated by it all, they pretty much accepted whatever they were told. So long as they got their kid. To those parents, he and his wife were heroes. If any of the couples were suspicious, they certainly hadn't shown it.

Most amazing, they didn't even care about the exorbitant cost. Vera had justified the fee by reminding them that they got children in perfect health and in the race they requested. Besides, Vera had deliberately picked people who could afford their rate. For wealthy people, a hundred and fifty thousand dollars didn't sound like much for a perfect baby.

For a split second, Doug thought of the parents whose children he and Vera had abducted. He shrugged. The way he saw it, he had actually done those people a favor. He had purposely taken kids on the downside of the economic food chain. Those families couldn't afford the kids anyway. They would be better off without the expenses of a child.

And the kids? Definitely better for them. They would enjoy their more luxurious surroundings. Two parents in each home. An abundance of money. Country club living. All the advantages. What kid could complain about that?

He stared at Burke Anderson's house. This kid didn't quite fit the profile like the others. But that couldn't be helped. He had promised to deliver the children over the weekend. If he didn't, one couple might want to know what happened. They might go to Vera's agency, start asking questions. That could cause trouble.

So he couldn't wait. He had to take another, and he had to do it tonight. If Rusty Redder hadn't gotten a case of the guilts and screwed up the scheme, he wouldn't need Burke Anderson's child. But as it was, he had no choice. Burke Anderson's baby it would be. After that, he and his wife would shut it down. A half a million, that's all they wanted. No reason to get greedy.

"We need to let the last of this rain pass," he said, peering through the windshield. "It's still coming down pretty heavy out there."

Vera rolled her eyes at him. "No way, man," she said. "The worse the storm, the better for us. No one else is out. Let's get it done and get out of here." She unsnapped her seat belt and leaned toward the door.

Doug grabbed her by the arm. "But we don't even know if the kid's in there."

Vera shrugged but didn't budge. "Only one way to find out."

Knowing he couldn't stop her if she was determined, he let go of her arm. "Okay," he said, rocking back and forth in his seat. "We'll try the room with the light. If someone's up, we might as well know it right off."

Vera pulled her cap lower, reached to the floorboard behind her seat, grabbed a screwdriver from the tool box sitting there, then stepped out of the van into the whirling winds. Not more than three minutes later, using the screwdriver, she pried the screen off the window outside the lighted room. Within another two minutes, the same screwdriver had slipped through the wood frame on the top of the window and pried open the lock. Pleased with her progress, Vera stepped back and beckoned Doug to inspect her work.

The sound of his movements blanketed by the falling rain, Doug edged around her, raised the window, and peered inside. To his great relief, he spotted a night lamp burning on a table beside a crib. "It's the nursery," he whispered, turning back to Vera. "I'm going in. You stay here."

His pulse quickening, he lifted a leg and threw it across the window sill. Within seconds, he crossed the carpeted floor and reached the crib. Without pausing, he dipped over, lifted the sleeping child out of her blankets and turned back to the window.

Easy, he thought, so easy. Though his plans called for him to take his money, close down their operation, and leave the state, he might have to reconsider. Almost half a million dollars for three children. Making childless couples happy. Rescuing poor children from lives of despair. Everyone came out on top.

Pleased with himself, Doug reached the window and leaned out, ready to hand the baby girl to Vera.

The instant Doug's feet had landed in the nursery, Debbi opened her eyes. Though not sure, she thought she heard something—not really a thud, but something thumping softly on the floor. She wondered about Burke's mom. Had she gotten up? Not likely. The woman slept even harder than Burke did.

Debbi rolled over. Was the noise something from outside, blown against the house by the storm? Probably so. The wind was picking up again, becoming more furious, as if it had a mind to get more and more angry.

Debbi fluffed up her pillow and told herself to calm down. She missed Burke, that was all. She didn't like it that he was out so late on such a bad night. New-mom jitters, she told herself. She inhaled slowly, trying to relax.

There! The floor creaked. Something—or someone—was moving in the house. She knew it in her bones.

Had Burke gotten home? She waited for the sound of his footsteps moving from the garage into the kitchen, from the kitchen toward the bedroom.

But no sound came from the garage. If not Burke, then what?

Debbi sat up and grabbed her robe from the foot of the bed. Maybe it was silly, but she felt something was wrong in the house. Moving from the bed, she walked to the closet and reached for the Beretta she kept on the closet shelf. But it wasn't there. Then she remembered—she had given it to Burke.

Debbi stepped out of the closet and stopped still in the room, listening. Above the wind and the rain, she thought she heard a whimper, just one short second of a tiny cry. She knew instantly what that meant. Elizabeth Joy was awake!

That made no sense at all. In her short life, Elizabeth Joy had never awakened in the middle of the night unless it was time to eat. But the three o'clock feeding was at least an hour away.

It took her only seconds to reach the nursery. Her fists clenched with tension, Debbi pushed back the door. A gust of wet wind whipped into her face, and she saw the back of a bald man standing

   *Dark Road to Daylight*

by the window. For a moment, she stood there, too stunned to move. The man held her baby in his arms. He shoved Elizabeth Joy through the window.

With a scream that ripped through the increasingly heavy wind, Debbi yanked the lamp off the table by the crib and threw herself across the room toward the man. Her face contorted with rage in the now dark room, she smashed the lamp across the back of the intruder's head. Though stunned, he turned around quickly and fought back, trying to jerk the lamp away from Debbi. But she wouldn't let go.

Suddenly, he did. He dropped his fingers from the lamp and reached for Debbi's throat. His fingers closed around her windpipe. She gagged. He squeezed tighter and tighter. She dropped the lamp to the floor at his feet, and her green eyes glazed over.

For a second, she hung between consciousness and coma. The man's fingers clawed into her skin. The pain felt hot, sharp and piercing. It bore into her, a smothering inferno. Debbi felt herself blacking out, giving in to the pain.

Outside, a blaze of lightning bit through the air, and Debbi thought of Elizabeth Joy out in the storm. If she gave up, her baby would be hurt, maybe even killed.

Debbi fought back. Her eyes focused again, and she lifted her fingers to the intruder's face. With the ferocity of a lioness protecting her cubs, she dug her nails into his skin. He grunted in pain but didn't let go of her throat. Still digging with her nails, she lifted her right leg. The blow hit him in the genitals. He groaned and doubled over, his hands releasing her neck.

Still gagging for air, Debbi reached again for the lamp. She lifted it off the floor and raised it over her head. She crashed it down against the man's bald head. The lamp shattered and the kidnapper collapsed to the floor, his head in his hands, groaning in pain.

Yelling her baby's name, Debbi rushed past the man, away from him, headed for the window. The bald man reached out, grabbing for her ankle.

Driving like a man possessed, Burke almost rolled the Jeep as he rounded a sharp corner about five miles from his house. Over the last half hour he had spent almost equal amounts of time blaming himself for what had happened and praying to God that no harm would come to his wife and child.

He should have gone to the police the moment he found out about Redder, he lamented to himself. No matter what his suspicions about Cleve Chapman.

Fighting off the self-recriminations, Burke forced himself to think positively. Maybe the kidnappers had no thought of taking Elizabeth Joy. Perhaps they just threw his wallet on the ground and the wind blew his baby's picture away. Even if they did plan to take her, Debbi would stop them. Stealing a child right out of a house certainly wasn't easy. A thousand things could go wrong. He might get there before they did. The storm might slow them down. They might lose their way and give it up.

Hoping and praying that he was right, he ran through a red light and turned left. Only three more miles to his house.

The road snaked to the right and up an incline. Trees whipped side to side like windshield wipers against a giant sky. Burke whizzed the Jeep through an intersection and past a row of parked cars. Only a half-mile to go now.

He careened through a turn. The wind outside picked up steam and lightning flashed continually, a fantastic light show. The Jeep tilted to the side, its left wheels leaving the ground for a split instant. Suddenly, from the sky above, a wave of rain washed down to the earth. With the rain, a roar like a locomotive rumbled through the air. The tornado touched down not a hundred yards away, its whipping wind a monster grabbing for the tires of Burke's Jeep. The monster grabbed the tires and tossed them into the air. The tornado threw the Jeep in a spiral, end over end across the street.

Inside the vehicle, Burke gripped the steering wheel and held on for dear life. His head hit the steering wheel, and a splash of blood bounced down into his eyes. Slowly, like a fighter feeling a delayed reaction from a punch, he felt himself losing consciousness. Though he fought against it, he lost the battle. He thought about Debbi and Elizabeth Joy as is eyes closed and his head rolled sideways. The Jeep came to rest upside down against a pine tree less than a quarter mile from his dear family.

Outside Burke's house, the wind had become a howling rage, and the rain now washed down in an incredible torrent. Staring through the downpour into the nursery, Vera held the baby against her chest and watched, dumbstruck, as her husband collapsed under the blow of the heavy lamp the woman had smashed into his skull. Blood now poured from her husband's head as he fought for his life.

The sight of the blood startled Vera into action. She had to help Doug! She had to get him out of there.

Moving quickly, Vera lowered Elizabeth Joy to the ground and sprinted back to the van. She had a gun there. Though she hated to do it, she would protect her husband.

Before Debbi reached the window, the man on the floor lunged at her and grabbed her ankle. He twisted it, and she toppled to the carpet beside him. In a squat, he pulled her toward him, his hands reaching for her throat again. Frantic, she quickly scanned the room, looking for a weapon. If he managed to get her by the throat again, she didn't know that she could fight him off. She saw the shattered lamp to her left. No good anymore. She didn't see anything else. The man's fingers touched her throat. She pushed against his chest, struggling to keep away from his grip. He locked one hand around her windpipe and raised the other.

She dropped her head, still searching for a weapon. She saw a gun in the man's belt. A Beretta. Her gun.

The man must have gotten it from Burke. But how—what did he have to do with Burke? Was Burke okay, or had the man killed her husband with the very gun she had insisted that he carry?

Spurred by anger and fear, Debbi arched her back away from the man's grasping hands. At the same time, she reached for the Beretta in his belt. She closed her hand on the gun and yanked it out.

The man dropped his hands from her throat and reached for the gun too. He grasped her wrist and bent it backward. The gun now pointed directly at the ceiling.

Burke stayed unconscious less than two minutes. When he awoke, he immediately climbed out of the Jeep and began to run. In spite of the pounding rain, he could get there within a couple of minutes if nothing else went wrong. He prayed he wasn't too late. Driven by fear, he moved into a dead sprint. To his great joy, the wind was behind him.

In the black van, Vera grabbed her gun from under the seat on the passenger side. Her finger on the trigger, she rushed back toward Burke Anderson's front porch. One step away from the porch, she felt the wind lift her off the ground. At the same moment, the tornado ripped a twelve-foot dogwood tree out of the yard twenty feet away.

The wind threw her upside down. It rolled her over and over, head up, then down, head up, then down. It played with her like a cat with a ball of string. It yanked her away from the house and toward the dogwood tree, spinning her and the tree through the night. Vera had never heard such a noise. It sounded as if the hinges holding the earth in place were breaking.

Ten feet away from the porch, Vera and the dogwood tree came together. The tree trunk crunched into her ribs and knocked the air from her lungs. The pistol in her hands disappeared into the black night, knocked away and blown upward by the fierce wind. Her baseball hat zipped off her head and dipped like a crazy kite into the black sky. Her hair, long and blonde, dropped out of the hat and billowed around her face, blanketing her closed eyes.

Suddenly, as if tired of the game, the tornado lifted its snaking tail and moved away, ejecting her and the dogwood tree from its grasp at the same time. The two of them landed together—the dogwood sitting upright against the detached garage by Burke Anderson's house and Vera resting in the crook of its split branches, her blonde hair now matted against her blood-smeared face.

Burke ran into the yard just in time to see the woman and the tree fall to the ground. With a quick glance he saw that she wasn't a

threat anymore. He moved past her into his house. The storm had taken care of the woman. But where was her partner?

Yelling at the top of his lungs, Burke burst through the living room and down the hall. He heard a gunshot, and his scream became louder. He flew into the nursery, and his eyes fell on Debbi and the man in the rain slicker rolling over and over each other on the floor. The man had a gun in his hand and he was lifting it to take aim at Debbi.

In an instant that seemed to last forever, Burke searched the room for a weapon. To his right he spotted Elizabeth Joy's broomstick horse, the one his dad had made for her. A black mane at the throat. A pink ribbon around its neck.

Burke grabbed the horse, slid his hands to the end opposite the head, and pounced across the nursery.

The man had pinned Debbi to the floor with his knees. He pointed the gun at her face.

From three feet away, Burke swung the horse like a baseball bat, its head cutting through the air at the bald man's skull. The horse made a direct hit. A sliver of blood poured out of the man's right temple. He toppled over, falling to Debbi's right, the Beretta dropping to the floor.

Still gripping the horse, ready to swing it again if the man moved, Burke inched over to Debbi. Squatting, he stared down into her emerald green eyes.

She reached out to him, her arms open. Incredibly relieved, he grabbed her by the hands and pulled her into his arms. Shaking from the rush of adrenaline, both of them stood still in the room, Burke hugging Debbi gently and rubbing her back. They stood there for several seconds, the sound of their breathing the only thing disturbing the quiet of the room. The rain and wind from the storm had completely ceased, as if tired out from the energy it had exerted.

Burke heard a whimper. Startled, he pulled away from Debbi and tilted his head toward the window. Elizabeth Joy?

"The baby!" yelled Debbi, moving to the window. "The woman took Elizabeth Joy."

"She's outside!" called Burke, already moving.

"By the window!" yelled Debbi, right beside him.

Thirty seconds later, Burke bent down and lifted his daughter off the wet ground and into his arms. Though soaked from head to toe, she looked fine. Wiping water from her face, Burke handed her to Debbi. Together, the three of them sloshed back across the muddy yard, back past the porch, and into the house.

Burke picked up a phone and dialed 911. He had saved his child. Was it too late for Stacy and Taylor?

Sunday
August 31

CHAPTER FORTY

6:45 P.M.

Leaving Elizabeth Joy with his mom, Burke and Debbi visited Jackie Broadus at Murphy Memorial right after supper. For the first time in the three days since she was shot, they found her sitting up in bed. After they both gave her a long hug, Debbi took a seat at the foot of the bed, and Burke pulled up a chair. Jackie, her dark hair pinned back and her face still a blanched white, smiled her pleasure at their visit.

"You've been here every day," she said.

"And you've improved every day," Debbi said.

"Almost good as new," Jackie agreed.

"Better off than that kidnapper, Vera Klick," said Burke. "She's at West End Hospital. Better trauma surgeons there. Her head injuries are severe. Doctors don't know yet if she'll live."

"What about the husband?" asked Jackie. "What's the latest on him? They've kept me in the dark to protect my health, according to Patrick."

"He has a concussion," said Burke. "I swing a pretty mean stick. But he's okay. The doctors checked him out, then let your guys have him. He gave us some wonderful news."

"Yeah, I heard it on television," said Jackie, taking Debbi's hand and squeezing it. "Both Stacy Chapman and Taylor Bradford are okay. They're already back with their parents."

"Bethany Chapman called me right after the news report," said Burke. "She had been living in her mother's car, hiding from the authorities. But she's back at the trailer now, relieved that it's all over. The amazing thing is, she said she really had planned to take Stacy and run from Cleve. That was her plan, scary as it was. That's why she took the money out of the bank on Friday."

"But Rusty Redder beat her to it."

"Exactly."

"She survived pretty well for a lady who was supposed to be so weak. Guess your time with her was well spent." Jackie smiled at Burke.

Uncomfortable with the praise, Burke changed the subject. "Klick is a retired military guy," Burke said, repeating what the news report had said. "And he actually had a baby-sitter at his house keeping the kidnapped children!"

"The sitter, a sixteen-year-old girl, didn't know about any of this," said Debbi. "Klick told her the kids were his niece and nephew. He couldn't leave them alone, he said, didn't want anything to happen to them. Needed them perfect, he said. People paying top dollar deserve children in perfect health."

"But he's not connected to the dead child," interjected Burke, parroting the information Debbi's paper had gathered.

"No, apparently not. Nothing ties him to it. It's a totally different kind of act."

"That girl looks like the victim of some kind of cult sacrifice," interjected Jackie. "We're still investigating it. Trying to find that Hector character. We think that's who shot me. Patrick has at least told me that much."

Burke started to voice another opinion, to say that Cleve could just as easily have shot her as anyone else. From the abusive example he had demonstrated in his past and his newfound interest in Satanism, it certainly sounded like he was capable of it. But he had no proof. For now, he would keep his suspicions quiet. But he would keep his eyes and ears open too.

"Klick's wife worked with an adoption firm," said Debbi, interrupting Burke's thoughts. "For over six years. Got the idea for the kidnappings a year or so ago. The plan was to find wealthy people who wanted kids but who couldn't go through the normal system of adoption for one reason or another. The wife could make it all look legitimate, provide all the correct paperwork. The people getting the children would never know. A couple of strokes of the keyboard, and the original identity of the children disappears. The kids are too young to remember where they came from, and the new parents don't tell them they're adopted until years from now, if ever. Everything is beautiful, everyone is happy."

"Except for the people who lose their kids," suggested Burke, thinking of the fear he felt when he thought he might lose Elizabeth Joy.

"Sure, except for them. But Klick even had an answer for that. Said he figured he was doing the parents a favor. Relieving them of a burden they really couldn't afford."

"I guess he tried to soothe his conscience with that," suggested Jackie.

"Apparently so."

"They did it for the money," said Debbi, her tone disbelieving.

"Sure, people do all kinds of terrible things for money," said Jackie.

"I can't imagine many worse things than this," said Debbi.

For several moments, all three of them became quiet. The late afternoon sun burned through the window. Burke stood up and walked over to it. He rubbed his palms on his pants pockets and took a deep breath.

"Don't you get tired of it?" he asked Jackie, staring into the hospital yard. "The endless, vicious pain people inflict on each other? The rapes, robberies, kidnappings, murders. Don't you want to throw up your hands, admit that you're helpless and throw in the towel?"

Jackie raised herself higher in her bed. "Look at me, Burke Anderson," she said. "Look at me."

Slowly, reluctantly, Burke pivoted to face her. She motioned for him to come to the bed. He obeyed, taking a spot right beside Debbi. Jackie took his right hand in hers and patted it.

"Listen," she said. "You met me about four years ago. At that time I felt exactly like you do now. I felt like the bad guys had gotten the upper hand, that I was holding my finger in a dike that was inevitably going to collapse. I've even felt that way in the last few weeks. I've thought about taking my little finger out of that dike and letting someone else do it if they wanted. If they didn't, okay, I was going to quit anyway. But, guess what? Since I got shot, I've spent quite a few hours thinking about all this. And guess what I've decided? I've decided that the faith you told me about and that I embraced for myself last year prevents me from thinking that the bad guys are going to win.

"If what I now believe about God is right, then in the end, sin doesn't win. We've already won. You know that. We've already won. What we're doing now is a mopping-up operation. Isn't that what the cross was all about? The good guy winning, winning for all of us? Showing us that if we stand with God, we win too?"

She paused and took a breath, her face alive with conviction. Staring at her, Burke suddenly chuckled. A Christian for less than a year, Jackie was already encouraging him, her former mentor.

"You sound like a preacher," he said, smiling.

"A preacher telling the truth," agreed Debbi.

Jackie pinched his hand. "Nope, not me," she said. "I'm a cop. That's what I am and what I always want to be."

"What about that wife and mother thing?" asked Burke, teasing her.

"Hopefully that too. Someday soon. But until then, I think I'll just keep my finger in the dike."

"We'll lend our fingers too," said Debbi, putting her hand in Burke's and on top of Jackie's. "Together, we've got thirty fingers. That'll stop up a lot of holes." Debbi and Burke smiled at Jackie. And all three of them knew it all at once—they *had* won. They truly had.

Dark Road to Daylight

Sunday
September 14

CHAPTER FORTY-ONE

11:07 A.M.

Dressed in his Sunday outfit, a traditional navy suit with subtle windowpane squares, a starched white pinpoint cotton shirt, and a red-and-blue tie with horizontal stripes, Burke took several slow breaths and told himself to calm down. The service had just begun, the organ piping out the prelude, a rousing rendition of "How Great Thou Art."

Turning to Debbi, he took her hand. She looked radiant. A burgundy dress that made her green eyes stand out like double emeralds. Her hair up in a sophisticated wavy arrangement that he especially liked. Gold earrings, but not big ones. Understated class, Burke called them.

"Everyone is here," she whispered, looking up from her examination of the bulletin.

Burke scanned the row beside them. He sat on the aisle seat. Debbi beside him. Then Jackie Broadus and Aaron Hans. Past them, Bethany Chapman and Stacy, both of them the picture of health. As if feeling his gaze, Bethany leaned over and gave him a thumbs-up sign.

The organ stopped playing and a minister, robed and silver-haired, stepped to the pulpit and began to pray.

Burke offered a silent prayer of thanksgiving for Bethany and Stacy Chapman. How wonderful to see Bethany so happy, he thought. And her mom was doing better. Not recovered yet, but out of her coma and in therapy now for the paralysis on her right side.

The prayer ended and Burke opened his eyes. Smiling, he

squeezed Debbi's hand. He couldn't imagine a more glorious morning.

The minister on the platform began to speak. A woman entered from the side of the sanctuary, holding a small baby girl in her arms.

Burke heard the minister calling his name, then Debbi's. He stood, pulling Debbi up with him. Stepping back to let her lead the way, he followed her up the aisle onto the platform of the Commerce Street Methodist Church.

Stopping beside their pastor, Burke stared out at the congregation. His friends at the church. Molly, his secretary from the clinic. His mom and dad from Birmingham. Even Richard, his older brother, had come from Jacksonville.

The woman with the baby stepped onto the platform also and walked over to them. She handed the baby to Debbi. Debbi cradled her in her arms and Burke leaned down, close to his baby's face, and a smile as wide as Texas broke out across his cheeks.

Dressed in a white gown, with a white ribbon in her dark hair, Elizabeth Joy stared back up at him and Debbi, her eyes as green as her mother's, her little mouth twitching, her hands opening and closing as if trying to milk a cow.

The minister began to speak again. Burke, still leaning close to his child, listened carefully to what he said. "We come today as a church family to dedicate this dear child, Elizabeth Joy Anderson, to the God who created her. At the same time, we come to pray for her parents and offer our love to them. In addition, we come to commit ourselves to serve them as their spiritual family, making sure that we provide an atmosphere of Christian example to both parents and child. We do this because God loved the children. You may recall that Jesus showed the love of God for children. You remember what Jesus did the day they brought the children to him. He took the children in his lap, and he blessed them. Jesus said, 'Let the little children come to Me. . . . For of such is the kingdom of heaven. . . .'"

As the minister said these last words, Elizabeth Joy Anderson grinned hugely, reached out with her tiny right hand and grabbed her daddy by the nose. And her daddy laughed.

ABOUT THE AUTHOR

GARY E. PARKER has a Ph.D. from Baylor University and is a national consultant for theological education and Baptist principles. He is former pastor of First Baptist Church in Jefferson City, Missouri. He lives in Suwanee, Georgia, with his wife and two daughters. He is the author of seven books, including the novels *Death Stalks a Holiday, Beyond a Reasonable Doubt,* and *Desert Water.*

Other great thrillers from Gary E. Parker!

Beyond A Reasonable Doubt

A young pastor is implicated in a homicide—but he can't remember where he was at the time of the murder. This fast-paced thriller follows Pastor Burke Anderson on a trail through temptation to the liberating truth.

0-8407-4148-0 • Paperback • 256 pages

Death Stalks A Holiday

Four women are murdered on four consecutive Sundays, and only Burke Anderson can see the connection. A former pastor, Anderson can tell that the wounds the women have sustained are identical to the wounds of Jesus from the crucifixion. Now he must discover the identity of the killer before another woman loses her life.

0-7852-7784-6 • Paperback • 288 pages